TIME ON THEIR HANDS

BY

RICHARD F JONES

To my wife Meg and our friends Ken and Dee whose tireless efforts made the publication of this book possible.

ISBN: 978-1-291-55008-5

PROLOGUE

Men with time on their hands can get themselves into all sorts of trouble. Brains, that throughout life have been used for positive purposes, like work, can sometimes stagnate when idle and seek other outlets on which to germinate.

A tall plumpish, ordinary looking man, with dark hair, going rapidly grey, wearing a white short sleeved shirt, with a red patterned tie and dark blue trousers is playing roulette in a busy city centre casino in the middle of the afternoon. For the past half an hour he's been winning big money on every roll of the wheel. A dizzy blonde clings onto his arm and shrieks with delight each time he gathers in another pile of winning chips. Beads of perspiration are beginning to form on his brow. News of his winnings has spread around the room. A sizeable crowd of onlookers is jostling close to him, increasing the pressure. The last roll of the wheel was his sixth straight win in a row. The chips in front of him now add up to thousands of pounds. He's praying he can still remember the system. The previous evening he'd gone over it in his head a hundred times, chanting the formula to himself, hoping he could recall it all when it mattered.

Carefully he places a neatly stacked pile of chips on a straight ten. The croupier looks at him disarmingly. 'No more bets,' he says, with a degree of irritation, and spins the wheel. The onlookers go silent, the blonde moves in closer, looping her arm through his. He can feel his body shaking. He closes his eyes and waits.

A huge cheer tells him he has won again. Relieved, he opens his eyes to smiling, laughing faces. The blonde shrieks 'that's fantastic.' People slap his back. The croupier's face is like thunder.

CHAPTER ONE

It's early morning in late summer. An eerie silence hangs over an empty golf course. The semblance of a heat haze mingles with a sea mist at the far end of the dunes. When Ginger gets out of his car a rabbit scurries across the eighteenth green. The little creature stops, looks at Ginger, pricks his ears, then continues with his journey, unconcerned.

Ginger is always the first of the group to arrive. Partly out of necessity, partly out of habit. His name isn't really Ginger, his name is Talbot Reardon, but nobody locally calls anybody Talbot. He possesses a tall, thickset body and close cropped, curly ginger hair. By birth he's from Scotland, but that was a long time ago. He needs to arrive early to use the toilet. Two years back, his elderly mother-in-law moved in with him and his wife, Caroline, and since then from seven in the morning, until he leaves home for golf, they both commandeer the bathroom, forcing Ginger to complete his ablutions in the changing room at the clubhouse.

Jimmy usually arrives next. That annoys Ginger. In fact, Jimmy often annoys Ginger. Jimmy is short, with pointy features; a pointy nose, a pointy face and short dark hair, which comes to a point in the centre of his forehead. Jimmy is Irish and takes great delight in riling Ginger. The Irish are like that with the Scots and visa-versa. Now Ginger is a hefty man. At least sixteen stone and well over six feet tall. With a driver, he can hit a golf ball the best part of two hundred and seventy yards, almost twice the distance Jimmy can manage. And occasionally, Ginger longs to hit Jimmy. He's big enough to hit Jimmy into next week, but he can't, and Jimmy knows he can't, because Ginger's mother-in-law, Mrs Hetherington, has cancer. Just after she moved in with Ginger and his wife, Ginger broke his toe. Stubbed it on a slab in the garden, when walking barefoot. Jimmy lived off that for months. He still never lets Ginger forget it. At the time, Mrs Hetherington was visiting hospital three times a week, for radium treatment. Ginger's wife Caroline can't drive; Mrs Hetherington was too ill to drive and Ginger's foot was in plaster, so he couldn't drive. For five weeks Jimmy drove them all to the hospital, twenty miles there and twenty miles back and he wouldn't take a penny. 'If you can't help a pal, who can you help?' he'd say, grinning. So as much as Ginger sometimes wants to hit Jimmy, he knows he can't.

More often than not Ginger is still in the toilet when Jimmy enters the changing room. Every time, in that situation, Jimmy will call out, 'Fore. Keep your bowels open Ging.' Ginger can set his watch by it. The words annoy him so much, he never bothers to reply and remains in the cubicle until Stan arrives.

Stan is Welsh, well sort of Welsh anyway. He's from Cardiff, which according to Jimmy isn't really Welsh. 'Just like London now, all suits and bankers,' Jimmy would say. At moments like that Stan and Ginger would just look at each other and make no reply.

'His nibs is in with the Pope,' Jimmy said, when Stan came in through the changing room door that day; another of his regular phrases.

'Looks as though it's going to be fine for once,' Stan said, ignoring Jimmy's remark.

'It does that. The barometer's high,' Jimmy replied.

For eighty years there's been a golf club on that windy peninsular. Over those years the changing room has acquired a permanent odour of damp must; a humid concoction of old wood, sand and salt sea air. On the wooden bench they were both sat upon, there were hundreds of tiny holes in the timber, caused by decades of studded golf shoe laces being tied on its surface. 'Part of our heritage here,' Jimmy remarked one day, pointing at the holes. 'Like putting your shoe in somebody else's footprints.'

Stan was attending to his laces. When he'd finished tying the bows he said, 'Something strange turned up in the post today,' and extracted a letter from his trouser pocket before handed it to Jimmy. It was computer written and from his building society.

'Good God,' Jimmy said after he'd read it. 'You're in the money then.'

'Well, that's what's strange,' Stan replied. 'I'm not actually.' The letter was from the Provincial Building Society. It was addressed to Mr and Mrs Stanley Gladstone Richards, his full name and their correct address and postcode were on the top. The letter said, 'We are in receipt of your remittance for two hundred and fifty thousand pounds and as requested we have credited this amount to your Instant Access Account.'

The toilet flushed. Hearing Stan's voice, Ginger felt safe to extract himself from the cubicle. He walked to the basin and began to wash his hands.

'Well it says here the money's yours,' Jimmy said, still marvelling at the amount.

'That's the problem Jim. I don't know anything about it. I haven't got that sort of money.'

'What do you think of this Ging?' Jimmy said. Ginger was drying his hands on a paper towel. 'You know about these sort of things,' Jimmy continued. 'Stan's in the money I'd say.' Ginger was a retired bank manager. He'd finished his career quite nicely thank you, as the local manager at this seaside holiday town. On financial matters therefore, he tended to laud it over the other lads. Ginger's family had been wealthy. He was educated at Gordonstoun and throughout his banking career he had constantly used his old boy connections to bluff his way through to the best jobs. He slumped down on the bench, puffed out a catarrhal snortle, snatched the letter from Jimmy's hands, pushed his glasses down onto the bridge of his nose, and read it.

'Obviously a mistake,' he said without hesitation.

'Come on now Ging. Give Stan a bit of respect. He didn't bank with you. How do you know how much money he's got? He might have been left the money.'

'I heard him say it wasn't his,' Ginger replied impatiently. Stan cut in.

'That's right. I don't know anything about it. Came in the post this morning. Picked it up off the mat on my way here, opened it up and there it was, quarter of a million smackers. Took the wind out of my sails, I can tell you.'

By then the other three, Toby, Scott and Colin began to arrive. Every Monday, Wednesday and Friday, at eight fifteen, the first tee was always booked for the six of them. Regular as clockwork, foul weather or fair, they would play in two groups of three. Before starting, one of them would throw six golf balls, belonging to each of them, into the air, to see who'd play with who. The balls that landed nearest to each other would play together. 'It's a balls up,' Jimmy would always remark while the balls were in the air; another comment, according to the others, that had also long ago passed its sell-by-date. Unfortunately, even with this system, Ginger always seemed to end up playing in the same group as Jimmy and that annoyed him. Now as I said before, Ginger can hit the ball a long way. Normally on the longer holes its take Jimmy three shots to Ginger's two, to get the ball to the green. But Jimmy isn't normal and he can chip and putt like a demon. From off the green or on it, when he's chipping or putting, he tends to stand over his ball and say 'I have a feeling this is going in, Ging;' a remark that also annoys Ginger intensely. And Jimmy's chipping stroke is such an awkward little punch of a movement, Ginger becomes irritated just watching it. It bears no resemblance to a proper golf shot; a jumpy, jerky twitch is the best way to describe it. But somehow, like a piece of metal attracted to a magnet, Jimmy's ball almost always seems to home in on the hole. That leaves Ginger fuming. Then when Ginger's standing over his ball, just as he is about to hit it, Jimmy always says, 'This is for the hole then Ging.' Ginger fumes some more and of course his shot misses. And that's how it is.

Time was pressing; eight fifteen was approaching. Briefly the letter was handed around. The other three made similar comments of surprise, before it was given back to Stan. Then they all marched off, with their metal spikes clicking on the steeply sloping concrete path, sounding like a troupe of cavalry horses on parade, towards the first tee. That day Jimmy was paired with Ginger and Stan. By the time they reached the sixth tee, Jimmy, much to Ginger's agitation had already parred three of the first five holes. But more than that Jimmy's brain was in ferment.

The sixth tee is a popular resting place. The flat surface there commands a fine view out across the bay. The difficult early holes have been completed and the fresh breeze off the sea usually invigorates those who are flagging. It's about forty minutes out from the first; enough time for early morning tea, or other breakfast liquids to have worked through the system. On one side of the tee there is a good blackthorn hedge, behind which, those who wish to relieve themselves, can do so, out of sight of the rest of the course.

'I've been thinking about that letter of Stan's,' Jimmy said as he unzipped his fly. Ginger sighed. He'd been waiting for Jimmy to say something about it, his only doubt had been how long it would take, so he made no reply. 'It would serve those buggers right to lose that money,' Jimmy continued.

'Which buggers are we talking about?' Ginger replied, farting while beginning to pee.

'The building society,' Jimmy retorted. 'They buggered me about for years,' he added belligerently. 'Charged me about twice as much interest as everybody else when I had a mortgage, then when I retired, paid me bugger all on my savings.'

Ginger had heard all this before many times. The view from the sixth tee was something he looked forward to each morning. It was one of the pleasures of playing that course. By then the early mist had cleared. A faint breeze, like a violin concerto was creeping over the blackthorn, cooling his perspiring brow. The cliffs at the end of the bay stood out grand, like a stately monument, dominating the vista. 'You could have shopped around for a better rate,' Ginger said, hoping that would shut Jimmy up. They began to walk back to the tee box where Stan was patiently waiting.

'That's not the point though,' Jimmy said, zipping up his fly as they walked. 'It's all right for you to say that. You're educated that way. Bank manager and all that. You know all about that sort of stuff. Clever bugger you are. The rest of us though, we have to get by best we can. I just think it'd be nice to put one over on those bastards for once.'

'What have you got in mind?' Ginger scoffed and picked the driver out of his golf bag. 'It's at least five years nowadays for fraud.'

Stan was munching on a Mars bar, listening and becoming impatient to get on with the game. Having won the last hole Jimmy was first to drive. He picked a three wood out of his golf bag, took a couple of disjointed practice swings while he continued to talk. 'We were talking about your letter Stan.'

'*You* were talking about Stan's letter,' Ginger corrected. Jimmy lined up against his ball, wiggled his arse and the club a few times and fired the golf ball straight down the middle of the fairway.

'Good shot,' Stan said. Ginger remained silent. Jimmy held his follow through, posing, as he watched the ball skip along the fairway, scattering two magpies, who'd been happily grazing on the green-keepers freshly laid grass seed.

'Pretty good eh?' Jimmy said, looking at Ginger. 'I was only saying Stan, that it would be nice to get one over on those financial bastards for a change. How much interest are you getting on your money?'

'Oh I don't know, the missus looks after that,' Stan replied. 'About two percent I think.'

'There you are then, a pittance. Keeping some bugger like Ginger here in a job, you are,' Jimmy said. Ginger wasn't going to rise to that bait either. He'd been hooked too many times before on that one. That morning he'd wanted to enjoy his golf.

Stan was tall and slightly rotund, in a comfortable sort of way. He looked younger than his sixty four years. An ex British Telecom engineer by trade. 'Well I can't steal it Jim,' he said. 'The missus would kill me.'

'I'm not suggesting you steal it Stan,' Jimmy said. Ginger was lining up his drive, something he was meticulous about. He'd pick a spot on the horizon, point his club at it, then angle the club back down on the same line to his feet. Usually it took some time to accomplish this to his satisfaction. Then, standing over the ball he'd waggle his arse, flick the club back and fore several times, before settling into his stance. 'Unnecessary arrogant nonsense,' Jimmy used to say to the others, out of Ginger's earshot.

'What are you suggesting he does then?' Ginger said, unable to resist the temptation to reply as he hovered over his ball. This was one of his favourite shots on the course. The sixth was a good driving hole; four hundred and eighty yards long, with a reasonably wide fairway. It gave him the opportunity to really let it rip. If he caught the ball perfectly, he could be more than a hundred yards ahead of Jimmy on the first shot. He was about to hit when Jimmy spoke again.

'I think we ought to do what you buggers have been doing for years, Ging,' he said. 'I think we ought to borrow it for a while, invest it, then when we've made some money, let them have it back for a small fee.' In his anger Ginger lashed at the golf ball like a demented woodchopper hacking at a tree trunk. The ball flew off the tee peg at a right angle, gathering pace in a banana like trajectory over the adjacent fifth fairway. At the end of its flight it hit a pinnacle of a rock, then catapulted off again towards the calm, blue sea, where it finally landed with a spectacular splash, reminiscent of a gannet's dive into water.

'Fucking   hell!!'   Ginger   yelled.

CHAPTER TWO

With our group there were many, many golf days like this. Days when, during a round, Jimmy would say something that upset Ginger, or got on his nerves. But that day, after watching his drive off the sixth tee find a watery grave, Ginger was fuming uncontrollably. He waved his driver furiously at Jimmy in time to his words. 'I have repeatedly asked you not to talk when I'm playing a shot,' Ginger hollered.

'Oh, sorry Ging,' Jimmy replied looking abashed. Stan stood silent and still, smirking, unable to decide what stage this particular contretemps had reached.

'It's just that you asked and so I thought you wanted to know,' Jimmy said, still looking sheepish. 'I'm sorry about your shot.'

'Of course I don't want to know,' Ginger responded. 'I've never heard such a harebrained idea in my life. I'm here to play golf. To do that properly I need quiet to concentrate. If I don't have quiet, I can't play. If I can't play, it ruins my day. Do you understand? Have I made myself clear?'

'Perfectly clear Ging. I'm sorry. You won't hear another word, not out of me anyway.'

'Good,' Ginger said. 'You'd better play your shot Stan and I'll play three off the tee afterwards.'

And so that's how it was for the next three hours. Nobody spoke much. Ginger's game deteriorated into a sad collection of missed putts and poorly hit shots, all accompanied by a cacophony of foul and abusive language. Jimmy played, well, as Jimmy always plays. He holed outrageous putts; chipped in from off the green and and drove straight down the middle of the fairway, going about his game as though nothing had happened. Except this morning he kept quiet, very, very quiet. Poor Stan was caught in the middle. He realised that it was his letter that had caused the trouble in the first place. He kept his head down and concentrated on his own game, uncertain whether to speak or not.

By the time they reached the eighteenth green a heavy cloud had darkened the sky overhead. Misty drizzle was beginning to drift in off the sea. Jimmy won the three ball by a street. At the finish they all just about managed a cursory handshake, but nothing else was said. That morning there were no congratulations, or commiserations. Usually somebody said, 'Well played' or 'Hard luck', or something more cynical, but not on this day.

'I don't think I'll come in for a drink,' Ginger said gruffly and stalked off towards his car. Jimmy and Stan looked at each other, gathered their golf bags and headed for the clubhouse.

The golfer's bar is a decorative hotch-potch of contemporary and old. A glass cabinet, profusely stocked with prize winning silverware dominates one wall. Two other walls are panelled in heavy austere oak, on which boards, depicting the names of past prize winners are displayed. The south aspect consists of sliding patio doors, leading to a verandah, with tables and chairs overlooking the eighteenth green. With a pint of beer in hand Jimmy and Stan settle around one of the many glass top tables. While they are talking the other three enter the bar.

'I've upset his nibs,' Jimmy said when they were in earshot.

'No, not again?' Toby responded sarcastically. Being in his seventies he was the oldest of the six. For most of his life Toby had been a fireman. Then, when he retired, he sailed a boat around the world. He sported a voluminous walrus moustache, shaggy greying hair and wore clothes that always looked baggy and about half a size too big. He possessed a resounding laugh and enjoyed his food and drink, which showed in his generous waistline. Now, mainly to ease his retirement boredom, he was a church warden, a town councillor and actively involved in almost every local charity and social advisory board.

'Yes, but I've upset him good and proper this time,' Jimmy replied to Toby's remark. 'Put my big foot in it, right up to the proverbial. It's Stan's fault, we were discussing his letter.'

'Don't blame me. You were the one who upset him. I know better than to talk when he's about to hit a shot,' Stan replied.

'We beat him though didn't we Stan? He's a toffee nosed bugger,' Jimmy retorted. Stan just smiled. Toby guffawed.

'What did you say to upset him this time?' Colin cut in. Colin was quieter, more studious than the others. Tall, with dark hair, he'd been a lecturer in mathematics, at Cardiff University, before retiring to West Wales.

The other three all bought drinks, then they all squeezed round the same table. Beer was already spilled on the table top;

crisp packets, some opened, some still to be opened, messily cluttered the space between the glasses. Their usual format after golf, involved a bar meal, followed by a game of snooker; doubles when the six of them played.

'I only suggested that we give these banks and building societies a run for their money,' Jimmy said when they had all settled.

'You should know that's a dicey subject with him,' Scott said. He was the youngest of them all, a retired dentist. Retired to a pot of gold by all accounts. He drove a flash Porsche car, lived in an expensive house, with a trophy wife. He was tall with jet black hair and twinkling eyes. Women swooned at him regularly. 'Like bitches on heat when he's around,' Jimmy commented often.

'I know, I know. I'll make it up to him. I'll let him win next time.' Jimmy said, chortled and took a slug of his beer. 'It's just that while we were playing an idea came to me about Stan's letter.'

'What idea's that then Jim?' Toby said. His face creased into a smile, which made him look like a pet Labrador about to be presented with a bone. He loved it when Jimmy had one of his ideas. 'What devious plan has that crooked little mind of yours cooked up this time?' Toby added. Jimmy beckoned them all to move in closer. The other four pulled up their chairs and angled their heads over the table.

'Well as I see it,' Jimmy began in hushed tones, 'we all know that the money doesn't belong to Stan.' Stan nodded in agreement while he munched crisps. The salty residue of those he'd already eaten was coating his lips. 'So, he can't take the money for keeps,' Jimmy continued. 'But at this moment in time only Stan and us here know about it.' He paused for his words to sink in. 'The building society won't know, until somebody else, who's money it is, shouts. Do you all agree on that?'

'The building society may know already,' Colin cut in. 'There may be a stop on the account now.' He picked up his beer, drained the remains of his glass, and smacked his lips as he put it back on the table.

'That may be the situation, I'll grant you that Colin. But let's assume for the moment it isn't.' Colin sat back in his chair and folded his arms. Jimmy continued.

'What I tried to say to Ging, before he blew his top, was that we should just borrow the money for a while, invest it in something with a quick turnaround, then put it back before anybody notices, having taken the profit.' They all sniggered. Toby guffawed louder than anybody else and got up out of his seat. 'And how do you propose to do that my little Irish genius? I'm thirsty, anybody else for a refill?' Colin and Stan held out their empty glasses. That day it was only the five of them in the bar, plus John, the steward, who was flitting back and fore to the kitchen, so Toby could still hear Jimmy from the bar counter. He pinged the little bell to attract John's attention.

'Well, what I spotted on Stan's letter,' Jimmy continued, emphasising his words with the index finger of his right hand, 'was that this account could be used as a telephone account. Isn't that right Stan?' Stan didn't know the answer to that. His wife looked after such matters. He fished in his trouser pocket for the letter. By then it was crumpled and creased. He flattened it out with his palm on the table and reread it.

'You're right Jim. It does say that, down here at the bottom. I hadn't spotted it.'

'You see, there you are, I'm not as stupid as you all think I am.'

'That's a matter of opinion,' Scott said. His eyes were twinkling, just as they did when he was looking at a voluptuous blonde. Jimmy's index finger rose again.

'Just you listen Mister Cleverdick, don't you be too hasty. That was Ginger's trouble this morning. He was too hasty, wouldn't listen. Pity, 'cos we could have done with his expertise on this. I'll have a pint please Toby, while you're there.' Toby looked back at him with an expression of exasperation and sloped wearily back from the bar to the table for Jimmy's glass.

'From what I saw in that letter,' Jimmy continued, 'you must already be an account holder with that lot?' He pointed at the letter in Stan's hand.

'That's right,' Stan responded. 'Used to have my mortgage with them. Now what little savings I have is still there.' Jimmy nodded. By then Toby had returned with the beer. He spilt a bit on Jimmy's leg as he put his glass on the table.

'That's what I thought. It's all right Tobe, I've got another pair at home,' he said, brushing the beer off his trousers with his hand. 'So if you've got the same type of account, you'll have a password or an ID number?' They all fell silent and looked at Stan.

'I don't know. I expect so. As I said the missus does that sort of thing. I haven't got a clue.'

'Well let's just say you have.' Suddenly they were all looking again at Jimmy. He had their undivided attention now. 'Let me have another look at that letter Stan,' he said. Stan passed it over.

'That's what I thought. It's an instant access account. Which means you can draw the money on demand. And it says here at the bottom that it's a telephone account. So you don't have to send off the passbook for a withdrawal. You can do it all over the phone, using a password.' Stan put down his beer glass.

'Now hang on a minute Jim. I said I don't know whether I've got a password or not. I'm not looking for any trouble over this. The missus would kill me if I got into any trouble.'

'Let him finish Stan,' Scott interrupted. 'Don't worry we won't let you get into trouble Stan. But let's hear what the little leprechaun has in mind.'

'Do you guys want to order any food?' John called out obstinately from the bar.

'Just a minute John,' Toby replied. 'We'll be there now.'

'Well you'd better be quick. I'm going to close the kitchen soon,' the steward said and stomped back into his cooking lair.

'Go on Jim, finish what you have in mind,' Toby said. The froth from his beer was gathered on his moustache like snow on a mountain.

'Well, as I see it, and it's only an idea mind,' Jimmy began, pointing again with his index finger. 'Seeing how this money is in limbo, we could draw it out, invest it in something that has a quick turnaround, take the profit, split it between us, or use it as a fund for social occasions.' Jimmy took a swig of his new pint. The others remained silent for quite a few moments before Colin interrupted.

'We'd never get away with that Jim. That's fraud. That's a criminal offence. We'd all end up in jail.' Jimmy was about to answer, but Scott cut in again.

'What could we invest it in that would have a quick enough turnaround to make some real money?' he said.

'That's where we need young Ginger,' Jimmy said. 'He knows

about these sort of things. I wish I hadn't upset him earlier. And he's a gambler, he'd take a chance.' Ginger was well known amongst the group as a punter. On the horses mainly, but he also dabbled a bit in shares. Nothing big, just an odd flutter here and there when the mood took him. By all accounts he was quite successful.

Jimmy tidied up some of the spilt beer on the table with his beer mat, then said, 'These financial set ups nowadays are so inefficient. It'll be weeks before they get round to Stan's nest egg. You wouldn't believe the trouble I had with a standing order. Months it took them to sort it out. By the time they've got around to this, the money will be all tucked up again in Stan's account.'

'Do you lot want any food!!? This is your last chance!' John shouted out from the bar.

Their empty stomachs were grumbling so John's impatience curtailed the discussion.

Afterwards the dissection of their individual scores that day, involving a division of money, caused a heated diversion. A pound each was always paid to the day's best individual score, on a stableford system; Jimmy, that day. And another fifty pence was distributed for the best first nine holes, Jimmy again, and the same amount for the best second nine holes, Colin. There was also a fifty pence prize for the longest drive on the eighteenth; Scott that morning. All these financial transactions had to be accounted for, before they paid John for the food. This, as you can imagine, took considerable time and involved not a little argument. By the time the food arrived, Jimmy's idea had, therefore, been put on a back burner. Sides also still had to be agreed for the snooker game. This, was compounded with difficulty, as there were only five of them, not the usual six, which meant they were going to have to play snooker as a three against two; which confused further the allocation of the prize money for that event, as according to Scott, it would change the odds. 'Whoever the two are, should have a handicap, otherwise it's unfair,' he suggested. All this resulted in a prolonged disagreement, which became even more inflamed when Colin admitted he had forgotten to bring any money with him that day. Matters therefore, got a little out of hand. Eventually, the snooker game ended up as two against two when Colin took umbrage at being called 'a tight fisted git' by Scott and left in a huff after his meal.

'I didn't deliberately not bring any money Scott,' Colin said. 'I just forgot in the rush this morning. I had to take the dog out as the wife was going to her sisters.' So for the time being, Jimmy's idea lay in abeyance.

CHAPTER THREE

On his way home from the golf club Toby often made a detour no-one else knew about. His own house, which he shared with his wife Margaret, a large detached, villa type property was at the top end of town, overlooking the sea. But instead of taking the route from the clubhouse back into town, Toby would often head down the coast in the opposite direction, towards the village of Saren. A tin mine had once been its claim to fame. Defunct now since before the first World War, only the surrounding agriculture provided any sort of local employment. Most of it was seasonal, back breaking and poorly paid. The village was really only a strip of a dozen or so bungalows, alongside the main road. There was also a farm, a garage repair business, with one petrol pump and at the end of the village, jammed together in an unattractive small close, littered with parked cars, were twenty five scruffy council houses, all occupied by inhabitants of indeterminate means. Social Security housing in other words.

Toby pulled up in front of number seventeen. A battered Ford Fiesta was parked outside. In the tiny front garden, all grass, except for a hydrangea bush under the front window, was a toddler's play bike, a coloured plastic football and a red garden slide. The front door was open.

'Are you in?' Toby called out as he walked inside. In response a little boy with blonde curly hair ran down the hallway to greet him, shouting 'Tiad,' as he ran. Toby crouched expectantly and the toddler charged into his arms. 'Mark, my little pumpkin,' Toby said as they embraced. He ruffled the boy's soft hair, then kissed him on his head.

From the kitchen, a tall, slim, mousy-blonde girl, of medium height, in her late twenties appeared, wearing a hooped, pale blue and white T shirt and light blue jeans. 'He's been a little bugger these last few days,' she said, brushing her hair off her forehead with her hand. She had a glowing, intelligent, fresh looking face.

'At this age they all are,' Toby replied, lifting the boy up. 'He's putting on weight.' He carried the boy into an untidy lounge. Toys and the child's clothes were scattered everywhere. Washing was drying on a clothes-horse by the front window.

'We're going to have to do something with him,' the girl said. Mark had learning difficulties. He was bright enough, but just couldn't retain anything. Even though he was five years old, his vocabulary was limited to words about his mother and his reading skills were non-existent.

'Catryn I know that,' Toby said impatiently. 'I've spoken to the Welfare people. The local place is not suitable. They say he will have to go to Carmarthen.'

'How can I afford to take him there. That's forty miles. How much will that cost in petrol?' the girl said angrily, while picking some of the clothes off the floor.

'There'll probably be a bus,' Toby argued back. 'The Council usually put on a special bus for those who need it.'

'But that goes round all the villages. It'll take hours to get to Carmarthen. You know I have to get to work. I can't wait around half the day for that. If I lose my job I'm done for. There isn't anything else around here.'

'We'll sort something out Catryn.'

'You make sure you bloody well do,' Catryn snapped back. Toby was still holding the boy. He stared at her, put the boy down and walked towards her and placed his hands on her shoulders. Then he kissed her on the forehead.

'I know it's hard for you. I know you must be tired,' he said. They stood facing each other in silence for a few moments, while Mark tugged at Toby's trouser leg. The girl picked up the boy. Toby extracted his wallet from his back pocket and drew out five ten pound notes and gave them to the girl.

* * * * *

West Wales weather is as unpredictable as the service provided by the local plumbers, electricians and builders. When expecting a tradesman to call, there is an oft used Pembrokeshire remark, referring to a 'Pembrokeshire promise'. Most times the appointment is not kept, hence the tradition of the phrase. The weather in the area is similarly fickle. Expert forecasters regularly predict fine, dry days, hoping perhaps to encourage a migration of tourists to the area's beautiful beaches and rugged cliffs. Regrettably however, an isobaric low always seems to hover unseen, somewhere around the Irish Sea, perpetually waiting to catch everybody out with storms and gales. On those occasions campsites are flooded, caravans are evacuated and once happy tourists flee back down the M4, to the drier weather of their homes and garden barbecues.

That evening Jimmy was sitting in his lounge. A gale was howling in the chimney, while rain lashed on the window pane. He was conjecturing on how a day, which started with such promise, had deteriorated so badly as the weather closed in. The morning forecast had been good, there was every hope of a fine, dry round. The early holes were combative fun, until he'd become involved in that fracas with Ginger. To quell his melancholia, he'd resorted to an LP record of Maria Callas and a large Irish whisky, when the phone rang.

'Jimmy my old fruit, how are they hanging?' the voice at the other end said. It was Scott.

'Oh not so dusty after today,' Jimmy replied.

'That's why I'm phoning,' Scott said. His voice sounded enthusiastic. 'I've been thinking a bit more about that idea of yours. Do you really think we could get our hands on that money?'

'I'm sure it could be done,' Jimmy replied. 'Persuading Stan would be the problem. He may be too scared to do anything about it.'

'Never mind about that. I've an idea how we could get around him. But do you really believe we could get the money out.' Scott's enthusiasm was infectious, Jimmy could imagine his eyes twinkling as he spoke.

'I don't see why not. It's all systems nowadays. There's very little human involvement. If you can get round the system, as I said this morning, it would be weeks before they caught up with what we'd done. With any luck we'd have put the money back by then.'

'Yes, yes,' Scott said. 'But you really think we could get it out?'

'The letter said we could.' Jimmy replied. 'I repeat, it's just persuading Stan that's the problem. You know what he's like. Proper stick in the mud.'

'H'm,' Scott said. Jimmy could hear him breathing down the phone. 'You leave Stan to me. I've already spoken to him this evening and I've persuaded him not to do anything about the money until we meet up again. Are we all playing on Wednesday?'

'I guess so,' Jimmy said. 'Don't know about Ginger though. Depends on whether he'll put up with me again.'

'Course he will. He loves you as though you were normal really. Whatever you do don't mention anything when we're out on the course. When we get Stan back to the bar we can really have a go at him there. I'll speak to the other two. Keep your pecker up Jim. Just keep on thinking little man, that's what you're good at,' Scott said and rang off.

Jimmy had never been a hundred percent sure of Scott. Bit of a wide boy he thought. Too clever by half, despite the fact he'd been a dentist. 'Glad he hadn't done my teeth,' Jimmy had once said to Iris, his wife.

'Why do you say that?' Iris had replied.

"cause he'd have probably put in cut price fillings. Bought cheap from Russia or somewhere like that.' Jimmy said. Iris had laughed.

Jimmy sat back in his armchair, took another slug of his whisky and wondered why Scott had been so enthusiastic. Normally he dismissed Jimmy's ideas as mischievous Irish nonsense. Mind you he'd never come up with an idea involving a quarter of a million pounds before.

CHAPTER FOUR

Scott Lambert was brought up in Wood Green, North London. Near enough to White Hart Lane to be a Tottenham Hotspur supporter. His father had been a second hand car dealer, owning a garage at Muswell Hill. By the time he was thirteen, Scott could tune most cars, strip an engine and drive a Mercedes. The lad really wanted to be a mechanic, but his father wasn't having any of that. A proper profession was what he wanted for his son. At birth, his name was put down for nearby Harrow. A doctor, was his father's wish, but young Scott wasn't an academic. He was clever enough, but wouldn't apply himself to school work. Trading in car spare parts and chasing girls took up too much of his time to achieve any sort of scholastic record. At sixteen he was expelled for siphoning petrol from the headmaster's car.

Dentistry was therefore the nearest occupation, with any sort of medical association, he could aspire to. In many ways being a dental technician had similarities to a mechanic; you tinkered with tools and repaired broken parts that moved. Young Scott's dental college, being next to a training hospital for doctors and nurses, also offered an unlimited supply of girls. Even at that age his sexual attraction was formidable and his conquests legendary. By day he honed his art in molars, and at night he similarly developed his skills between the sheets.

Once qualified though, the problems began. Let loose in a dental practice, amongst female patients, whose gums he was permitted to massage, was a recipe for disaster. And disaster surely occurred. In his first posting, a busy national health centre in Acton, the female clientele increased by fifty per cent in six months. But once irate husbands started ringing up to complain, he had to go. It was a similar story at his next appointment, but worse was to follow.

His first dabble into private practice was a total catastrophe. It wasn't that he was not a good dentist. As a technician he was superb. The clients loved him, the women literally. And by and large the partners mostly considered him an acquisition. He attracted new business, he was good at the job and he got through the work quickly and efficiently, without any mishaps.

But at Simon Khan's up market dentistry in Fulham, there was the most attractive blonde dental assistant, Carole Young. She was a peach and naturally succumbed to Scott's charms. Unfortunately, Simon Khan also had a very attractive wife, Sonia, who also found our young dentist equally irresistible. Scott, of course, was more than happy to oblige, on both counts without a second thought. But somehow or another the two women found out about each other. Instantly they became jealous. The result was a fight between the two of them, in the surgery, causing damage to expensive equipment. Scott Lambert had to go and so it went on.

There were at least half a dozen or more similar episodes at other practices around North London. Eventually, enough was enough. Scott's father got wind of it all and to save everybody a lot of trouble he set his son up in practice, with a middle aged man as a partner, and two of the most manly looking female assistants his father could find. Matters didn't change a lot though. The female clients came in droves and Scott fornicated with a great number of them. Now though, he had to sort out his own messes. Yet somehow his business thrived. As the years went on he became more adept at getting himself out of tight corners and the practice survived.

When he was in his early thirties he met Anne Barrett, three years his junior. Like many of his conquests, she was blonde, beautiful and voluptuous. But as well as being single and beautiful, Anne also had something else to offer to tie young Scott down; she had money, or at least her family did. She and Scott were married a year after they met.

Her parents were property developers, in London South West One. They moved in high places, had connections with moneyed people. Exactly what our Scott was looking for. Soon, with Anne's help and some of her money he moved his practice to a wealthy part of Mayfair. There he really took off. He was one of the first practitioners into dental makeovers. Pop stars, TV presenters, fashion models; glamorous people who wanted to improve their smile flocked in. He loved his work and the clients loved him.

Now, Anne wasn't stupid. She knew what Scott was like. She knew about his philandering, but she was clever too. The glamorous life by itself was not enough for her alone. Just being on his arm at parties and receptions didn't satisfy her. She was used to money and wanted more. Everything with her had to be new. The latest car, the biggest house, the most expensive clothes, the newest gadgets. If something was slightly old hat, Anne would want it changed. To make more money she persuaded him to invest in property. To begin with they started in a small way; buying a couple of flats and renting them out. Then it became terraced houses, then apartment blocks. To fund it they were borrowing money in a big way. Anne ran it all from home. She had the background, she had the family connections. Builders, estate agents, bankers, finance people, they were all familiar to her and her family. Scott was too busy fixing teeth and looking after his ladies every need to get involved.

For the best part of twenty years things were fine. Then, the eighties came and the property bubble burst. At the time they were heavily borrowed; interest rates went up; Nigel Lawson resigned and Anne and Scott's empire crumbled down, like one of their apartment blocks with chronic subsidence.

Trouble closed in, the vultures were gathering. They'd become too greedy. Suddenly rents weren't covering the loan interest and creditors were hammering on the door. It took quite a few years to sort it out. If it hadn't been for Anne's parents they'd have gone bankrupt. Eventually though, one by one, the properties were sold and the debts paid. But it all took its toll on Scott's health. During the worst years, he had to work night and day to survive. Then, in his late forties he suffered a heart attack. By the time they were clear, he'd had enough. Fortunately for him, the one thing he'd managed to preserve, was his pension. While he was earning good money he'd salted a lot away. Even when he was in trouble, he kept up his pension payments. So, when he reached fifty, he packed it in and sold up. The practice was still worth quite a lot of money. At the time property prices in West Wales were cheap, and he and Anne retired there, on what looked, to the locals, like a veritable pot of gold.

They had never produced any children, so after they'd moved to West Wales and partly to stop herself from going mental, in such a rural backwater, Anne ran Yoga classes, while Scott tried to laud it over everybody, playing golf and generally enjoying himself. He also reverted to tinkering with cars. At last, he was able to realize his childhood ambition. Partly to help pass the time and partly to make some beer money, he purchased clapped out Porsches, Mercedes and Ferraris. He'd drive them as his own for a time, until they were restored. Then he'd sell them on for a healthy profit. On the proceeds, in the winter, when the damp and the wet set into West Wales, they'd both jet off to Spain and Florida, to play golf and live the high life.

* * * * *

Jimmy was still wondering about Scott's telephone call when he arrived for golf on the Wednesday morning. He was relieved to see Ginger's car in the car park. Despite their differences, the last thing he wanted was to cause a rift. They were all his pals and he needed them in the same way they needed his Irish wit, his chirpiness and on occasions his downright cussedness.

'Morning Ging,' he called out in the clubhouse changing room, omitting his usual remark.

'Oh morning Jim,' he heard Ginger growl from inside the toilet cubicle. At least they were on speaking terms Jimmy thought. He said nothing more till Stan arrived.

'Looks like it's going to be a good one,' he said to Stan, when his chubby face appeared around the changing room door. Jimmy had made a vow with himself not to mention anything about the building society account until they were all back safely in the clubhouse bar, afterwards. Hearing Stan's voice, Ginger risked vacating the haven of the toilet seat and the three of them conversed, in the middle of the changing room, as though Monday hadn't happened.

'The monthly medal is on this Saturday,' Ginger said. 'Are we going to make an appearance?' The other two looked apprehensive.

'Why, are you looking to spoil your weekend?' Jimmy replied.

'Well I expect young Lambert will want to show off again,' Ginger said, while stamping his feet into his golf shoes. 'If he wins this one, that'll be the third time this year. We can't let him get away with that.'

'Those that have, shall continue to have,' Jimmy said.

'We'll see what the others say,' Stan said. He was pulling on a blue and white check pullover. Each time he tried he kept getting his head stuck in the armhole; the other two were beginning to snigger. When Stan's head caught again, Jimmy pulled it on tighter, causing it to stick more. Jimmy was pleased to see a smile back on Ginger's face.

One by one the others arrived. Guarded insults were exchanged, partners were drawn and like men going off to battle, they trouped off in single file to the first tee. To everybody's relief, Jimmy was drawn with Colin and Toby. While they were waiting to play though and no matter how hard he tried, Jimmy still couldn't resist advising Ginger to 'look out for the water on the sixth'. Ginger grunted, then hit his first drive straight down the middle.

Very occasionally, there are days in West Wales when the setting and the climate resemble the ocean grandeur of the Caribbean. Sometimes, if the wind is in the right direction, the residue of the Gulf Stream drifts in that way. On days like that, when an open blue sky mingles with the white sandy beaches and the mustard yellow of a rape crop, you could be induced into feeling you were somewhere near paradise. Kestrels hover tantalisingly over the dunes and even golf shots appear to go straight. Let it be said, those occasions are few and very far between, but they do occur.

That day, our lads had a golf day they wouldn't forget. Ginger scored forty four points, beating his personal record by four. Jimmy, Stan and Scott also hit forty, while Colin had three two's on the par threes and Toby went round, for the first time, without losing a golf ball. Their voices positively chirped as they made their way from the eighteenth to the clubhouse. This time, winnings were paid without acrimony. Beer was consumed with haste. Food was ordered promptly and they all sat around the same table, chorusing, like the winning team at the Ryder Cup.

For two days Scott had patiently waited for just such a moment and he knew the lines he had to deliver. Two and a half pints into their luncheon fun, he calculated, was about spot on the mark. 'Now Jim,' he began, 'have you thought any more about your idea for Stan's money?' The others went quiet. Jimmy was in the middle of supping. The forty points he'd scored that morning, although he would never admit it, was near his personal best. Savouring his golf round, with the finest that Worthington could brew, was at that particular moment more important than any claptrap his mates could muster. But he also knew he had his audience in the palm of his hand. Like an actor about to deliver the final oration, he delayed his reply, dragging out the ritual of his quaffing, until he reached the final dregs. Eventually, he held up the empty pint glass like a trophy.

'Wonderful,' he said and rested the glass on the table. 'Funny you should mention that Scott, 'cause I have actually been giving the matter a lot of thought.' At that moment John arrived with their lunches.

'You lot want to shove some of those glasses out the way,' he said, with no particular manner of courtesy. It took a while for the assorted meals, all with chips, to be distributed, before Jimmy could recommence.

'As I see it Scott,' Jimmy said when John had gone away, 'we, or should I really say, Stan, should not look a gift horse in the mouth. I mean, on how many other occasions is he going to have a quarter of a million smackers in his savings account?'

'You're not still going on about that nonsense,' Ginger interrupted.

'Well it might be nonsense in your eyes Ging, but Scott and I see it as making the most of our opportunities. We're not going to steal the money. We'll just borrow it, use it for a while, then put it back. After all that's what you lot have been doing with our money for years.' Ginger was forking some chips into his mouth. He'd put too many on his fork and they were spilling on to his lap.

'Tosh!!' he replied sarcastically. 'The bank is the custodian of your money. You sign custody over when you open the account. Nobody is going to do anything illegal with your money in a bank.' He picked the errant chips off his trousers with his fingers and stuffed them into his mouth. Jimmy had been anticipating that sort of response.

'You try telling that to the customers of Barings Bank then. And what about the Equitable Life people. They didn't think anything would happen to their money either, but it did.' Ginger looked irritated.

'That's different. Anyway Scott or Stan don't want to go to jail. Nick Leeson, went to jail!'

'Oh Christ the missus would kill me,' Stan said, laughing exaggeratedly.

'She couldn't if you were in jail,' Jimmy said, chuckling.

Scott cut in. 'Just think what an opportunity this is for us to get one over on those people for a change,' he said and leaned his head over the table. 'We've got some good brains here. What a challenge it would be if we could beat the so called pundits on investment growth.' Ginger averted his eyes away from Scott, grumbled and carried on eating.

'I agree with Scott,' Jimmy began. 'What I had in mind, was that today we all go away from here and at home and in our own time, come up with an idea of how best to make the most of this little, what shall we say, windfall. Just as an exercise. Report back here on Friday with our ideas. Let's see what's possible.' They all looked at the little Irishman.

'Hey, I'm not saying I'm prepared to go along with this,' Stan said interjected. He put his knife and fork down on his empty plate and wiped his mouth with his napkin. 'It's my name that's on the account. I'd be the one that would catch it if anything went wrong.' Scott had been waiting for that.

'But you haven't done anything wrong Stan, old son,' he said. 'They're the ones, the building society, are the ones that have done the wrong. They've loused up somebody's money and they've told you, in writing, that you've got two hundred and fifty thousand quid. You've done absolutely nothing wrong. There's no need whatsoever for you to be on the defensive. They're the ones that have erred and they should be made to pay.'

'I just don't want any trouble,' Stan said.

'There won't be,' Jimmy said. 'Come on let's all try and think of a scheme by Friday. It'll be a bit of fun anyway. Something to occupy our tiny little minds for a few days. Come on Stan, just as a laugh. Let's at least go that far. You keep looking at that quarter of a million pounds against your name old son.'

And so the dye was caste.

* * * * * *

Stanley Gladstone Richards, was Cardiff born and Cardiff bred. He attended school at Canton High, two miles west of the city centre. As a youngster, he played football for Cardiff Corries and when he became too old for that, on Saturday afternoons, he travelled a mile or two down the road, to Ninian Park, to watch Cardiff City play football. His wife Rosemary, was from the slightly upper class suburb of Roath Park, two miles east of the city centre. In marrying her, Stan, in effect, crossed over the tracks and for the rest of their lives together she never let him forget it.

In Rosemary's eyes everything Stan did was never quite good enough. No matter what, no matter how trivial, his every action required some alteration to accommodate her whims. Now in his early sixties he'd learnt to live with her fastidiousness. Earlier on in their marriage, their two children, Paul and Heather, provided a distraction. But since they'd left home and he and his wife were on their own again and particularly living down there in 'West Wales, of all places,' as Rosemary often remarked, her attention was able to focus once more on Stan's shortcomings. Hence golf, three days a week, and the prolonged lunch time clubhouse session.

His career, not a glittering success by any stretch of the imagination, as a telephone engineer, was competent, attaining the position of area supervisor. He was accurate and conscientious. Unfortunately his inferiority complex prevented higher elevation, but he was well liked and a respected employee.

Until they moved to West Wales, Stan and Rosemary lived most of their married life in a substantial, Victorian, three story semi-detached house by Roath Park lake, a quarter of a mile from Rosemary's former family home. Their children attended the same school as she had and until they left for university. The family all worshipped at the Congregational Church, two hundred yards from their house. Stan though, had one vice that Rosemary knew nothing about. The guilt of it from time to time gnawed at his mind. Unbeknown to her, for twenty five years, every week, Stan indulged in his secret. If Rosemary had known about it, all hell would have broken loose. His one and only vice entailed a flutter on the horses. Never very much. His total outlay had always been five pounds. Whatever the race, whatever the temptation, five pounds was his absolute maximum. In fact Rosemary always gave him the money. From the time when they were first married, she'd handled the finances. The five pounds she gave him each week was supposed to be his beer money. 'A man's got to have money in his pocket', he'd said, the first time they sat down to work out the weekly bills. So Rosemary gave him five pounds. 'That's your lot my boy. You won't get anymore, so don't ask,' she'd said. And so every week, for twenty five years, she gave him five pounds, which at the end of the week, if it wasn't required for other purposes, Stan spent at the bookies.

On the odd occasions when he won, he was so riddled with guilt, he usually ended up buying Rosemary a present. 'Where did you get the money for this,' she would say when he brought the gift home. Most times it was a pot plant or a vase, even occasionally a jumper. 'We had a sweepstake at work and I won', was his favoured response. That evening, after golf, he was sitting at home with Rosemary, watching television, when the phone rang.

'Scott here,' the voice said excitedly, when Stan picked up the receiver.

'Oh hiya,' Stan replied. He was surprised. He didn't usually get calls from Scott. Scott and Anne tended to move in more affluent circles than Stan and Rosemary. The only time Stan would get a call from Scott, was when one of his cars was out of action and he wanted to cadge a lift to the golf course.

'Some game we had today,' Scott said. 'Haven't seen you come in with such a good score in a long while.'

'The moon must be in the right quarter,' Stan replied. 'By the law of averages it's got to happen once in a while.' Stan wasn't a particularly good golfer. His twenty handicap illustrated that. Competent was a way to sum up his play; he could get round without too many disasters. Scott and Ginger were the low handicap players. Toby could play well when the mood struck him. Colin was very accurate, but didn't hit it long, and Jimmy, well, was just Jimmy. With his swing, all things being equal, he should never score at all, but he did and often he won.

'Tell you why I was ringing,' Scott said, with the hint of excitement still in his voice. 'Anne was wondering if you and Rosemary would like to come here for dinner on Saturday night. It's been a long time since we've seen you both.' Stan couldn't believe his ears. He was sure Scott had never invited either him or Rosemary to dinner before.

'That would be very nice Scott. Just let me check with my managing director, she's sitting here.' Stan regularly referred to Rosemary as such and occasionally even as 'executive management.' The others weren't sure if he meant it as a form of sarcasm or endearment. Rosemary always felt Anne ignored her. 'I'm not wealthy or glamorous enough for her to bother with', she often said to Stan. Anyway, that evening she was so shocked by their invitation she stammered out her agreement.

'Yes we'd love to come.' Stan replied to Scott. 'Is there any special occasion to celebrate?'

'No, just your sweet company,' Scott replied. 'Oh and Stan, you hang on to that building society account until we've all had a good think about it, old son. Don't rush into owning up yet. I think Anne's got an idea she wants to tell you about.'

'Oh,' was all Stan could manage in response. He still wasn't happy about getting involved in anything underhand. By then he was wishing he'd never mentioned the letter. But it was too late now, the cat was out of the bag. 'We'll look forward to it,' Stan continued. 'What time?'

'Oh, about seven o'clock,' Scott said and rang off.

Since they had all known each other, Stan had developed a bit of a crush on Anne. Heaven knows she was attractive enough for any man to have a crush on. Blonde hair, tanned shapely figure and long legs, would give most males the goose-bumps. But Stan had it bad. Whenever she was around he got excited, tongue-tied and sometimes stammered. Anne, who was more than aware of his affection, would tease him mercilessly. And Scott noticed too. Rosemary didn't of course. She believed no other woman in the world but her would put up with Stan. 'Well that's a surprise,' Stan said when he put down the phone.

'Stan, I haven't got anything smart to wear to go there. You know what she'll be dressed like,' Rosemary said.

Stan sighed and sat back in his armchair.

CHAPTER FIVE

Toby had been worried after his visit to see the girl, Catryn. When he'd telephoned early next morning she had sounded vague, diffident, not at all like the chirpy happy, girl she'd recently become. On impulse he drove to her house. Her car was parked outside, but the front room curtains were drawn. It was just after eleven o'clock and he wondered why she wasn't in work. Twice he knocked on the front door, to no avail. He walked round to the rear of the house and tried the back door. It opened. 'Catryn,' he called out loudly as he went inside.

In the kitchen, the accumulation of two meals worth of dirty dishes remained unwashed in the sink. Cupboard doors had been left open. Two pairs of shoes, hers and the childs, were scattered across the floor. There was a sweet pungent smell in the air and he knew what that was. Dope!

One of Toby's many part time local duties was as a counsellor for young people on drugs. Catryn was one of the cases he'd helped rehabilitate. Up until then she had responded well. She'd got back on track again, if you like. 'Catryn,' he called out again and moved into the hallway. One of Mark's play-bikes was lying on its side. 'Catryn, are you in?' he shouted and started to climb the stairs. Her bedroom door was half-open, he pushed it wider and looked inside. The curtains were drawn, the same acrid smell filled the air. He walked into the bedroom and there on top of the duvet, in her bra and pants, lay Catryn, prone and asleep. 'Ach,' Toby sighed as he looked at her dishevelled form. 'Catryn come on get up,' he said and began shaking her by the shoulders. She stirred and made to push him away, then slumped back down again. He went to the bathroom, soaked a flannel and picked up a towel. 'Come on Catryn,' he said, as he rubbed the flannel on her face. 'You've got to get yourself out of this.' The water from the flannel wetted her hair and ran down her cheeks.

'Go away,' she said, spitting the water off her lips. She grabbed Toby's hand that held the flannel and pushed it away. 'Leave me alone.'

'Catryn where's Mark?' Toby said.

'He's gone to school. Joyce down the road took him. I'm not well.' There was an ashtray on the bedside table. Two joint ends were stubbed out in the bowl.

'I thought we'd been through this before. We agreed that smoking your way out of problems doesn't work. I thought we agreed about that,' Toby said. She remained lying down with her eyes closed.

'Well I've changed my mind.' The words choked out of her mouth like a smoker's cough.

Toby was sitting on the edge of the bed. 'But why? You were doing so well?' he said.

'Cos it's better this way,' she replied, half screaming. Desperately he wanted to touch, hold her, but he knew that would do no good.

'No it's not. You know that. You've got Mark. You've got your work. Surely that's better than this.'

'I haven't got my work. They don't want me any more. I couldn't work enough hours. They've got somebody who can. Someone who's not lumbered with a kid.'

* * * * *

Professor Colin Mordecai, to give him his correct title, was a boffin. He had been a lecturer in Mathematics at Cardiff University and all his life he'd had a fascination with figures. 'Figures can be proved,' he would say. 'You know where you stand with figures. With figures they either add up or they don't. If they don't you know you're wrong.'

Colin and his wife Veronica and their labrador dog, Dudley, lived in a large country house overlooking Carmarthen Bay. Twice a year the four acres of cultivated garden that sloped gently down to a sandy bay, were open to the public, to raise funds for charitable purposes. Both of them were experts in the propagation of shrubs peculiar to the salt winds of the seaside. On the two days their garden was available for public viewing, the traffic would be parked half a mile back on the roadside, much to the irritation of their neighbours. Calculators were another of Colin's fascinations. Inside the elegant nineteenth century manor house was a veritable museum of contraptions that added, divided, converted or computerised figures. On shelves, on tables, on landings, forced into every nook and cranny, all manner of calculators, large, small and some minute, were kept in perfect working order. At one time or another he would use all of them, to calculate or check his sums, quantify his theorems and debate a hypothesis. His head, like his day, was full of equations needing to be solved. Therefore, Jimmy's idea about Stan's windfall was just as much of a challenge to him as Pythagarus' theorem, or the splitting of the atom. Much as he disagreed with the principle of misappropriating money, his brain could not resist the conundrum of possibilities the problem presented. It had taxed his mind since their lunchtime session at the golf club.

Retirement hadn't retarded Colin's faculties. If anything the reverse was true. Without the daily pressure of students and lectures to confront, his brain was free to wander into areas he'd never had the opportunity to explore before. During retirement he'd become a dabbler in stock market investments. Not in the way Ginger dabbled. Ginger's financial gambling was more of a flutter. Usually an amateurish punt on some tip he'd been given, or collected through his old-boy grapevine. Professor Mordecai however, approached his speculation through mathematics. Daily he studied the Financial Times and from the diminutive print of its pink pages, he constructed charts, drew graphs and followed linears of figures, in an attempt to maximise the residue of his retirement savings.

Recently, he'd discovered a method, using algorithms, he considered almost foolproof. Hedging in futures and options, he'd found provided a pay out irrespective of whether the markets rose or fell and you could even bet on the possibilities of both at the same time. To Colin the process was magical. When he did lose money, he put it down to his own inefficiency in timing, not the basis of his system. So that evening he rang Jimmy at his home.

'Sorry to bother you Jim,' he began. Whenever Colin was unsure, he always started by apologizing. 'This idea you had at the golf club. Do you really think we could get our hands on that money?' Jimmy was halfway through his second, post dinner, brandy. That evening, his wife Iris had cooked his favourite Irish stew and while she was engrossed in the intricacies of the early evening 'soap', he was curled up on the sofa, drifting off nicely into a little shut-eye, before taking the dog out. It was a struggle therefore, to get his brain into any sort of working order in response to Colin's question.

'Well I don't think it would be a problem Colin,' Jimmy

replied hazily. 'Stan could be the problem though. It's his money and he would actually have to make the call.' Colin interrupted quickly.

'Yes, yes, I appreciate that. But wouldn't they query an amount of that nature?' Jimmy's mind was still sluggish, but gradually the cogs in his brain began to loosen.

'Not nowadays. Two hundred and fifty thousand isn't such a large amount nowadays. The average house price in the South of England is about that amount. And all these telephone accounts are computerised now. Even the voice that replies is mechanical. It's all pre-recorded.'

'H'm,' Colin said. 'I don't mean to be a nuisance on this Jim, but if we got the money out, how long do think we'd have it available to use?' Jimmy hesitated. Colin usually took very little notice of Jimmy's musings. It was unlike him to follow up one of his ideas, so this time Jimmy was careful in what he said.

'Couple of weeks, I guess. That's if we do it straight away. The longer it goes on though, the more likely it is that someone will shout for their money.'

'Couple of weeks eh,' Colin said. 'What do we do if someone shouts in that time?'

'Blame it all on Stan. Plead ignorance,' Jimmy said rather flippantly. 'No, I'm only joking. We'd have to devise a reasonable excuse. Say he was expecting some money from an aunt's will, something like that. All a big mistake. Drew it out, thinking it was his inheritance. The thing about all this is that Stan isn't the one who's made the mistake. The building society is the one that's made the mistake.'

'H'm,' Colin said. 'But you think we could use it for about a fortnight or more?'

'It's possible, if the other customer doesn't query about his money in that time,' Jimmy replied. 'With the speed the financial institutions deal with these things nowadays, I'd say we had at least that. Why, have you got an idea for an investment?'

'I'm working on it Jim. I'm sorry to have troubled you at this late hour.'

'Well let's hear about it on Friday Colin. The more ideas we can throw at Stan, the more disposed he's likely to be. But I repeat, if we're going to do it, we've got to strike while the iron's hot.'

'I'll see what I can come up with. My apologies to Iris for disturbing you,' Colin said and rang off. When Jimmy put the phone down he looked across at his wife.

'Colin sends his regards,' he said. Iris was still engrossed in the 'soap'. She nodded and didn't reply.

Colin had been at his desk in his study, active on his computer, throughout all that evening. It was his favourite room in the whole house. In there he could be alone with his computations. The study was situated on the west side, across the hallway from the other living rooms. A bay window provided a view over the garden and down the cliffs to the sea. Often, the orange glow of the most incredible sunsets would edge across his desk. And from the same direction, he could watch the approaching westerly storms, before they began battering on the sash panes of the window in front of him. The walls of the room were wood panelled and so was the floor. Shelves, bursting with books lined a back wall. Leather chairs and a leather top desk made it comfortable and moneyed in appearance. Veronica, his second wife, would never disturb him in his study and the grandchildren were similarly banished. Only Dudley was allowed in the room and he would lie under the desk at Colin's feet and sleep. Even in a dire emergency, to contact him, Veronica would buzz through on the internal phone that roamed the big old house. After speaking to Jimmy, Colin updated the data from that day's Financial Times and recalculated the adjustments to his pension nest egg.

CHAPTER SIX

The next day wasn't a golf day. Normally the six of them didn't meet up on a non-golf day. Ginger would say 'I see enough of that little Irish bastard three days a week, without having to put up with him on any other.' But after Colin's call to him the previous evening, Jimmy began to worry about Stan getting cold feet on the matter in hand. To begin with, in the clubhouse, Jimmy had suggested the idea almost as a joke; a source of amusement; something for them all to argue about over their drinks. Colin's serious involvement however, changed all that. Colin was a clever guy. They all knew his head was often in the clouds, but when he really applied himself to something, he did it for real. There were no half measures with Colin.

And then there was also Scott. They all had their opinions about Scott. To Toby, an elder of the church and a lay preacher, he was a serial adulterer, who was destined for Hell. To Ginger, he was one of his up market cronies. Someone to impress; someone to show off to. Someone he could lay out the same jingoism with; someone whose wife he'd like to get across. To Colin, there was a grudging affinity. They both loved machinery and spent hours verbally dismantling parts and refitting replacements. To Stan, well Stan was just mesmerised by Anne. She was his every desire, his schoolboy dream. So if Scott was part of the package he'd go along with it to please Anne. To Jimmy, Scott was just a laugh. But for him to ring up the other evening and get personally involved with one of his ideas was unusual. So he considered what he'd suggested was not so pie in the sky after all. Therefore, that morning, Jimmy made an excuse to call round at Stan's home.

Stan and Rosemary's house was situated at the far end of a middle class estate, about a mile and a half from the sea. Decorated immaculately, to Rosemary's pedantic taste, their retirement haven should have been a romantic idyll. But nothing ever completely satisfied Rosemary. Constantly, there was always something that needed changing. 'It looks fine to me. Why are we changing it?' Stan would often say. 'Cos it doesn't look right,' Rosemary would reply. Stan bore the brunt of her nagging, mostly with a deferential fortitude, but when it all got too much his escape was to his garage. He was quite good with his hands and carpentry had become a retirement hobby. Nothing he constructed of course was ever good enough for Rosemary's house, but he made quite acceptable cabinets, chairs, small tables and the like and he'd sell them at the local car boot sales. When Jimmy drove up to Stan's house he could see the garage door was half open. Inside, he could hear Stan's electric saw buzzing like a bee. Stan saw him approach and switched it off.

'Thought I might catch you in here, nose down, arse up,' Jimmy said.

'You're a stranger in these parts,' Stan replied.

'I know. Only come when I want something,' Jimmy said. In his hand he was carrying his pitching wedge. He held it up for Stan to see. 'I chipped it on a stone the other day. Wonder if you could put it on the grinder for me?'

'It'll cost you,' Stan said.

'Doesn't everything,' Jimmy replied. Stan took took the club from him, inspected the damage, plugged in the grinder, donned his goggles and proceeded to eliminate the scar. Sparks flew everywhere. Jimmy stood well back and watched.

'There we are. Thirty quid to you,' Stan said when he'd finished and handed the club back to Jimmy.

'Phew, bloody hell. I'll buy you a pint on Friday,' Jimmy said after inspecting the wedge. 'Colin phoned me last night,' he continued. Stan made no reply. 'Baffled me a bit he did. You know what he's like, all computors and formulas. He's much too technical for me. Anyway, it seems he's come up with this red hot plan for your money.'

'Oh I don't know about that Jim, I've told you all, I'm not looking for trouble. Rosemary would kill me if I got into any trouble.'

'There'll be no trouble Stan. Do you think Colin would get involved in anything that would cause trouble. He's a doctor or something.'

'Professor actually,' Stan said. 'But it's not his name that's on the account, Jim, it's in mine. That makes me the one that who would get the trouble.'

'All I'm saying at this juncture is just to wait and hear what he comes up with. You know how clever he is. Look what he did on his computer with that eclectic tournament for the Seniors. Brilliant it was. Don't look a gift horse in the mouth Stan. None of us get money presented to us these days. I repeat, this thing isn't your doing. If you ring up the building society today, will they give you any thanks? No. I guarantee that all you'll get is some snotty nosed girl, who won't even appreciate the trouble you've gone to in phoning her. Believe me I've dealt with these people before.'

Stan looked at him. Little did Jimmy know, but at that moment, his words about a 'gift horse' did strike home. Stan hadn't had a decent winner now, in his betting, for over six months. He could badly do with a change of fortune. And over the past few weeks Rosemary had been going on and on about wanting a new kitchen. Stan couldn't see anything wrong with the existing one. It had everything you could possibly want in a kitchen and he just couldn't afford to go laying out thousands of pounds for a change of colour scheme. He'd wanted to go away for a little holiday, but Rosemary had said. 'If we can't afford a kitchen, we definitely can't afford a holiday.'

'I know,' Stan replied to Jimmy's remarks. 'We can't break the law though. I can't take what isn't mine.'

'Of course you can't Stan. Will you just listen though to what Colin has to say. You know him, he won't lead you astray.'

'I'll think about it Jim. That's all. I'm not promising.' At that moment Rosemary came into the garage.

'There you are Stanley. I've been looking all over the place for you,' she said, ignoring Jimmy. 'You haven't forgotten we have an important appointment in town in half an hour?' Rosemary wore glasses. They were perched on the end of her nose. She looked at Jimmy over the top of them, as though he was some vermin the cat had brought in.

'No dear,' Stan replied. 'I'll be there now.' Rosemary left the garage without a word to Jimmy. Stan looked at him with a resigned, weary expression.

'Dentist appointment,' Stan said and began putting away his tools. Jimmy smiled.

'Right, I'll see you on Friday then mate,' Jimmy said. 'Don't forget what I've said. Let's at least give Colin a chance.' Stan made no reply and Jimmy headed out to his car.

To say Toby Ballard lived an active retirement would be an understatement of gigantic proportions. He was a local councilor, a magistrate, a social worker for homeless people, a returning officer for elections, the treasurer of the local lifeboat, a Scout Commissioner, and a Church Warden, amongst other things. Whatever event took place in the area, Toby would appear in one capacity or another. His wife Margaret was of a similar nature. She was also a County Golf Player and a member of the local bowls team. To find them in together, daytime or evening therefore, was an occasion you could mark on the calendar.

Before West Wales, Toby and Margaret had lived in the West Midlands, where he worked for the Fire Brigade. Since a boy it was all he ever wanted to do. Eventually he rose to the position of deputy head of a station; a role he hated. Tackling fires was what he loved. An aspect of the job he performed with gusto and heroics. He'd lost count of the number of awards he'd received for bravery. Something he would constantly put down to 'just doing my job'. In the end, because of his age, they had to force him to stop. A high ranking desk job was on offer, but that was of no interest to Toby. When they stopped him fighting fires, he packed it in, bought a boat and sailed around the world. For some of the way, Margaret sailed with him; their two boys, Tim and Gavin, who by then were in their late twenties, turned up on selected other passages during their holidays, while other friends crewed for a few legs of the voyage. But Toby sailed almost a quarter of the distance by himself. The whole trip took two and a half years and once he had been home for six months only Margaret's intervention and pleading prevented him doing it all over again. So, to stop himself from going round the bend, he immersed himself in everything that needed doing in the locality. Living by the sea, and being restricted to being a mere landlubber, sometimes made it harder to cope. Many a morning when he saw a clear horizon, the lure of the ocean would get to him. Then he had to immerse himself in one of his local tasks to hold on.

Jimmy's prattle about Stan's money had struck a chord in his mind though. Not that he gave a damn about the machinations of the financial services industry and Jimmy's vendetta on its shortcomings. Nor for that matter did he want any form of personal monetary gain. What stimulated his interest was the Scout Hall roof. The dilapidated building at the lower end of town, by the harbour, was originally nothing more than a corrugated hut. Over the years, bit by bit and mainly due to the public spiritedness of local builders, they had managed to replace the walls and the floor, but the original tin roof was still in place. Now, years of damp and regular buffeting gales had taken their toll; there were more bits of patching up than original. Finding the labour locally to replace the roof wasn't a problem. Tiles and timber were the expense and the troupe was having difficulty raising the money. A fete in the Spring had yielded a miserable sum, due to bad weather, and that year every other fund raising activity seemed to be affected by something or another.

The situation caused Toby to do something he rarely did; call in on Jimmy at his home. Like the others, three days of the little Irishman was enough to test his patience, but the thought of winter approaching, with that roof in the same condition, spurred Toby towards Jimmy's terraced house near the harbour. Originally it hadn't been much more than a two up, two down, fisherman's cottage. However, with the aid of improvement grants and a flood of incomers, who now purchased similar cottages as holiday homes, Jimmy's early nineteen fifties speculation had turned into a well maintained, respectable, little pot of gold.

Jimmy's working life was spent at sea. Well, the Irish Sea anyway. Born in Wexford, Southern Ireland, he started work on the fishing boats that put out from that town's windswept harbour. 'A miserable existence', he claimed, when he talked about it. 'Wet, smelly, backbreaking, bloody cold and hardly any pay', was his added description to anybody who listened. Later on he found work on a steamer, carrying coal back and fore to Scotland, which he maintained was only marginally better. But his big break came when he obtained a job on the Irish ferries. They came into West Wales and that's how he met his wife, Iris. Eventually they married and settled in their current home. Four children followed. Now much to Jim's gratitude they were all married and spread about the four corners of the British Isles. 'All far enough away to make it difficult for them to come sponging off me every week, thank God,' he would add.

Iris answered the front door when Toby rattled the highly polished brass knocker. It always amazed Toby that a woman as large as Iris would marry 'a little squirt like Jimmy'. Iris was at least six foot, to Jimmy's five foot five and whereas Jimmy couldn't be much more than nine stone, Iris must have been at least fourteen. She wasn't really fat, it was just that she was about twice as big as Jimmy. 'Is he in, my dear?' Toby asked, before Iris had a chance to say anything. She was wearing a red jumper, on which a string of decorative pearls hung, and a green plaid skirt. Her skin was clear, her brown hair, still almost untroubled by grey and her figure, allowing for her size and age, remarkably well kept. Not at all what you would expect if you'd met Jimmy by himself.

'He is. Guess where?' Iris replied.

'Around the back,' Toby said. She nodded her head and Toby set off, along the pavement to a lane at the end of the terrace, which provided the rear access to the properties. There, each house had a garage of sorts. Jimmy had converted half of his into a loft for his racing pigeons. Toby hammered on the garage door with his fist.

'I don't know how your neighbours put up with the racket these damn birds of yours make,' he said, when Jimmy slid the door aside.

'They don't squawk as much as some of the women round here,' Jimmy replied. 'You wouldn't believe what I hear up here.' He was dressed in a set of blue overalls. On his head was a blue baseball cap, liberally splattered with what looked like pigeon excreta. Jimmy guided Toby up a homemade staircase to the pigeon loft. There, in a wire cage, Jimmy's pride and joy, fluttered and cooed enthusiastically.

'This lot must cost a pretty penny to keep James,' Toby said. Jimmy smiled, his green eyes sparkled like a pair of emeralds.

'It's a completely self supporting venture,' Jimmy replied. 'This dovecote contains the finest racing pigeons in Pembrokeshire. There's the prize money I win. Then I breed and sell, and you know Tobe, I even occasionally have the odd bet with the other racers.' The smile grew wider.

'You're bloody incorrigible,' Toby said. 'You'll never go to heaven.'

'I know. That's why I intend to have a good time while I'm down here.'

Toby laughed. 'Look Jim,' he said. 'What I've come about is this business of Stan's illicit money you keep prattling on about. I'm not interested in how you're going to do it or whatever. That doesn't concern me. In fact in my position I'd prefer not to know.' Jimmy said nothing, his smile just broadened, so Toby continued. 'It's just that I'm sure you've noticed that the Scout Hall needs a new roof. The truth of the matter is we haven't got the money to do it.'

'Ah now.' Jimmy began, still smiling. 'The works of the devil are tolerated if it's all in a good cause, is that it Tobe?' Toby sighed.

'Well let's just say it's looked on more leniently. A sinner who repents and does good for others is always forgiven.' Toby twirled the curled ends of his moustache with the fingers of his right hand and looked Jimmy straight in the eye. 'Come on Jim, you know what it's like round here. There's nowhere much for the kids to go at the best of times. At least if we can herd them into the Scout Hall a couple of times a week there's a chance they might start off with some of the right values.'

Jimmy scratched his head through his baseball cap. 'As I said before, the problem's going to be in persuading Stan. Getting our hands on the money, or doing something useful with it, won't be a problem with all you clever dicks on board. It's convincing Stan and making sure he doesn't tell his missus is the difficult bit. If he tells her the baby will be dead in the water. That's why it's important we all butter him up tomorrow.' The pigeons were becoming active. While Jimmy and Toby were talking they'd begun to fly at the wire cage, flapping their wings and squawking.

'This lot are getting restless.' Toby said and stood back.

'They're itching to get out and fly Tobe. Highly trained they are. Champing at the bit for the starter's gun.'

Toby looked at the expression on Jimmy's face and smiled. 'I'd just be happier about it all if the money was being used for a good cause Jim.'

'Well, I repeat, the whole thing starts off with Stan. He's got to be our target tomorrow at golf. Let him win if necessary. If we can't persuade Stan, you can forget your new roof.'

* * * * *

In that part of the country the prevailing westerly wind is a dominant factor in much of what you do outdoors. On the Friday, gusts buffeted the golf course like the slipstream of a passing lorry, making a pullover a necessity. The course, being a links type is built on sand and has the advantage of drying out fairly quickly after rain. In summer, the hard pressed green-keeping staff save time, and manpower, by letting the rough off the fairway grow long. At that time of year, therefore, any errant shot is usually severely punished and often results in a lost ball. Jimmy rarely encounters such problems as he hits a golf ball fairly straight and Stan, being steady, is much the same. The others, however, do tend to spread it about a bit and at such times tempers can get frayed.

That morning the round started with everybody in good humour. The other five, knowing they were trying to keep in Stan's good books, ignored long running points of contention and made their best efforts to sound agreeable. Stan was partnered with Jimmy and Colin. Jimmy winked at the others, behind Stan's back, after he had driven off the first tee. Into the round Jimmy and Colin engaged Stan in a constant dialogue about his favourite subject, sport. By the fifth hole, the format of the England cricket team, the current state of football and the shortcomings of Welsh rugby had all been dissected, analysed and debated. Uncharacteristically, Jimmy even gave Stan some short putts. 'It's only a game,' he was heard to utter when conceding on one occasion. Colin looked on in amazement.

Now, whether it was the uninterrupted chatter, or the shock of not having to make some vital putts, or even maybe the argument Stan had that morning with Rosemary about a new kitchen, we'll never know. But suddenly, and without warning, on the sixth tee, Stan's game began to disintegrate. They'd had their usual break for natural causes, then Stan sliced his drive into much the same locality as Ginger had found the other day. The crosswind accentuated his slice, only his ball didn't quite make the cliffs. Instead it plummeted like an injured bird into two foot high grass, beyond the adjacent fifth fairway.

'Don't worry about that, play another,' Jimmy said instantly.

'I can't do that. I'll have to look for it first.' Stan said. 'It won't be fair on the others. We're playing for money.'

'Don't worry about them, we won't tell them, will we Colin?' Jimmy said winking across at Colin. Colin said nothing, just nodded his head.

'No, I can't do that,' Stan said. 'I'll play another one as a provisional. But I'll have to go over and look for the first one.' And so Stan played another ball, which like an arrow, went straight down the middle. Then he went over to the rough ground to look for the original, with Jimmy chastising him all the way 'about being silly'. 'I can't cheat, not on my pals,' Stan said as they walked over. And after a few minutes searching, he found his first ball. It was deeply buried in a jungle of matted wet, long, grass, almost undetectable, for the twisted and curled vegetation encompassing it.

'Why don't you leave it and play your second? You're in good shape there,' Jimmy said, anticipating what was going to happen next.

'I can't do that Jim. You know the rules. If you find it you've got to play it.'

The three of them surveyed the permutations of extracting the little white object from its tangled lie. From whatever angle they looked, the task looked nigh impossible, so Jimmy spoke again.

'Look Stan, we'll just say we couldn't find it. Go and play your second. Nobody's going to see it here,' Colin kept nodding in agreement.

'I just couldn't do that Jim. It's the etiquette of the game isn't it.' The other two looked resigned. The choice of club required to extract the ball from its lair provided a long topic of conversation. Colin reckoned a pitching wedge would do it. 'Give you some distance, if you manage to get it out,' he said, attempting to apply mathematical calculations to the matter.

'I think you'd be better off with a brush cutter,' Jimmy said jokingly.

Eventually Stan chose a sand wedge. Neither of the other two agreed, but they were not about to upset their man further, so a sand wedge it was. Stan stood, pondering the distance to the nearest flat, clear patch of the fifth fairway, then took a couple of practise swings. Making contact with the stringy, long grass, nearly dislocated his wrists, even without hitting the ball. Then he bounced up and down on the balls of his feet, trying to create enough bodily momentum to hack it out. His first real effort of a proper shot, made no contact with the ball whatsoever, although it shifted a chunk of grass, thick enough to feed a goat on for a day. Retaking his tiptoed position, he lined up for another go. Jimmy interrupted. 'Why don't you leave it Stan. You're not going to score on this hole. Just pick it up, play your provisional and we can get onto the next hole. The others are on the tee.' By then Ginger, Toby and Scott were watching all of this from the sixth tee and waiting to play.

'I'll not be beaten by it,' Stan said. 'It's only a golf ball. Question of mind over matter. If I can just get it out from here I'll feel better about it.' And he swung again, and again and again. Everything else around the ball moved, but the little white object remained obstinately motionless. Sweat began to pour off his brow. The other two stood well back to avoid the lumps of grass, which constantly flew by them.

'Fore!' Ginger bellowed from the sixth tee.

'Come on Stan, leave it, you'll injure yourself,' Jimmy said as Stan kept swinging.

'According to David Leadbetter's video, if I hold the club open at this angle,' Stan demonstrated, showing the open face of his sand wedge. 'It should come out no matter what the lie.' Stan replaced the club back on the grass and attempted more heaves. Still the ball wouldn't move. By then he'd cleared quite a large area of grass around it. His face had become a lather of perspiration; blades of grass and bits of foliage were stuck to his pullover; his wrists, arms and hands were beginning to ache.

'I should ask for your money back on that video if I were you Stan,' Jimmy said.

'I just don't understand it. He was quite clear in what he said. I practised it for an hour in the garden the other night and it worked there every time.'

'Fore!' They heard Ginger bellow again.

'Come on Stan. Let's go,' Jimmy repeated

Stan was still adamant his theory would work. More agricultural hacks were attempted, more perspiration and grass flew in the wind. By then the other two had walked on to where their golf balls lay. In the meantime Ginger played his drive, ignoring Jimmy and Colin, who were standing in the middle of the fairway, attempting their second shots. Ginger's ball bounced past Jimmy, nearly hitting him, just as he was about to play. He turned round and stuck two fingers in the air, back at Ginger.

The seventh tee is adjacent to the sixth green. 'Don't you buggers know the etiquette of the game,' Ginger shouted when he reached the green.

'Don't you!' Jimmy retorted. 'You shouldn't hit a shot when someone's in front of you trying to play.'

'You're allowed five minutes for a lost ball, then you should either call the game behind through, or move on.'

'It wasn't a lost ball. Stan could see his ball, he just couldn't get it out.'

Ginger marched over to the tee, his face glaring. 'So what are we supposed to do, stand there all fucking day while Stan practices his technique.' Stan looked sheepish.

'Acquire a little patience. You're not the only person on this course,' Jimmy said.

Ginger stalked back to the green. Stan, Jimmy and Colin took their drives in silence, but the spell had been broken. Any chance of a peaceful, argument free round, was gone. Stan's shirt was soaked with sweat. He wiped his brow and gulped water before attempting his drive. They could still hear Ginger grumbling away to his two partners behind them on the green. The rest of the round was a series of disasters. They'd all lost their rhythm; the incident had upset their composure. Thereafter, every swing became an ungainly lunge. Golf balls flew in all directions. Very few in the direction they were aimed. Stan hardly scored another point; the others fared little better. Scott and Toby who were not really involved in the fracas, were affected by Ginger's agitated mentality. For the six of them, it was a round of golf to forget. When they gathered on the eighteenth, Ginger stormed off the green. 'I don't know why I play with you fuckers,' he said, slamming his putter into his golf bag.

'Well let's all go and have a drink and forget about it,' Jimmy said, subtly winking at Ginger, trying to remind him of their pact. Ginger however, was too deep in his own mire of self pity, to pick up any nuances from Jimmy.

Stan was feeling abashed, having caused the altercation. 'Look I'm sorry I held you up Ging,' he said. 'My mind was elsewhere. Rosemary's been going on about a new kitchen and I spent ten quid on a David Leadbetter video and that shot worked perfectly in the garden. It's me you should blame not the others.'

'H'h', Ginger grunted. 'Well all that waiting about broke up my tempo completely.' On any other day Jimmy would have certainly made some sarcastic crack about Ginger's tempo, but that day he was out to keep the peace.

'Let's go and have a drink and think about something nice, like Stan's quarter of a million pounds,' Jimmy said. Ginger grunted again. The others all kept their heads down and together they trudged off to the clubhouse, not saying very much. In the locker room Jimmy kept pointing at Stan, behind his back, to the others. Ginger who wasn't that fussed about the idea anyway tried to ignore him. In the bar, drinks were purchased and they settled at their usual table. Scott had cleaned up most of the money at the golf, the others hardly figuring at all.

'Now guys, have we been able to give any thought to our little enterprise?' Jimmy began after an initial bout of supping.

'You're not still harping on about that are you?' Ginger cut in.

'Why shouldn't we give you financial buggers a run for your money. You've never given us poor suckers anything.' Jimmy knew very well that such a remark would rile Ginger into some form of response.

'What's that supposed to mean?' Ginger replied irritably.

'Well you don't do you. What about the millions of pounds you banks have floating round in the clearing system? Days go by without you paying us a penny. You lot earn millions on that.'

'What are you on about?' Ginger said, picked up his pint and took a large slurp, to try and appease his aggravation.

Jimmy had made his opening though. 'Nowadays it doesn't take three days to clear a cheque, it's all done electronically. So why is it three days before you can draw on a cheque you pay in and how much money are your lot making on it in the meantime? Complete rip off if you ask me. If it was anybody else but a bank, they'd be accused of fraud.'

Ginger put his pint down on the table and thought for a minute. He was debating whether to respond or not, but the bait Jimmy dangled was just too much of a temptation. 'The clearing system has to be paid for Jim.'

'Cor, they earn more than that on the balances overnight. Daylight bloody robbery it is. In France you can draw on the money next day. If they can do it there why can't we here? That's all I'm saying. I'm not suggesting we steal Stan's money. I'm just saying we should borrow it for a while. Use it to make a bit, then give it back, just like your mates do.' The others all sniggered.

'Your argument has some economic validity,' Colin cut in. He rubbed the side of his nose as he talked; a habit he had when his mind really got into something. During his lecturing days he wore away a sore patch on the right side of his nose doing the very same thing. 'As I see it,' he said, continuing to rub. 'At the moment that money is earning nothing for anybody but the building society. It's not Stan's money, so when it's discovered he'll get no benefit. The person whose money it is, at the moment isn't getting any benefit either and so, as Jimmy says, the only people who are benefiting from the money is the building society. Technically it's part of their liquid assets.'

'There you are Mister Clever Clogs, see,' Jimmy said pointing at Ginger. 'You listen to the professor.'

'But they're going to have to pay the right person the interest, from day one eventually,' Ginger said looking at Colin, then taking another large swig of his beer.

'Oh indeed,' Colin replied. 'But in the meantime, as Jimmy says, theoretically the money at the moment is theirs to use. I mean the real owner might have wanted to withdraw it by now, but he hasn't had the facility to do so, 'cause the money isn't in his name. He hasn't the benefit of the amenity value of the money, so Jim has a good point.' Jimmy nodded his head in an exaggerated gesture at Ginger. The others remained silent.

'I understand you have some ideas about investing the money?' Jimmy said looking at Colin.

Colin rubbed the side of his nose again. 'Well they're only ideas.' He looked up. All the others were now looking at him. 'Nowadays, you can invest in the market if it rises or falls. In the old days when you bought some shares and they went down you lost money. Now if you keep a close eye on the market, you can invest on a fall in price as well as a rise. For something like this, where we only may have the money for a short time, like a few weeks, it's a good thing to do. You can even specify a date to get out, which would suit this admirably. Futures and options, it's called. It's a specialist thing, but I've been trying it out myself now, for about nine months and it does work, if you're careful. You have to keep monitoring it every day though.' Colin sat back and took a sip of his beer.

Jimmy's eyes lit up. 'Excellent. There, can you beat that mister bank manager?' he said and looked again hard at Ginger. All eyes turned to Ginger. His status as a financial guru was now under challenge, he felt he had to suggest something, if only to hang on to his reputation.

'That's very interesting Colin,' he began tentatively. 'Certainly an idea worth considering.' He drained the remaining beer from his glass, belched and sat back. 'Last week I had a tip from an old school chum. He's the managing director now of a chemical company, in Hampshire. First class brain.' The others looked at each other knowingly. 'The company's going public in a couple of weeks, it'll all be in the FT,' Ginger added pompously. 'It's a new issue, an IPO. If we got in on the ground floor, we could sell next day and make a big profit. Mum's the word on this mind. I wouldn't have said anything, 'cept I know you all so well. You mustn't say anything to anybody though, or you'll blow it.' He looked at Jimmy. He knew telling Jimmy anything was like printing it in the West Wales Gazette; the whole of the county would know about it by the end of the week. 'All this gassing's made me thirsty. Anyone else for another?' They all finished their pints and headed to the bar. Once they'd ordered food, they reconvened back at their table.

'I've got a friend who dabbles in currency,' Scott said when they'd all sat down again. Walking five miles round a golf course and the excitement of what they were talking about had made him warm. He began to remove the red V-neck pullover he'd been wearing. Underneath, he sported a gaudy, canary yellow shirt that clashed horribly with the pair of turquoise slacks he had on. Stan, who was sitting opposite him lifted up his arms in mock horror, to shield his eyes. The others laughed.

'Your missus been buying your clothes again,' Jimmy said. Scott fingered his shirt collar and sniggered.

'What we could do with the money,' he continued, without responding to the jibes, 'is buy into a currency. At the moment euros have a better exchange rate than the pound. We could open an account with it, in say somewhere like Spain, then transfer back the original amount, leaving the profit for us to spend when we are next in that country.'

'If you did that you'd be transferring the same amount back. There'd be no profit,' Ginger scoffed and took a slurp of his beer. Toby was enjoying all this. He'd made no comment in response to all these suggestions. He just laughed and guffawed at each one of them.

'You'd have to leave the money for a week or so,' Scott replied. 'Watch the currency movements, do it when the time is right. There's a different buying and selling price anyway.'

'Oh, I don't know about that,' Ginger said mockingly.

'They're only ideas Ging,' Jimmy added quickly. 'At this juncture we just wanted ideas. They can all be amended to suit the needs at the time. What about you Stan, you're the one with the money?'

Stan shook his head. 'I don't know Jim. I'm still not sure if I want to get involved. The missus does all this financial malarkey. I've said before she'd kill me if she knew about this.'

'Toby?' Jimmy said, looking across at him.

'Don't involve me in your skullduggery. I may have to be on the Bench when you lot come up before the beak. The less I know the better. All I do know is that the Scout Hall needs a new roof. If you spend your ill gotten gains on that, there's a chance you may go to the Open Prison at Gloucester, rather than the 'Scrubs'. For a few moments they all went silent and supped on their beer.

'What about you little man?' Scott said. 'What's your idea?' Jimmy took a second draw of his pint and the others waited.

'Well now my friends,' he began. 'I have a friend across the water, who knows a man, who knows another man, who owns a racehorse.' They all groaned. 'Now this wee fellah tells me that this horse is being prepared, very quietly, for a big race at Kempton Park and they reckon he's an absolute cert. Better than Shergar.' Sarcastic laughter resounded round the table.

'Oh bloody hell, look out,' Stan said. Just then, John brought the food.

CHAPTER SEVEN

Indulging themselves in golf on a Monday, Wednesday and Friday, meant Scott, Stan and occasionally Toby were usually under standing orders on a Saturday to take their wives out shopping and often lunch. Colin didn't get involved in such frivolities, being too busy with his wife at the weekend, cultivating their garden. Ginger's wife would never take her husband shopping anywhere, as he would embarrass her to death with his bombastic nature and Jimmy, well Jimmy did what he wanted to do anyway. Scott didn't actually shop with Anne. Her spending capacity was far too extravagant for his blood pressure. Facing the Visa bill once a month was enough of a nightmare, without actually seeing the money disappearing, bit by bit, before his eyes. Their usual arrangement was that he would drop her in town and then go on elsewhere to sort out the spare parts he needed for his various automobiles, amongst other things. Later, they'd meet up for lunch in one of the smart restaurants near the harbour. There, only the crutch of alcohol prevented his apoplexy, as Anne recounted her purchases over their meal.

That morning the day was bright and clear. A southerly breeze had blown away yesterdays cloud. It was a day for summer dresses, light shirts and slacks. On those rare occasions when the weather obliged the town adopted the ambiance of a small, balmy, Mediterranean port. Boats drifted leisurely in and out of the harbour. Tourists strolled nonchalantly along the narrow streets, garbed in anything from shorts to full hiking gear. Children in prams sucked on ice creams. Pedestrians walked everywhere but on the pavement. Whilst the motorists drove round and round, bad temperedly looking for somewhere to park.

Stan had left Rosemary in the dress shop, pondering over which of the six outfits they agreed on would suit her best for the evening's soirée at Scott's house. 'I'm happy with any of those. You decide,' he said when he became weary of his wife's indecision. 'I just want to nip down to Smith's. I'll be back in a few minutes.'

Now, there are only three main shopping streets in town, so it's not unusual to bump into someone you know. Halfway down

High Street, Anne spotted Stan walking in front of her. She scurried to catch up. 'Stan,' she said, when she was alongside. 'You're just the man I'm looking for.' He turned, to be greeted by Anne's best gushing smile.

'Anne, how nice to see you,' he stuttered. Her effervescence threatened to overpower him; being close up to her was a rare event. She placed her hand on his arm. She was wearing a red dress, with lots of cleavage, displaying a burnished all-over tan. Her legs were bare and, as far as Stan could see, no bra either. A pair of cream sandals completed the summery effect.

'Stan, can you give me five minutes?' Her smiling blue eyes illuminated the tanned face.

Five minutes, Stan thought, I'd give her the rest of my life if I could. 'Of course,' he replied.

'Follow me,' she said, still holding onto his arm. She guided him through the maze of pavement shoppers to one of the narrow little side streets, repeating all the way, 'I promise you this won't take long.' She stopped outside a shop with small, mullion squared window panes; a shop Stan had never noticed before. The window display was set back, so you almost had to put your nose up against the glass to see anything inside. Above the window, was a fascia sign with the words 'Ooh-La-La' painted florally in blue letters on a red background. Stan was already beginning to feel warm. Having Anne next to him, holding onto his arm, was enough on its own to induce a roaring temperature, but on this occasion his mind was running wild as well.

'It's Scott's birthday next week,' Anne began breathlessly. 'I want to wear something as a treat, you know, something that'll turn you men on. Don't worry, just the thought of it will be too much for him. I've got an idea of the type of thing I want, but if I had a man's confirmation, I'd know I had the right item. It'll only take five minutes.' Before he could begin to formulate a reply Anne had dragged him in through the shop door. Suddenly he was standing in the middle of the tiny emporium, surrounded by slinky bras, panties, knickers and all manner of other garments he'd never seen before in his life. Anne was holding onto his left arm as though they were husband and wife. From behind a lace curtain, a nubile twenty something, with shiny, jet black hair, bare waist, studded belly button, tank top and mini skirt appeared. Stan felt more uncomfortable by the second.

'I'm looking for some underwear to turn my husband on,' Anne said to the girl, who looked at Stan, smiled, then delved into the bottom half of the glass fronted counter. From it, she extracted numerous bras, panties, basques and suspender belts; some lace, some with straps, others with garters. Anne held each of them up in front of Stan's face, felt the texture, modelled them next to her body, stroked or crumpled each one with her hands, and each time asked Stan what he thought. Mostly he could only nod. His verbal replies alternated between 'fine', and 'Oh yes'.

'I think I'll try these,' Anne said holding up a black lace bra, panties and a suspender belt. 'What do you think Stan? Can you see me in these?' She held the bra up against her chest, then down below, the panties and the belt.

Stan could hardly look. 'Oh yes,' he repeated shakily.

'Are they all right?' He nodded back his affirmation. Anne handed the garments back to the girl, who wrapped them up, then smiled at Stan while Anne signed the Visa receipt. Soon they were outside on the pavement.

'You've been an angel,' Anne said planting a kiss on Stan's cheek. 'Without you I wouldn't have got the right thing. I needed to see the expression on a man's face first. Now you won't be late tonight will you?'

When they parted Stan wandered slowly in a daze back to the dress shop, where Rosemary was waiting impatiently. 'Where the hell have you been?' was her greeting. He'd completely forgotten whatever it was he wanted from Smith's. Three quarters of the way home Stan suddenly remembered, he hadn't actually wanted anything from Smith's. Smith's was next to the betting shop. Needing to visit Smith's was the excuse he gave to Rosemary each week, once he was sure she was engrossed in something else. Then he would place his weekly wager. He was angry with himself. That week, a horse was running at Chepstow at fifty to one. By his limited evaluation, it might have a chance. Now it was too late. He wouldn't dare ring from home; Rosemary might hear. Suddenly he thought of Jimmy's words, about his tip from Ireland. If only, Stan wondered. No I'd never have the courage, he told himself. When they got into the house Rosemary's first words were, 'Oh this kitchen does depress me.'

To escape from more domestic aggravation he spent the afternoon in the garden. Mowing, digging, weeding, raking. Anything and everything physical, to try to rid his mind and body of his lust for Anne. At five o'clock, on the pretext of checking the cricket scores, he came indoors. Instead of cricket, he turned the Ceefax pages on the television to the racing results. And there, to complete his misery, he saw his horse, 'Redoubtable', had come home first at Chepstow, at fifty five to one. Stabbing the remote off in anger he heard Rosemary call out.

'Don't forget Stan, we're going to Anne and Scott's tonight.'

* * * * *

Jane Kirby was the co-owner of The Ship Inn, a boisterous little pub, by the harbour wall that provides a watering hole for a rowdy crowd of locals and tourists. Tall, very busty, with long blonde hair, Jane was Scott's primary local female dalliance. The Ship had become his local since moving to the area. Its bawdy clientele provided ideal company for his almost perpetual dialogue of one-upmanship. Theirs had been an almost permanent affair from the moment Jane revealed to him her well-rounded breasts, while stooping to pull the first pint of Real Ale he'd consumed at her hostelry. She was a tough as teak Yorkshire lass who'd moved to the West Wales Coast when her first marriage culminated in divorce. With her share of the divorce settlement she'd bought a half share in The Ship from Bill Summerbee, the existing landlord. At the time Summerbee was on his financial knees. Over the years he'd managed to drink away most of the pub's profits. An ex-sea captain, he and Jane soon shacked up together, but in time the drink took it's toll and as the years rolled on he faded more into the background, leaving Jane to run the place. Being ten years older than her and almost an alcoholic also caused a decline in Bill's sexual powers, which made Scott a welcome visitor to Jane's home.

Bill also owned a little boat and most mornings, at the crack of dawn, when the tide was right, and after seeing to the early morning delivery by the brewery lorry, he would set off into the bay for a days fishing. Later in the morning, having dropped Anne off in town to shop, Scott would make The Ship Inn his first call. The bar wasn't open that early and Jane was almost always still attired in her night clothes. It therefore didn't take long or a lot of effort to manoeuvre themselves into a promiscuous entanglement. The two of them seemed to give each other immense satisfaction and its distraction helped Scott bear the burden of his wife's expensive shopping forays a little more pragmatically.

'We ought to go away somewhere and do this in a more relaxed manner,' Scott said, that morning, as they lay in each other's arms afterwards. She nuzzled his shoulder with her lips, while her hand wandered down his chest.

'When would I have time to go away,' Jane said. 'If I left the pub for a day, Bill and his cronies would drink away all the profit.'

'What about your son, couldn't he take over for a few days?' Jane had two sons by her first marriage. One was a Rugby League player in the North of England, the other worked in a nightclub in nearby Carmarthen and spent his days on the golf course.

'He could, but Bill would never take orders from him.' Her hand reached a spot somewhere around Scott's groin. He gasped a lung full of air before he spoke again.

'I wondered perhaps we could have a couple of days in Spain,' he panted. 'There's a golfing trip coming up. Anne won't want to come. We could make a twosome. It's only four days. Come on what do you say?' His breathing was becoming laboured.

'Oh Scott I don't know,' she said. 'We're so busy at the moment. The summer season's just getting going.' Slowly Jane's lips moved down Scott's body to where her hand had been. When they reached his swollen member, talk for both of them became impossible. Scott moaned joyously. At that moment all he could visualise was Jane doing that to him on some sun kissed Iberian beach.

Like a young man, about to go on his first date, Stan was as nervous as hell as he and Rosemary drove over to Scott and Anne's house that evening. So much so, he'd accidentally banged his head on his car when ducking into the driver's seat, before they set off. A small lump had formed on his forehead and all the way there he kept fussing with it in the driver's mirror.

'Who do you think is going to be looking at that?' Rosemary

berated every time he glanced up to the mirror. 'I just hope my dress is suitable. I expect Anne will be in some exotic creation,' she repeated at least five times during the journey. In the dress shop she had settled for a purple, floral print dress in classical style, which made her look very smart.

The approach to Scott's house had been renovated to replicate something out of the American TV series 'Dallas'. Tall, black, wrought iron gates and a fence, with the top spikes tipped in gold paint, announced the entrance. A wide tarmacadam drive led to a stone water fountain, which acted as a turnaround, by a pillared portico. In its modest surroundings of ordinary middle class homes, it all looked completely over the top. Strategically placed outside a massive double garage were Scott's Porsche Boxer, with the number plate SL 1 and Anne's huge up-market SUV. After assisting Rosemary from the car, Stan approached the highly veneered, double front doors with trepidation. Scott answered a door chime, which played a mini instrumental version of Queen's 'Bohemian Rhapsody'. He stood in the open doorway looking resplendent in a yellow and blue polkadot shirt and red slacks.

'Well there you are. You found us then? Rosemary you look divine,' Scott said before kissing her cheek. She handed him a bottle of champagne. Stan was clutching a posy of flowers he'd bought for Anne. The scent of Scott's cologne nearly overpowered him as he walked past. 'Stanley you old devil, I didn't know you cared,' Scott remarked, when he spotted the flowers.

Anne was waiting in the centre of a spacious marble tiled hall, directly under a dramatic candle bulb chandelier. The reflected light accentuated the highlights she'd added to her blonde hair and sparkled on the sequins of the shimmer effect, dark blue bodice top she wore. Tight black trousers and a tall pair of black, high heeled shoes, completed the outfit. Stan held out his offering of flowers and in his nervous state nearly fell into her arms to receive his welcome kiss. Her stoop revealed the bra she had purchased that morning. 'Are these for me? They're my favourites,' she said.

Once they were comfortably inside Scott led them all on a guided tour of 'Lambert Towers' as he continually referred to their home. Anne kept close to Stan, gently nudging or taking his arm when they changed direction. Rosemary repeated, 'Oh how wonderful,' at every audacious household fitting. 'That's just what I want Stan to put in for me. Stan are you looking?' Scott answered most of Rosemary's double talk with the phrase, 'her ladyship wanted that.' Eventually they settled in a lounge of Hollywood movie set proportions. Tall glasses, jugs of Pimms and Bucks Fizz and assorted nibbles were on an adjacent table. Anne sat next to Stan on a white leather settee, continually crossing and uncrossing her legs. The soft swishing sound the material of her trousers made, was, for Stan, another step down the road to purgatory. Scott had his own special armchair, which swivelled and tilted on his command, at the press of a button on the side. Rosemary was ensconced on another expensive chair, making animated, hypocritical, small talk about their 'beautiful home', which was 'just as she had always wanted hers'. 'Are you listening Stan,' she would add, after Scott had described the practicalities of the installation of each item. Stan would just nod while desperately trying keep his hands from touching Anne's body.

'I understand you've had a little windfall,' Anne whispered to him, while Rosemary and Scott were talking interior decorations.

'Mum's the word on that.' Stan replied quietly, nodding in Rosemary's direction. Anne shuffled up closer and put her hand on his thigh.

'It's just that Scott said you may be looking for ideas,' her eyes widened, her smile broadened, she was talking in a whisper. 'I've got one that might interest you. Perhaps we can meet up, somewhere alone, so I can tell you about it.' Her hand moved on his thigh, his blood pressure rose several metres. He gulped, swallowed hard but no words came out; all he could manage was a nod of his head in acknowledgment.

Throughout their meal, and for the rest of that evening, Anne paid Stan particular attention. To serve him food, she would bend close, letting her hair brush his cheek. The view he was given confirmed she was wearing the black bra he'd seen that morning. When Anne sat down to eat, her knee rested permanently against his leg. Constantly he kept looking across at Rosemary. Fortunately, Scott was entertaining her with a barrage of nonsense about house fittings. When the time came to leave and while Scott was helping Rosemary on with her jacket, Anne whispered in Stan's ear, 'Now don't forget,' and winked at him. On his way out Scott also winked at him and gave him a thumbs up.

All the way home Rosemary kept up a constant prattle about Scott and Anne's house. 'Yes dear' and 'no dear' were his intermittent replies while his imagination played with the possibilities of Anne's invitation. On Sunday morning a Church visit was an essential. He hoped prayer and submission would drive all those carnal thoughts from his mind. After lunch he took to his garden. Thrashed his way through a jungle of weeds, cut a hedge and re-mowed the lawn, but still the mental agony continued. By bedtime, he'd decided not to go to golf next morning.

CHAPTER EIGHT

Jimmy usually spent Sunday mornings either training or racing his pigeons. After breakfast he drove north, with the birds in boxes, to an open spot on the coast road, south of Fishguard. On a windswept cliff top bend, he stopped the car, removed the boxes and with a flourish opened the cage for them to escape. 'Home my beauties,' he called as they winged skywards.

Afterwards he sat in the front seat of his beat up old Mercedes, lit a cigarette and took in the view. Ahead, the rocky coastline meandered around indented bays until it reached the white projection of the lighthouse at Strumble Head. Hedgerows, brightly coloured with thrift, arabis and michaelmas, dazzled in a riot of early summer extravaganza. Cliff top fields of barley, wheat and corn edged down to innumerable rocky coves. Fulmars, shag and choughs dived and whirled in the blue overhead. Crests of foamy white sea water splashed up against the jutting cliffs. 'Paradise,' Jimmy said to himself while puffing on his cigarette.

In a sheltered cove further along the road was a village, well just about a village. Six small cottages, mostly holiday homes, a pub and a farm at the top of the hill, to be more exact. He started the Mercedes and drove down to the pub. The Myrtle Inn was his Sunday watering hole. A lime and mortar roof, rotting wooden window shutters and faded, pale cream paint work presented a rustic exterior. Inside some attempt at modernisation, in terms of seating and tables, was evident, but apart from that the rest of the bar had retained its nineteenth century clutter and charm. Dark furniture and maritime related ornaments prevailed. Despite the warmth of the day, a coal fire welcomed at the far end.

In the corner, at a small table by the fire, yet close to the bar, sat the man Jimmy had come to see. Dougal Slattery had a pint of real ale and a whisky chaser in front of him and was reading the Sporting Life. With tousled red hair, he was dressed in an old, heavily darned fisherman's sweater, a pair of dirty brown corduroy trousers and green wellington boots. Lying on the floor, asleep at his feet, was a grey whippet dog.

'Have you let those damn pigeons go?' Dougal said when Jimmy stood in front of him.

'I have,' Jimmy said. 'They'll be home before me now. Will you have another?' He asked pointing at Dougal's drinks.

'Of course I'll bloody well have another,' Dougal Slattery said, passing up his whisky glass. Years ago, Dougal had worked with Jimmy on the Irish Sea ferries. They'd been mates on board for the best part of twenty years. Dougal had also had married a Welsh girl and settled locally. On retirement he'd purchased a cottage twenty yards from The Myrtle Inn, acquired a fishing boat and trawled the adjacent little bays for mackerel, crab and lobster. Whereas Jimmy's family in Ireland had all died or moved on, Dougal still had brothers and cousins alive in the South, and one of them knew a man, who knew another man, who owned a race horse. Jimmy bought a pint for himself and a whisky for Dougal.

'What sort of time have you had this week?' he said to Dougal, as he sat down alongside him at the table.

'Och they've had me this week right enough, they have,' Dougal replied folding up his Sporting Life. 'There was a little beauty at Bath on Monday. But she came in fifth, just ran out of steam in the last furlong. Wednesday, I won a pony on a cert at Sandown. Friday I went down the pan with a one legged donkey at York. Lost twenty notes on that one.'

'It's a bad business, it is Doug,' Jimmy responded. 'There's no form at all. You just can't rely on the nags these days.' Dougal took a sip of his whisky and winced when it hit the back of his throat. He reached in his pocket, took out a tin and began to roll a cigarette. The whippet sat up.

'I think it's all fixed nowadays, Jim. Ever since those Far Eastern bookies came in on the internet. I reckon everybody's bribed to fix the result now.' He snapped off the loose ends of the rolled cigarette. The whippet was anticipating the move and jumped up to devour the bits before they touched the ground.

'You could be right there mate,' Jimmy said and took a lengthy gulp of his pint. 'What's the news on our little venture?'

'Everything going to plan, according to my cousin. I phoned him this week. They've had the big man out on the gallops, over the distance, and he's going great. As long as he doesn't catch a cold or twist something, I tell you he's a cert. Have you got your money organized.'

'I have something new on that. I may have found a big new

source,' Jimmy said. The bar door opened, a couple walked in and a downdraft of smoke belched from the fireplace. The dog got up.

'Sit down Eamonn,' Dougal growled. 'Really, how much?' he continued.

'Well I'm not counting on it, but it may be a quarter of a million.' Dougal's green eyes lit up and he sat up in his chair. 'Jesus, Lord, where?'

'That I cannot say. It's a pal, a golf pal. Trouble is, it's not exactly his money. Persuading him to get involved is the problem.' Dougal leaned his head over the table towards Jimmy.

'Do you want me to see him. Tell him straight from the horse's mouth so to speak.'

'I don't want you to go anywhere near him. You'd frighten him off. I've got to be very careful with this one. One or two of my pals are working on him as well.'

'Jesus, Jimmy, you can't let that amount go. That's exactly the sort of money the syndicate needs. Bloody hell man, we'll all be millionaires if we could add that to the pile.'

'I know, I know. You'll have to leave it to me though. I think I may have sussed out his weakness.'

'What is it?'

'I wouldn't bloody well tell you.'

'Oh, bugger off then. Drink up it's my round.'

* * * * *

Toby Ballard's Sundays were always chock-a-block with commitments. In the morning he had to be at church at ten for Matins. When his church warden duties were completed, he would cross town to pick up an elderly relative from the nursing home. Every Sunday, he and Margaret treated Mrs Watson, Margaret's aunt to lunch. Then, later he had to get down to the Scout Hall, for Sunday school, take Mrs Watson back to the nursing home, have his own tea and be back at Church for Evensong at seven. Those events, on a Sunday were sacrosanct, embedded permanently like the sunrise and sunset, in his personal diary. Once he had returned Mrs Watson to the Grange nursing home however, Toby always called in at Catryn's house in Saren.

Mark, Catryn's boy, was Toby and Catryn's love child and nobody but the two of them knew. Toby had supported Catryn through her drug rehabilitation. She'd been a runaway on crack. When she was clean he found her work and helped to stabilize her life, but the resulting attraction was just too great for them both. Toby became the father, the friend, counsellor, and in time the lover she'd never had throughout her short life. Catryn was bright, intelligent, fun loving, attractive and brave, but wayward. She was from a broken home. Her father used to beat her. In the two years Toby spent rearranging her life she became dependent on him. In time their affair was like a runaway train. The result was Mark. Toby was a pensioner, nearly forty years older than her. But he'd brought light into her life, where there had been darkness, tranquillity where there was chaos, humour where there was sorrow. And she'd given him vitality in looming old age and purpose when apathy and fear were creeping in.

Catryn was still in a bad state that Sunday when he called. Her temper was short, her mood inconsolable. Losing her job had depressed her. Toby guessed she was still resorting to drugs. His enquiries on that matter fell on stony ground. Mark seemed to have changed as well. The once normally happy, contented child had become tetchy. He cried a lot. Toby looked at Catryn's face and knew at once that he had to get the boy away to the special school that week.

* * * * *

'Aren't you going to golf today?' Rosemary said to Stan, when she came downstairs early on Monday morning and found him sitting at the kitchen table.

'My back's playing up a bit,' he replied, then gulped down the remainder of his coffee. 'I've phoned Ginger and told him.' Rosemary began rattling cups and plates in the kitchen cupboard.

'Well I hope you're not going to get under my feet around here today. Monday is my cleaning day, you know that.'

'No I'll not be under your feet. I've got to go into town later. I've put your breakfast things out here on the table,' he said, pointing at the cup, saucer and plate he'd already laid on the check tablecloth.

'That cup doesn't look very clean to me,' Rosemary said, picking it up and inspecting it. Her face looked like sour cream and she replaced it with one she extracted from the cupboard.

Soon after nine Stan was organising to leave for town.

Rosemary was still at the breakfast table, reading her horoscope. He planted his customary peck on her cheek as he headed for the garage. 'Will you be back for lunch?' she said without paying him, or the kiss, much attention.

'I expect so. If I'm late, you go ahead by yourself. I'll get whatever I want myself,' he replied from the kitchen door.

Stan's trip to town had two purposes. Purpose one was to visit the betting shop. Last weeks unused five pounds was beginning to burn a hole in his pocket and there was a horse running at Ascot that day which had taken his fancy. The other task was to make a telephone call. Alongside the town car park, on the way into the High Street, was a red, old fashioned stand up phone box. In his trouser pocket was a bag full of change. His hands were shaking as he dialled the number.

'Hello,' he heard Anne answer. His heart was pounding. For a second he thought about replacing the receiver. 'Hello, who is that?' Anne said again and Stan clumsily forced some coins into the slots. Some of them were falling on the phone box floor as he fumbled.

'Anne, it's me, Stan,' he stuttered.

'Stan! I wondered who it was at this time of the day. Where are you?'

'I'm in a phone box in town. You said you may have an idea about the money on my statement. You said that we ought to meet up.' He could feel his whole body shaking as he spoke. He was hot in that telephone box and propped the door open with his foot.

'Why don't you call up to the house now,' Anne responded. 'Scott's gone to golf. He won't be back till this afternoon.' Stan gulped. He could feel sweat form on his brow.

'Will it be all right?'

'Of course it will be all right. I'll make us a gin sling.' At that moment Stan felt he could do with a bucket full of gin slings, but he agreed to be there in half an hour. He gathered his loose change from the floor and hurried onto the betting shop.

'Endless Night' was his chosen favourite, twenty to one were the odds. For many minutes he stood in the centre of the betting shop, pondering. 'Oh to hell with it,' he said to himself. Then, from his wallet he extracted the five pounds he always put in a separate compartment and added another five, from the compartment where he kept the rest of his money.

* * * * *

Anne was waiting at her front door as Stan drove up. A white three-quarter sleeve jersey top, with an embroidered front and taupe slacks, with shoes to match, made her look dynamite. The smile she gave, when he wound down the car window, took his breath away.

'Is it all right to park here?' he said nervously.

'You can park anywhere you like,' she replied, retaining the smile and spreading her left arm out in an arc to indicate the vast empty spaces in front of the house. He got out of his car and approached her tentatively. She held out her cheek for a welcome kiss. In his enthusiasm he nearly stumbled into her on its delivery. Her skin was smooth, her perfume intoxicating, she led the way into the lounge.

'I've made us a little drink,' she said, picking up a tall glass mixing decanter.

'It's a bit early for me,' he said, suddenly feeling completely unsure of himself. Anne stirred the contents of the decanter with a long spoon. Lemons and assorted fruits whirled round in the clear liquid.

'Oh go on Stan, live a little dangerously. One won't hurt you. I won't tell.' She tapped the spoon twice on the edge of the decanter, poured the liquid into two tall glasses, gave each one another stir with the spoon, then handed one to Stan and moved very close to him. He could feel her fingers on his hand as he took the glass. 'Here's to fun,' she said raising her glass in toast. They were standing two feet apart. Her blue eyes held out an invitation, his docile mind was afraid to accept.

'At the moment Anne, I just don't know about all this. I've never done anything dishonest in my life.'

'Of course you haven't. Shall we sit on the terrace?' He followed her outside, through open patio doors, to a raised verandah, overlooking a small swimming pool, tiled in blue. A dark blue and white striped, hammock style sun-lounger was alongside the pool and she patted on it, for him to sit beside her.

Anne began. 'I absolutely assure you I would never get involved with anything dishonest either,' she said and turned sideways to face him; their legs were touching. 'But you just can't look a gift horse in the mouth. Life's too short for that. If you don't look after yourself, nobody else is going to.'

'Maybe you're right,' Stan said, starting to feel unsure again. He took a sip of his drink and spluttered when its fire hit his throat. 'What's in that?' he coughed.

'Oh, just a few fruits and things. Nothing that'll do you any harm. Anyway, from what I've been told, nobody is going to steal this money. It's just a question of borrowing it, then putting it back. That's what people do when they buy a house.'

'That's different. That's all done legally, with solicitors and things.'

'Same principle though. And who wants to pay for solicitors nowadays.' She looked at him intently. He wanted to kiss her. 'Look Stan, do you like me?'

He sniggered, his face went red. 'Of course I do.'

'No, I mean really like me, 'cause I like you. I'd like to be alone with you, like we are now, just the two of us. Do you see what I mean?' Stan shuffled in the hammock, moved slightly away, she moved up to him in response. He swallowed hard.

'I see what you mean, but…'

Anne interrupted. 'There can't be any buts, if it's something you want.' She put her hand on his thigh. 'Nothing in life comes without effort. I am afraid there's no gain without pain.' He sat back in the hammock. Her hand remained on his knee.

'What's your idea then?' he said. She put down her drink glass on a small table beside the hammock. As she moved the sun lightened her bronzed skin.

'I have a system.'

Stan stared at her. 'What do you mean by a system?'

'At roulette.' He looked startled. 'Don't look surprised, it works, I've proved it. But so far, using only small money.'

Stan laughed. 'Come on Anne, nobody wins at roulette. Only the casino wins in the long run, everybody knows that.'

'But I do. I can beat the casino,' she said emphatically. 'I tell you I've proved it. I keep a book. I can show you my winnings. I do it by numbers, averages. Up to now I've only risked a few hundred pounds, but in total I've made over a thousand pounds.' He shook his head in disbelief.

'But if we lost all the money on my statement, we wouldn't be able to pay that amount back, then it would be stealing.' Her hand reached out for his and held it, tenderly, stroking his fingers while she talked.

'We wouldn't need all of it, just a small portion. Say ten thousand. With all the other schemes Scott told me about, you'd have to risk the lot. I agree with you that that could be big trouble, and I think a big withdrawal like that would draw attention at the building society. Nobody's going to look too closely at a ten thousand withdrawal on a quarter of a million balance. And anyway, with my system, we wouldn't lose anything. It's foolproof.' Anne kept stroking his hand.

'I can't accept that,' Stan said. 'Nothing's completely foolproof.'

'If you don't believe me I'll take you with me and show you, using my money. We'll take a hundred quid and I'll show you. You can stand by me and watch.' Stan turned his head and looked into her eyes. He thought the whole idea preposterous. Never, ever, would he allow himself to get involved in such nonsense. But there was this look of pleading innocence on Anne's face.

'Where does all this skullduggery take place?' he said, almost laughing.

'Oh, in Swansea, Cardiff, Bristol. I've deliberately moved around, and I've kept my total winnings at each place down to a few hundred pounds.'

'Are you serious?' Stan said.

'I'm really serious. I'll tell you what I'll do, to show you how serious I am. I'll arrange a bank loan for whatever amount we take out of your account. I'll show you the papers to prove that I've got the cover. Then, if by the tiniest, weeniest chance anything goes wrong, I'll have the money to pay you back.' She was still holding his hand. Stan was looking at her incredulously.

'I don't know what to say.'

'Don't say anything at this stage. Come and watch me play, then decide. We can do it this week if you want.' She turned his hand over and stroked his palm with her finger. 'Don't you see Stan, it's something we can have a bit of fun together with. Have a few laughs, let our hair down. Come on what do you say, before we get too old.' She leant forward towards him and kissed him full on the lips. The hairs on the back of his neck stood out; he felt his toes curl and he was lost, drunk in the perfume of her femininity. They held in that embrace for a long time.

'I don't know if we are doing the right thing,' he said eventually. Anne extracted herself from his arms, but left her face very close to his.

'Does anybody know what the right thing is?' she said. He sat back in the hammock and rubbed his brow with his hand.

'Maybe you're right. I don't know.'

Before he left her house, he'd agreed to accompany her to Cardiff, on Wednesday. All the way home, he kept ruminating on what he had got himself involved in. While sitting on the hammock she'd shown him the book she'd referred to. It was only a small notebook, the cover was red. On its lined pages, in neat and concise hand writing, were details of her outlay. All the bets on each turn of the wheel, and her winnings, recorded like a cricket score book. Her system, she'd said, entailed starting on the black and continuing to bet on it until it won. Then she continued with a long explanation of what happened next which left him completely confused.

'What about Scott?' he'd asked.

'Scott knows nothing about this,' she replied vehemently. 'This is my little secret. Up to this moment in time, only you and me know about this and I'd like to keep it that way please.'

'Oh God, what do I do now,' he said to himself, as he drove home with the sweet taste of gin sling and Anne's kiss still on his lips.

Lunch with Rosemary that day was difficult. His mind had been tainted irreversibly. Already he was looking at his wife in a different light. Afterwards, when she'd gone into town, shopping, he buried himself in the garage with his carpentry. At four thirty he went inside for the racing results. 'Endless Night' had come in first, at twenty to one.

'Oh bloody hell,' he muttered to himself.

* * * * *

Colin Mordecai was sitting in his study, glaring at his computer screen. Over the weekend he and Veronica had been busy with one of their open garden days. So much had been his involvement that there hadn't been time to look at his investments since the previous Thursday afternoon. There'd been golf on Friday morning, then, in the afternoon he had to cut all the grass in preparation for the weekend visitors. And well, the weekend had been just too busy with people who came and all their questions.

It was now late on Monday afternoon and having returned from his morning round of golf, there was, at last, time to settle into his other hobby. They'd all been disappointed by the non-appearance of Stan that morning. It was so unlike him to miss out, unless he was really ill. They wondered if perhaps they'd been putting too much pressure on him over this building society account business, but the consensus was still to pursue him on the matter. That morning there had still been lots of talk about not 'looking a gift horse in the mouth' and similar phrases. What confronted Colin however, when he looked at his computer screen, was complete disaster. Red was everywhere. Over the weekend, bad news about the OPEC oil figures and further trouble in the Middle East had caused an avalanche in the financial markets.

'Bloody hell,' Colin cursed to himself. All his hedges had moved completely the wrong way. Earlier in the week the market was going up and what he'd gambled on continuing to go up had sunk like a stone. And his defensive stocks, which he thought might go down, or at least stay the same, had all rocketed skywards. 'Bloody hell,' he kept repeating. His words about needing to keep a daily check on this form of investment were already beginning to haunt him.

When he took retirement Colin received a lump sum, a cash payment, from his pension, as well as the normal annual income from an annuity. At the time, rather than reinvest the lump sum in another annuity, he elected to use the cash for his own investment dabbling. Originally the amount involved was getting on for fifty thousand pounds. Since concentrating most of his investments into trading in hedges however, this sum had risen to somewhere in the region of seventy thousand pounds. There would of course be tax to pay on the gain, but up until that moment he was highly delighted with the way things had gone.Now, as he continued to stare at the computer screen, he was calculating a reduction of approaching thirty five thousand pounds on the most recent balance. All of a sudden, the round the world cruise he'd been promising Veronica and the new BMW he'd been eyeing up were a distant dream. If things remained as they were, they'd be lucky to have any change left from the redecoration job he'd just organised on the outside of the house.

'Bloody hell!' he repeated for the umpteenth time. Angrily, he pressed the computer keys for the CNN page. 'Bloody hell!' he reiterated once more, when the screen came up. Everything, everywhere was still bright red; stocks were plummeting world wide. He knew he would have to move quickly to prevent this situation getting worse. Back on his investment screen he tapped and keyed for a couple of hours, ignoring Veronica's buzzing on the intercom for his afternoon tea. When he was done, he hollered at Dudley for a walk, roughly affixed the lead around the dog's neck and stomped off on his usual afternoon trek, without saying a word to his wife.

CHAPTER NINE

Wednesday dawned bright, although there was a fresh south westerly gusting. Overnight rain had left the golf course wet underfoot. For once, the six of them all arrived in good time, which was unusual. The atmosphere on the first tee that morning was somewhat restrained. Everybody was pleasantly polite, but there wasn't quite the usual gladiatorial banter. Each man appeared preoccupied with his own thoughts.

During the early holes no mention was made of Stan's building society communication. The blustery wind and the damp clinging rough provided each golfer with sufficient challenge to contend with. Stan was playing with Jimmy and Colin, while Toby, Ginger and Scott made up the other three ball. It was Stan himself who eventually raised the subject after playing their drives on the thirteenth tee. That morning his golf had gone well. His customary accuracy had returned and on the stableford points system, he was, by that hole comfortably in the lead.

'You know I've been thinking some more about that money,' he said to Jimmy as they walked down the fourteenth fairway. Jimmy looked across at him somewhat surprised. 'I've still heard nothing from the building society,' Stan continued. 'It's well over a week now since the letter arrived.'

Jimmy was in the middle of devouring his third banana of the morning. The three unzipped layers of yellow skin were flaying about in the breeze in front of his face. 'What have you got in mind?' he said, in between chomping.

'Do you really think we could get that money out without any problems?' Stan ventured. Jimmy stopped walking, flung the banana skin deep into the rough and wiped his mouth with the back of his hand.

'Well, all we've got to do is try,' Jimmy replied. 'You get nowhere if you don't try.' They looked at each other.

'Well I just wouldn't know what do,' Stan said. 'I've told you before, Rosemary handles that sort of thing. I haven't a clue how the account works. If anything went wrong she'd kill me.' While they were talking, Colin was somewhere off to the right, well out of earshot; looking for his ball in the rough.

'Well if you want me to help, I will,' Jimmy said. 'Why don't you bring all the paperwork around to my house. We can be in private there.'

'I just don't know Jim, I'll see. Don't tell any of the others at this juncture. Let's keep it between you and me at this stage.'

Nothing more was said. Stan won the money that day. When they were back in the clubhouse a few of the others raised the subject, but Stan kept repeating that he still wasn't sure he wanted to get involved. Eventually the matter was dropped. They all ate lunch, played snooker and went home. Except in the car park, Jimmy said to Stan, 'Iris will be out tomorrow afternoon. Why don't you call round then. We can use my phone.' Stan was sitting in his car with the driver's window rolled down.

'I'll think about it,' he said, 'what do we do if we get the money out?'

'Let's worry about that if we get it out,' Jimmy said.

'I'll telephone you in the morning then Jim. I'm still not sure mind.' With that he drove away, tooting his horn as he departed.

For the remainder of the day Stan's mind was in turmoil.

* * * * *

'Where's our building society account papers?' Stan said to Rosemary that evening after their meal. What he wanted was the pack they'd received when the account was opened.

'What do you want them for?' Rosemary replied snappily. He still hadn't mentioned anything to her about the letter with the large credit. The morning it arrived, he'd met the postman in the driveway on his way to golf, and the missive was still in his trouser pocket.

'There's something I want to check,' he responded. 'I noticed in town one of the other lot is offering a better rate.' Rosemary stared at him. Never before in their married life had he raised such matters.

'Stan, I'm quite happy with the money where it is. We've been with them for over ten years. I don't want to change now.'

'I just want to look at it that's all. It's my money too you know.' Surprise etched Rosemary's face.

'It's in the bedroom drawer, but don't go messing that up, all my personal things are in there.'

That evening while Rosemary was watching her 'soap', Stan went upstairs and searched the bedroom drawer. The papers he found revealed that the account in question had been opened two years back, with an amount of five thousand pounds. Scribbled in the corner of the welcoming letter was their joint password, 'Cathays'. He hadn't remembered it, but it was the name of the school their children had attended. From his pocket he took out the letter with the £250,000 balance. He checked carefully and yes the account number was the same; their address identical and their joint names were correctly spelt on the top. He looked at the original opening account letter; 'either to sign' to withdraw it said and so did the recent letter. Both letters confirmed they were instant access accounts. Both had their joint bank account noted as a location for withdrawal. For many moments he stared at the two pieces of paper, comparing the balances. One amount glowed at him, like the bounty in Aladdin's cave. In contrast, the smaller sum looked forlorn, boring and conventional, just like he'd become, he thought.

All that night Stan hardly slept. He kept going over and over in his mind the consequences of drawing on that £250,000. Shame, prosecution, jail and more were some of his fears. Divorce, homelessness and poverty were the worst. During what little sleep he got, his dreams were filled with the colour of Anne's blue eyes, and her blonde hair. By morning he was exhausted.

'I've got to nip over to Jimmy's after lunch,' he told Rosemary at breakfast.

'I thought you saw enough of him at golf,' she replied, hardly lifting her head from the newspaper.

'I won't be long. Something to do with a new roof for the Scout Hall.'

'I thought Jimmy's hobby was pigeon racing.'

'Just shows, you can't be sure about everybody,' Stan said and began clearing away the breakfast things.

After lunch Rosemary went into town shopping. Stan watched her car leave their driveway, then dashed upstairs to the bedroom. From the dressing table drawer he extracted the pack of building society papers and gave Jimmy a call. In ten minutes he was rattling the brass knocker on the Irishman's front door.

'Come in, come in,' the little man said, as he ushered him inside.

'I'm still not sure about all this,' Stan uttered as they crossed in the hallway. The rooms in Jimmy's house were all small, cottage style, with low ceilings. Stan almost felt he had to duck as he walked into the lounge. The furniture was comfortable, warm and homely; everything was neat, tidy and inviting. The front window let in only a minimal amount of light; two table lamps were switched on in the corners, each side of the fireplace.

'Sit ye down,' Jimmy said. Stan chose the brown leather settee. A hand crocheted blanket was draped over the sitting area.

'What's the worse that can happen in all this Jim?' Stan said.

'They can query the withdrawal and we can say you made a mistake. You punched the wrong amounts in on the keyboard. It's usually all done with the buttons on the telephone. You don't normally have to say anything, except for your password. Do you know what that is?'

'Yes, yes. And my four digit security code. I always remember that. It's my birthday dates reversed.'

'Well then, I think we are going to need a little bit of Dutch courage to do this,' Jimmy said and moved to a drinks cabinet alongside the settee. When he opened the lid, coloured lights lit up the inside.

'Oh Jim, I don't know. It's a bit early for that,' Stan said.

'A wee nip won't hurt, especially if you're going to live dangerously.' Jimmy poured a large tot of Irish whisky into two crystal glasses. 'This is from over the water,' he said, handing one to Stan. 'Great medicinal benefits, it has. Do you good. Take it back in one is the best way,' he continued. Stan took a big gulp.

He gasped breathlessly, spluttering at the same time. 'What the hell's that?'

'Oh, just a wee drop of holy water that's all.' Stan's eyes became liquid. He dabbed at them with his handkerchief.

'Now what about making that call?' Jimmy said. 'Have you their telephone number?'

Stan fumbled with the papers in the envelope. He unfolded one of the letters, rubbed his eyes and peered up and down the page. 'Jim are you sure it'll be all right?' Jimmy nodded and reached for the phone. It was one of those cordless efforts, silver in colour, with more buttons than a computer terminal. He looked at Stan, who was still scanning the letter.

'Here it is. Savings and Investment telephone number,' Stan said, the piece of paper was shaking in his hands. Jimmy pressed the digits on the phone as Stan read out the number.

'Do you want to do it or shall I?' Jimmy said holding out the phone to Stan. Stan took it without replying. His hand was still shaking.

A recorded voice, saying 'welcome to the building society', answered. A menu list of numbers to press was next; number two was for withdrawals. Stan did as instructed. Then he had to key in his account number and his four digit security number. 'Please speak clearly and state your password,' was the next instruction. Stan said 'Cathays', not confidently, but loud enough for Jimmy to hear. There was a pause. Stan looked at Jimmy who was smiling.

'Your details have been verified,' the recorded voice stated, reverting Stan's attention to the task.

'Using your telephone keypad, key in the amount you wish to withdraw in pounds,' the voice on the phone said.

'How much shall I withdraw?' Stan asked Jimmy.

'You don't want to close it. That may cause problems. Put in two hundred thousand and let's see what happens,' Jimmy said. Stan looked at him for some moments, then down at the phone, then back at Jimmy, who was nodding his head. Eventually, very carefully, he typed out the amount. Two hundred thousand. All the noughts were a problem, but he got there in the end.

'Type out the pence,' the voice said. Stan complied, nought, nought. There was a pause, a long pause, Stan could feel his armpits sweating.

'You have requested a withdrawal of two hundred thousand pounds,' the voice said. 'If you wish this amount to go to your registered bank account, press one.' Stan's finger hovered over the button. He looked at Jimmy, who was still smiling. Stan looked away, across the room, and then back again at Jimmy. He could hear the clock ticking on Jimmy's mantelpiece.

'No, it's just no good Jim,' Stan said. 'I can't do it. I just can't, I'm sorry.' He pressed the off button on the phone and handed it back to Jimmy.

For half an hour or more Jimmy cajoled, he bullied, he spelt out many good reasons, but each time Stan kept repeating, 'I'm sorry Jim, I just can't do it.'

* * * * *

At home, Stan chose the sanctuary of the garage and the excuse of his woodwork to replay over in his mind the decision he had made about the building society account. As he planed and sawed he continually asked himself, why had he been so cautious? What did he really have to lose? All through the afternoon Jimmy had provided enough plausible reasons to mitigate their actions. At the time not one of them had registered with Stan. Now in the peace and quiet of his garage, with Rosemary still out, he went over each one, trying to pick holes in his decision. In the end he concluded that all his years of service, all his commitment to devotion and benevolence, had produced a built-in dependence mechanism of conformity. He thought about the other people he knew, whom he considered as 'chancers'. Scott was one and of course Jimmy too and probably Ginger. No matter what mischief they got up to, nothing untoward ever seemed to happen to *them* as a result of their misdemeanors. Thinking of Scott, made him think of Anne. He put down his saw. 'To hell with it,' he said to himself. Rosemary was still out. He went inside and rang Anne's telephone number. Fortunately she answered and seemed pleased to hear from him.

'I'd like to see your system at work,' he said after their preliminary preamble. For a second there was silence at the other end of the line. Anne was taken aback.

'Wonderful,' she said eventually. 'When?'

'How about tomorrow afternoon?'

'Fine by me,' she replied. 'We'll go to Cardiff. We'd better meet out of town though, you know what it's like around here. There's a service station on the outskirts of Swansea. Do you know the one?' He did and they arranged to meet at two o'clock. Later in the day he made some excuse to Rosemary about having to go to Swansea for some special timber.

'You and your woodwork,' she responded. 'What about my new kitchen?'

'One day, one day,' he said.

'I've heard that before,' she replied.

76

CHAPTER TEN

Toby's mind was addled. His brain had been revolving in diminishing circles regarding Catryn and Mark and it was driving him crazy. Problem solving was usually second nature to him. You can't sail a boat around the world without having the capacity to put right what's gone wrong. This was something different though. This time his judgement was riddled with guilt, angst, and annoyance. This time he was the cause of the trouble, he was the one to blame. He'd gone against his own principals, thrown overboard all his religious beliefs, like discarding an out of date sea manual. He'd always considered this type of problem would never happen to him, believing his life was embedded on a foundation of rock firm principles. That's why he had become a social worker. He could stand back and advise objectively. Now, in his own eyes, he was in the same boat as the people he was advising; someone in desperate need of help.

'I'll have to go out this evening,' he said to Margaret as they washed up after dinner. 'I'm having trouble with one of my social cases.'

'I hope you're not doing too much,' Margaret said. 'You shouldn't get so involved. Why don't you get some help, if it's become complicated.'

Toby sighed. 'Unfortunately this is one I thought was on the straight and narrow. But she's slipped off again. I can't leave it to anybody else otherwise she'll be back where she started.'

Driving over to Catryn's house he knew he couldn't involve somebody else. If he involved somebody else, the truth would come out and all hell would break loose. Outside her front door everything appeared quiet. He knocked but there was no reply. It took two further knocks before she eventually answered. Then she leant against the door- frame looking bleary eyed.

'How are you feeling?' he asked.

'Oh, OK, I guess.' she said and yawned.

'Where's Mark?'

'He's in bed.'

'Can I come in?'

'I don't know if it's convenient right now.'

'Well I'd like to see Mark please,' Toby said firmly.

'It's your choice,' Catryn replied. For the first time in their relationship there was a touch of insolence in her voice. She opened the door wide and stepped aside. As he walked through the hall he could see into the lounge. Sitting in there, on the settee, was a dark haired youth of Catryn's age. He was smoking something and the smell wasn't tobacco.

Toby ran up the stairs two at a time and pushed open the child's bedroom door. Lying peacefully in his bed, sucking his thumb was his son. He stood over him for many minutes. He could sense Catryn standing outside on the landing. He turned and walked towards her.

'Catryn I don't want to see you go downhill again. It's not fair on the child.'

'Is it fair on me?' she said. 'Have you ever asked yourself that?'

'You can't bring up a child and smoke dope. I thought you knew that. I thought you were happy as you were.'

'Happy. Ha, ha.' Her laugh was coarse, almost callous. 'The other day was just a bad day that's all. It won't happen again. I lost my job, I told you. How would you feel if you lost your job?'

'What about downstairs?'

'What about downstairs?' The insolence was back in her voice.

'He's smoking something.'

'He's just a guy who used to come in to the pub. He's called in to cheer me up.'

'I repeat you can't bring up a child with dope around.'

'I agree.' She brushed her hair from her face and tossed her head back. 'What are you going to do about it then?'

Toby stood and stared at her, then looked back at Mark. 'I'll call tomorrow,' he said, brushed past her and went down the stairs, looking in through the lounge door on his way out. The youth was still on the settee, smoking and watching TV. At the front door Toby turned and looked back at Catryn, who'd followed him down the stairs. 'I know it's not easy Catryn. Just be patient. I'll see if I can sort something out this week.'

She made no reply. She'd stopped by the lounge door. She looked so young he thought. How could he have inflicted all this on her? He closed the door quietly behind him.

* * * * *

Driving down the M4 towards Swansea, Stan already felt invigorated. He sang along with a cassette on the stereo, something he couldn't remember doing in years. Deliberately he'd set out early. There was a timber merchants he knew, just off the motorway. His first port of call was there, to purchase a few items, to justify his journey. Then he sat in the service station car park, awaiting Anne's arrival. His pulse rate accelerated when he spotted her dark blue Range Rover slink into the car park. He waved and she drew up alongside. Her smile possessed a startling vitality when she opened her car window.

'We'll take mine if you like. I know the way,' she said. Sitting next to her, as the Rover powered down the M4, talking happily about this, that and nothing in particular, was very easy, as though they'd done the same thing many times before. She was wearing a white polo shirt and tight fitting red slacks. When she wanted to emphasize a point she was making she would touch his arm, and that gave him goose-bumps. Soon they were pulling into the car park of the casino. Glitzy neon signs and lots of smoked glass adorned the front portico. Anne brandished a membership card at the reception desk, then a coloured bouncer of heavyweight proportions held open a heavy door.

'Good afternoon, sir, madam,' he said as he stood aside to let them through. Anne nodded a half smile; Stan shuffled in behind.

The large room was dark. Occasional spotlights and brightly-lit enclaves highlighted certain areas. It took a time for Stan's eyes to adjust. He followed Anne across the room to a small bar in the far corner.

'Now, as this is your first time, this is all on me,' Anne said. 'What would you like to drink?' He was feeling warm, settled for a small beer, then loosened his collar button. That morning he'd pondered on what he was expected to wear. Eventually, a white shirt and blue tie, with a pair of dark trousers seemed the most comfortable. The room was small. Tables for roulette and blackjack were scattered about on raised dais's. Around the side walls, upright and in line like a row of guardsmen, were innumerable one armed bandits and in the corners, not at that time in use, were alcoves with card tables. To Stan, the whole thing was a revelation. The last time he had been in a casino was about thirty years ago, on somebody's stag night, and it certainly hadn't been like this.

'Now, this is what it's all about,' Anne said, extracting the little red note book from her black shoulder bag. 'My system's all in here,' she added, brandishing it in front of Stan's face. 'All I have to do is follow this and we can't go wrong.' Then, in hushed tones, while they sipped at their drinks, she outlined again the details of how her system worked. Stan hardly understood a word, she'd lost him completely after the first few sentences. 'You don't have to do anything today,' she said when she'd finished explaining. 'Just watch me.' From her shoulder bag she produced an envelope and extracted a wad of five pound notes. 'A hundred pounds,' she said. 'Freshly minted today,' she added with a smile. He tried to chuckle, but it came out as a cough. He was really very nervous. Why he felt like a criminal he couldn't understand, but his knees were trembling as he followed her to a counter, where she changed her money into chips.

They moved on to a roulette table where five other people were already playing. A swarthy, short man, with slick backed dark hair, wearing a black dinner suit, was spinning the wheel. Anne consulted her notebook. Stan watched as she placed two chips on the black. The croupier spun the ball in the wheel. Number 34 red was its resting place. Flamboyantly the croupier scooped her chip away. Twice more, two chips were placed on black before the spinning ball obliged and lodged on a number of similar colour. 'Right we're away,' Anne said, referred to her little notebook and made some mark in it with a biro. Then she put more chips on an even number which won. Stan laughed. Everybody around the table looked at him and he felt embarrassed.

From that moment onwards Anne appeared to win on almost every alternate bet. Sometimes she would bet on the colour, sometimes a straight bet on a number, sometimes a split, other times, odd or even, it was all too complicated for Stan to follow. Occasionally, she'd bet more than before, then she usually won. After each bet she would always refer to the little red notebook and make a mark in it with the biro. Gradually, the pile of chips in front of her grew. Without realising it, Stan became excited like a schoolboy, almost jumping for joy at each successful bet.

'That's enough for today,' she said after about half an hour and scooped up the chips in front of her. She took Stan's arm and guided him towards the change counter. He said nothing and followed. When they were outside, bright sunlight hit his eyes like a stinging ray.

'How much have you won?' he asked as they walked towards her car.

'One hundred and thirty pounds. The original pot of a hundred is now two hundred and thirty.'

'Anne that's simply amazing. How did you do that?' She reached in her shoulder bag, extracted her little red book and held it up for him to see.

'All down to my system,' she said, smiling.

'Will you explain it again to me?' he said as they got into the Rover. 'I'm afraid I still haven't followed it properly.'

'If you'll join me in my little money making scheme, yes,' she said, looking across at him from the driver's seat. 'So far, these have only been small trials, testers if you like. As I said before, I want to keep my winnings at each casino to a small sum, until we're ready for some real gambling. Now if I had a backer with a few thousand pounds we could really go for broke. We'd only need to do it once. Once would be enough Stan. You've seen what I can do. Just imagine if we'd put on ten thousand pounds to bet today.'

'Doesn't bear thinking about,' Stan said, as he fastened his seat belt.

'Certainly enough for us to have some nice times together anyway,' she said and turned the ignition key. The Rover fired into life and with a screech of tyres they swished away towards the M4. 'If we made enough we could buy a luxury static caravan,' she said excitedly as she drove, 'somewhere on the west coast, where we could meet up. Somewhere where nobody would think of looking for us. What do you think about that idea?'

'It's a hell of a risk Anne. Toby said I could go to jail if it all went wrong.'

'It can't go wrong. I've told you already, I can borrow the money from my bank. If it went wrong, I'd bail you out. We'd only need to risk a small amount. Ten thousand pounds would do us nicely. You could explain that away as a mistake. And we wouldn't lose it all. We could set a limit, say five thousand. If the pot got down to five thousand then we'd stop. You'd be alongside me to keep a check on it. It would be a bit of fun. Something daring. Go on Stan, live dangerously for once. You can do it.'

When they parted at the service station, he leant over and kissed her on the cheek. 'I have enjoyed today,' he said, 'you're right, it's been fun.'

* * * * *

'You've been gone a long time for a few bits of wood,' Rosemary said when he arrived home. She was peeling potatoes at the kitchen sink.

'Have I? Oh, there was a kitchen warehouse near the timber yard,' he replied defensively. 'As you've been going on about it so much, I had a look in there as well.' Rosemary turned to face him; her eyes lit up.

'Well, what did you think?' she said.

'H'm, bit expensive I thought, but very nice. We'll have to see. I could take some cash from my pension.' Rosemary beamed. 'I'll think about it,' he continued. After dinner he retired to his garage with his new pieces of wood and mulled over the day. While Rosemary was watching her TV 'soaps', he chiselled and planed and daydreamed of sun filled days with Anne, on some white, sandy beach. In his mind's eye he could also see a cliff top field, overlooking the sea, with their caravan at its edge.

* * * * *

At the end of the week the weather turned stormy, making the lad's decision about playing golf or not as protracted as a United Nations vote on Iraq. For the previous three days torrential cyclonic downpours had interspersed with periods of fine, clear spells and blue skies. The local TV station's weather forecasting was for the most part unreliable. Floods occurred in some parts of the county, while, ten miles down the road holiday makers sunbathed on the beach.

'That bastard on the BBC hasn't got it right one day this week,' Jimmy said to Stan, when they spoke on the phone, the night before their intended game.

'Oh I watch the ITV. I think she's better,' Stan replied

'That's only 'cos you like her tits,' Jimmy chortled.

'You may be right there,' Stan said. 'The Professor says he

82

gets it straight from the Meteorological Office off the computer and according to them it's going to start off wet, but get brighter as the day goes on.'

'H'm,' Jimmy said. 'Him and his bloody computer. I wish he could find me a programme on there to improve my golf. Have you thought any more about our little venture? Time's getting on Stan. Somebody's going to miss that money soon.'

'I'll have a chat with you about that when we meet up,' Stan said.

'As you wish. I'd better give Ging a call, see if he wants to play. One of us will get back to you,' Jimmy said and rang off.

'Talbot Reardon!' Ginger's voice boomed in Jimmy's ear when he answered the phone.

'What do you think about golf tomorrow morning, Ging?' Jimmy asked.

'Looks to me as though it's going to piss down,' Ginger said. 'I've seen it on Sky. They've got a proper chart on there with a satellite picture. You can see it coming in off the Atlantic.'

'Colin told me the Met Office are saying there's going to be lots of bright periods. We may get away with it.'

'Fuck Colin and his Met Office. If you think I'm going to get stuck out there in one of those monsoons on the basis of what Colin's got off his computer, you're mistaken. Two inches fell in Newcastle Emlyn yesterday. They didn't forecast that.'

'Perhaps we'd better leave it 'til the morning to decide,' Jimmy said. So Jimmy rang Scott, who rang Colin, who rang Stan, who rang Toby, who rang Ginger, to say they were going to leave it until the morning for a decision.

'I know we are going to leave it to the fucking morning,' Ginger bellowed when he got Toby's call. 'It was my idea in the first place to leave it to the morning,' he continued to bellow and then slammed down the phone.

Next morning they all rose early. Jimmy spent some time in his pigeon loft gazing at the cloud formations. There had been a heavy downpour overnight which left everything wet and mucky to touch. Colin delivered his wife's early morning cup of tea in bed, then took his tea to his study and switched on the computer. Stan sat in his kitchen watching the breakfast TV, while Rosemary commandeered the shower. Scott was on his exercise bike on the bedroom balcony, while Anne lay in bed, drinking orange juice, with the TV on. And Toby was putting the final touches to the RNLI annual accounts while he ate his breakfast, when Stan's telephone call disturbed him.

'What do you think?' Stan said.

'The barometer's going up. Should be all right,' Toby replied.

'I'll ring Jimmy then. Will you ring Colin,' Stan said. Jimmy said he'd risk it. Colin wasn't sure. He'd ring Scott, who sounded game for it. Jimmy then rang Ginger.

'I think we are going to risk it,' Jimmy said to Ginger.

'Piss off,' Ginger replied, having already burnt one piece of bacon that morning, while concentrating on the weather forecast. 'If I am there, I'll be there and if I'm not, I won't be.'

Just as Jimmy was loading his clubs into the car, the phone rang. By the time he made it from the garage back into the house, it had stopped ringing. When he got back outside and was closing the boot, it rang again. This time Iris met him in the kitchen. 'It was Colin,' she said. 'He's going.' Jimmy just waved to her, turned and headed for his car.

By then Rosemary had vacated the shower and Stan was sitting on the toilet when his phone rang. 'It's Scott for you,' Rosemary called through the bathroom door.

'Can you take a message?' Stan called back. She was gone a couple of minutes before she returned.

'He said he's going to risk it,' Rosemary said on her return.

'Good,' Stan said.

'Is there any message?' Rosemary asked.

Stan sighed. 'Just tell him I'll be there,' he said.

Along the narrow, twisting, hedge lined lane that leads to the golf course there is a selection of medium sized hotels and guest houses. In the off season, the council dustcart only goes down the lane once a week and it can get through the gateways without too much problem. However, during the busy summer months such is the way of modern living that rubbish has to be removed every day. This procedure also involves a bigger dustcart, empowered with all the hydraulics to cope with the excess waste. It is also too wide to go through the gateways.

Now, the 'modus operandi' in the summer is for the cart to stop at each gateway, while the council operatives go down the driveway to retrieve the rubbish; the dustcart's bulk then takes up all of the lane. Numerous journeys back and fore are often required by the operatives and not inconsiderable effort is expanded on pulling and pushing large wheely bins, into which most of the trash has been tipped.

That particular morning, for once, Jimmy was the first of our group along the lane. Outside the gateway to the Atlantic Hotel he was halted by the massive bulk of the dustcart. Normally all our lads arrive early enough to be down the lane before the cart appears. But that day's protracted telephone calls and the extra accumulation of rubbish, due to the holiday season, had slowed both their and the dustcart's progress. The Atlantic, a four star hotel, is the largest along the lane. It's a nineteenth century structure, with two turreted wings, east and west, and accumulates the greatest amount of rubbish.

'We'll not keep you long,' one of the lads called out to Jimmy, who waved back through his open car window. So, Jimmy picked up the newspaper he always collected on his way to golf and studied the racing news. Suddenly, a car horn tooted from behind. In his rear view mirror he could see Ginger, waving his arms and telling everybody to get a move on. The guys at the dustcart stopped what they were doing, looked back at Ginger, ignored him and carried on working.

'They won't be long,' Jimmy called back through his open car window. Whether Ginger heard him or not he couldn't tell, but Ginger kept waving his arms and looking annoyed. Eventually, the dustmen all climbed on, or in the cart and it drove on up the lane. Jimmy looked in his rear-view mirror and could still see Ginger gesticulating and shouting to himself. Jimmy followed the cart and Ginger followed him.

One hundred yards down the lane, in an equally tight spot, is the Mariners Guest House. A former public house, now tastily converted into eight bedrooms and a spacious dining area, with good views of the sea. Usually it is fully booked for the season. By the time Jimmy and Ginger caught up, the dustcart was stopped outside its front gate, blocking the lane. This time Ginger sounded his horn aggressively and stuck his head out of the side window. 'Can't you chaps pull over and let us through,' he shouted at the group of workmen by the cart. They all looked back at him. Jimmy said nothing and reverted to his newspaper. The dustmen continued on down the driveway to the Mariners. Then, the driver got out of the dustcart cab and walked back towards Ginger's car, smiling at Jimmy as he passed. He was at least six foot tall, as wide as a house, with a shaven a head and bulging arms, heavily marked with tattoos.

'Can't you pull over and let us pass?' Ginger repeated at the approaching man.

'Listen mate,' he said, angling his head down to the level of Ginger's window. 'If you think you're capable of taking this juggernaut down into the ditch in this lane and getting it out again, you're welcome to try. Only, I'll tell you now, this is a hundred thousand pound machine and I don't aim to risk it. There's a big pull-in near the golf club. I'll pull over when we get there, if that's all right with you.'

Jimmy was watching all this in his mirror. The dustcart driver walked back to his vehicle, then he saw Ginger slam his hands down on the steering wheel and shake his head. Behind Ginger's car he could see Stan had arrived as well. It took another ten minutes for the dustcart to make its way, property by property, to the pull-in by the golf club entrance. Jimmy waved to the lads as he drove past; Ginger accelerated by in a cloud of dust, scattering road chippings everywhere; Stan followed at a more sedate pace. 'Ignorant buggers,' Ginger said to Jimmy as they alighted from their cars in the Golf Club car park. Stan, Ginger and Jimmy visited the changing room, then for ten minutes, the three of them waited on the first tee for the others to arrive.

'Oh come on, I'm not waiting any longer. They're obviously not coming,' Ginger said.

'I expect they're held up for the same reason we were,' Jimmy replied.

'Well I can't wait any longer, I've got things to do later on,' Ginger responded, took his driver out of his golf bag, then placed a ball on a tee peg. He indulged in a couple of ungainly practice swings, lined up against the ball and pulled the club back. At the very top of his back swing, just as he was about to begin his downward pivot, a car horn sounded in the car park, causing him to lunge at the ball. The result was a duck hook into the long, knee high grass rough, on the left hand side of the fairway. They all looked around. The other three had just arrived in the car park. They were all waving their arms and laughing.

'Bloody wankers,' Ginger said.

* * * * *

Battling a twenty mile an hour onshore wind, while attempting to achieve a reasonable golf score, is taxing enough without the added distraction of a contretemp to contend with. So conversation between the group that morning was sparse. Afterwards in the haven of the clubhouse, over post match beers, an exhausted peace still prevailed while scores were calculated and prize money allocated. Scott won most of the money that morning, leaving the others to wearily delve into their pockets for the cash, while he verbally bestowed praise upon himself. By the time the food arrived, a few beers had restored some vitality to their aching bodies and a semblance of joviality returned.

'Now what about this money Stan? Have you come to any conclusions on what you're going to do,' Jimmy said, while vigorously shaking the vinegar bottle over his chips.

'I hope there's going to be some vinegar left in that bottle for the rest of us.' Ginger cut in.

'You can never have too much vinegar, my dad used to say. According to him it had very therapeutic qualities.' Jimmy replied, stopped shaking the bottle, then added some more with an exaggerated flourish, before handing it over to Ginger.

'I'm still not sure I want to get involved.' Stan said, replying to Jimmy's original question. The other five all stopped eating and looked at him.

'Now you mustn't be hasty on this, Stan,' Colin said. He put down his knife and fork alongside his plate. 'Since we last spoke on the subject I've given the matter some more thought. I think you're quite within your rights to use that money. After all, you have been issued with an official receipt. I'm not saying you should keep the cash, but whilst it's in your name I don't see why you can't use it.'

'You're getting on dangerous ground there, Colin.' Toby said.

'Well that's what I think as well,' Stan replied. 'It's just too much of a risk. I accept all the things you're saying, but for an old dodderer like me the risk is too great. I'd never sleep at night. Every day I'd be expecting that knock on the door. If that happened Rosemary would go demented.' The other five who'd all resumed eating, stopped chewing and looked at him again. 'I think you're doing yourself an injustice Stanley,' Scott said. 'From what I've seen, there's still plenty of life in the old devil yet.' The others murmured their agreement. Stan could feel himself blush. At that moment he couldn't be sure if Anne had said anything to Scott about their liaison, or even if Scott had put her up to the whole escapade. So he looked down at his food.

Looks can be deceptive,' he said, trying to hide his embarrassment by stuffing a fork full of chips into his mouth.

'We'd all share the responsibility.' Ginger said. 'If anything went wrong, we'd all be in it together.'

Jimmy cut in. 'It gives me great comfort to hear you say that Ging. There's me been thinking all these years that you were just the archetypal bank manager. You know the sort, one who's happy to provide you with an umbrella in the sunshine, only to take it away when it rains.' The others sniggered. Ginger glowered at Jimmy, who quickly delved into his steak and kidney pie.

Stan spoke again. 'I hear what you're all saying and in many ways I agree with you, but I have to confess that that sort of thing is just not me, It's not in my make up.'

'Well next time you see some dunderhead driving around in a Rolls Royce just think that could have been you,' Scott interjected aggressively. 'How do you think those people make that sort of money. Certainly not by walking the straight and narrow.'

'I don't think I'd want to own a Rolls Royce,' Stan replied. Scott reacted quickly.

'That's not the point. There must be certain things you want and unfortunately nowadays they all cost money.'

'I know, I know,' Stan said and could feel himself blush again. 'Unfortunately that's just the way I am.'

Scott scowled at him. 'Tell him Jimmy,' he said.

'I've told him,' Jimmy said. 'He knows my feelings on it.'

So that's the way it was left. They finished their lunch, played their snooker and made for home, except Stan, who didn't go straight home like the others. In the clubhouse he hung back, pretending to check on some weekend competition on the notice board. Afterwards he slowly walked towards his car watching the others drive away. When he was sure they'd all gone, he got in his car, took out his mobile phone and dialled Anne.

'It's me,' he said in hushed tones, when she answered.

'Oh hello you,' she replied, sounding delighted.

'Anne, I've decided to take your advice. I'm going to draw out some money.'

'Stan that's wonderful. Are you really sure?'

'Yes I've thought about it a lot. I'm only going to draw out five thousand though. That amount, I can genuinely say is a mistake, as that's what I have in my legitimate account. That's all I'm going to risk Anne.' Anne hesitated before she replied. Stan was holding onto the phone, awaiting her reaction, praying she would be happy with that amount.

'That doesn't matter,' she said. 'It'll be great just to have a go. You have surprised me.' Her voice still sounded upbeat.

'Perhaps I've surprised myself,' he said.

'When do you want to do it?' she asked.

'Let's see what happens with the withdrawal first,' Stan said. 'When it's in my bank account, I'll let you know. I'd better go now, Scott will be home soon, he's just left here.'

'Oh, I don't expect he'll come here first,' Anne said. 'I'll probably see him when it's meal time.'

'I'll phone you when I have some news,' Stan said.

'I can't wait,' The excitement in her voice was infectious, Stan could feel his adrenaline begin to flow.

He switched off his phone, then sat for a long time in his car, in the golf club car park and wondered. Never in his life had he risked anything more than his weekly five pound bet on a horse. Now he was contemplating a fraudulent withdrawal not to mention an affair with the wife of his pal. This mixture of fear and excitement was something new to him. It vibrated through his veins like the strong dose of a drug. He started his car and with a screech of tyres accelerated out of the car park, just as he had seen Scott do many times before. He chuckled to himself as he sped down the lane and switched on the stereo.

CHAPTER ELEVEN

Next morning Stan received three telephone calls. The first one, very early on, was from Jimmy, fortunately Rosemary was still in bed.

'I haven't caught you on the nest have I?' the little Irishman began.

'No you haven't, I'm eating my breakfast,' Stan replied sharply, while putting down his coffee cup.

'Good,' Jimmy said. 'Now Stan, this race I was telling you about is coming up in just over a week. The price for our favourite is still way out. I promise you if you risked a bet, you could make a fortune.'

'And if it lost, I'd wind up in jail,' Stan said.

For the past week Jimmy had been on the phone to his pal Dougal and they'd been avidly totting up their fund, like a pair of stock market traders speculating on a new issue.

'I have a man coming in with a thousand,' Dougal had mentioned. 'That'll take us up to about ten in total. What about your big fish?'

'He's getting cold feet,' Jimmy said.

'Well you must keep at him James. This will be the biggest thing we've ever done.'

'Ay, ay, I will, I will,' Jimmy said.

Jimmy had also been telephoning Ireland. He was not the sort of man to take just one person's word on the amount of money he was speculating. He had distant relatives still living in the area and he'd persuaded some of them to visit the gallops. 'He's a fine looking animal,' one had said. 'He'll run a mile and nothing will catch him,' was the consensus opinion. So Jimmy had no doubts when he spoke to Stan.

'I keep telling you it can't lose,' he said, still trying to quell Stan's fears. 'This isn't over the jumps, it's a flat race. If the horse runs to form there's nothing that can go wrong.'

'And if he doesn't, run to form?'

'He's on top form. I tell you my family have seen him in training.'

'What happens if he's not well on the day?' Stan said.

'If he's not well, they won't run him. He'll be withdrawn and the money will be safe. I'm putting my money on it. I've told you that.'

'But I won't be putting what's not my money on it, Jim. If it was mine, I might take a risk. Not for large amount, but I might be tempted to have a little flutter. I just couldn't do that with somebody else's money though. That would be foolish.'

Stan heard Jimmy sigh at the other end of the phone.

'You're passing up the opportunity of a lifetime,' Jimmy said. 'You'll regret it when the rest of us are all millionaires.'

'No I won't. I don't want to be a millionaire anyway.' At that moment Rosemary came into the kitchen.

'Who are you talking to?' she said.

'It's only Jimmy,' he replied and cupped his hand over the mouthpiece.

'Oh him. What's all this about millionaires?' Her glasses were perched on the end of her nose, she was looking down at Stan over the top of them.

'Just one of his hair-brained schemes,' Stan said with his hand still over the mouthpiece.

'Don't you dare get involved in anything with him Stanley Richards. I warn you. Don't you even think about it.'

'I won't dear, don't worry.'

Jimmy was still firing off on the other end of the line about how he'd help Stan to phone up the building society, but Stan interrupted.

'No really Jim, I think I'll take a rain check on this one,' he said, then rang off.

'Stanley I'm very pleased to hear you say that. I don't know why you mix with such people,' Rosemary said. Stan reverted to buttering his toast.

Later on, in the early part of the morning, while Rosemary was upstairs in the shower, the phone rang again. This time it was Toby.

'I don't want you to take this the wrong way,' Toby said after they'd exchanged some banter about the previous day's golf. 'And I'd never be the one to put temptation in your way, but if you do decide to take Jimmy's advice and have a flutter with that money I'd come in with you for a small amount.'

Stan was taken aback.

'Toby, you of all people. You do surprise me. I thought you

didn't agree with such things.'

'I don't normally, but I mentioned to you before about the Scout Hall roof. I can't see any other way it's going to get done. If you decide to do anything, I'll put a few thousand of mine in with you.'

'Surely things can't be that desperate. Can't you get a grant or something? Anyway you shouldn't be taking a risk with your own money.'

'I doubt if we would get a grant and if we did it would take months, probably years. We need a new roof now, before the winter sets in. I'm not putting any pressure on you Stan. I'm just saying, if you decide to do something, on this occasion, I'll come in with you.'

Stan was silent for a moment.

'I really think it's all too big a risk,' he said eventually. 'I've decided to listen to your original advice. I don't really want to go to jail. I think I'll write to the building society and tell them of their error.'

There was another silent pause on the line.

'I'm sure you're doing the right thing Stan,' Toby said eventually. 'If you change your mind though, will you let me know?' Toby added and rang off.

While Rosemary was organising to go out shopping the phone rang again. She was near the phone and picked it up. It was Ginger. He dispensed a lot of false flattery and then asked if 'her lord and master was in'.

'It's Talbot. I don't know why you men can't make your arrangements on the golf course,' she said to Stan as she passed him the phone. 'I'm on my way anyway. I'll be back for lunch. Don't forget you've got to clean the bathroom.'

Stan waited until she reached the kitchen door, blew her a kiss, then spoke to Ginger.

'Sorry Ging. I was just seeing the missus off.'

'The devoted husband eh,' Ginger said sarcastically. 'Stan, I mentioned to you a week or so ago about this little share issue I knew about. It's really going to be a cracker this one. I was wondering if you were still thinking about dabbling with that ill gotten money of yours.'

'I don't really think so Ging. It's too risky for me.'

Ginger ignored Stan's reply and continued on as though Stan

hadn't said anything.

'You see, if we applied for a big amount we'd get a larger allocation. More profit for us then. I'd put in what I was going to invest, but with your big chunk on top it would make a world of difference at the other end. We could do it as a nominee account and split up the proceeds proportionally afterwards. What do you say?'

Stan sighed.

'I've already said Ging, I'm not going to do it, it's too risky.'

There was another period of silence on the line.

'Are you sure old chap? You're passing up the opportunity of a lifetime. I assure you this listing is gold plated. I've had it straight from the top. The Managing Director is a very good friend of mine. I wouldn't bullshit you Stan, you know me better than that.'

Unfortunately Stan did know Ginger better than that.

'I repeat Ging, I've decided against doing anything. I'm sure your investment is a good bet, but I'm not risking it, not with money that isn't mine anyway.'

Another moment's silence prevailed.

'Oh well please yourself then,' Ginger said off-handedly. 'Don't say I never thought of your welfare.'

'I won't ever say that Ging,' Stan said and he heard Ginger put down the phone.

Stan sat at the kitchen table going over in his mind everything he'd heard in the last hour. It seemed all his mates were prepared at various times to enter into some form of risk taking enterprise. Ginger and Colin with their speculative investments. Scott with his cars and goodness knows what else. Toby had sailed around the world. Jimmy, well Jimmy dabbled in everything. What have I done to bring a little colour, and excitement into my life, he thought. He did, of course, have his weekly flutter, but that wasn't really anything of any real excitement. On the spur of the moment he decided to telephone Anne. The sound of her husky voice excited him when she answered.

'Hiya. Are you free for an afternoon out?' he asked initially.

'Stan *you are* getting bold. I dread to think what you'll be asking me to do next.'

'Ha,' he sniggered. 'I thought maybe we could go and have a

look at some of those sea bays you mentioned. While we're there perhaps you could show me your system again. If you write it down on a piece of paper I may be able to follow it.'

'I couldn't think of anything that I'd like to do more. When have you in mind?' she said.

'How about now. Rosemary's just gone out. Where's Scott?'

'Oh, out somewhere, I never know where. Just as well I think sometimes. '

'Right, I'll leave in half an hour.'

'Excellent,' she replied. They talked some more and then he rang off.

He wrote a note for Rosemary. 'Have gone to buy some timber. Will be out for lunch. Might look at kitchen units while I'm there. Love S.'

Next he went upstairs. The building society pack was still in the bedroom drawer. He ran back down the stairs, fetched the phone and laid the contents of the pack on the bed alongside the letter with the quarter of a million pound balance. For some time he hesitated.

'Oh to hell with it,' he said eventually and dialled the number.

The same recorded voice answered. The same instructions on which keys to press followed as before. He gave his password. When it came to the amount in pounds he typed in five thousand. The amount he had on his original account. That way I can claim it was a genuine mistake he told himself. At the end the metallic voice asked him to press key one to activate the transfer. For many moments his finger hovered, he could feel his body shaking. Eventually, his digit came to rest on key one. He pressed it extra firmly. When he released it he detected a film of sweat form on his brow. 'Your transaction has been completed. The money will be in your bank account in three days', the recorded voice stated. Quickly he switched off the phone, tidied the papers back into the envelope, stuffed the recent missive into his pocket and put the envelope back in the dressing table drawer. Then carefully replaced the other items on top, in the order they'd been before.

* * * * *

That same day, Toby visited the special school at Carmarthen. All the previous evening and later on in bed he'd fretted about the situation, continuing to blame himself. The first 'no no' of the social security job, was 'don't get involved personally with the clients' and he had. Secondly, with every passing sleepless hour he realised he had committed an unforgivable sin. Every Sunday when he attended church he repeated the words 'thou shalt not commit adultery'. But he'd done that willingly, compliantly and without turning a hair. Unfortunately, once Catryn was off the drugs, her youth and her new found vivacity had carried him along on a path of unmitigated licentiousness, without a second thought. Desperate to cure her addiction, their romantic liaison had seemed like an extension of the treatment. Having Mark also brought Catryn a renewed sense of responsibility and she'd revelled in the challenge. That night as Toby lay on his bed, with Margaret alongside him, he watched the clock and the early hours tick by. Most of his thoughts were riddled with guilt. Guilt, in the way he had deceived Margaret. Guilt, in the way he'd abandoned all his principles in getting Catryn pregnant. Guilt, in the way he had abused his position in the job and most of all guilt that he was old enough to have known better. If anybody discovered the truth, he'd be disgraced. The crippling aspect was not being able to share his thoughts on the subject with anyone. Margaret was usually his sounding board, but in this instance that was out of the question.

* * * * *

Bill Witherspoon, the school's principal, greeted Toby like an old comrade, clasping his hand fondly when they met. Everybody in that corner of Wales, who worked in social security, education or local government knew Toby. Many, many times Toby had arranged for difficult pupils to attend Witherspoon's establishment. The warm greeting added to Toby's despair, deepening his guilt, widened his shame.

'How are you my friend?' Witherspoon said. He was a tall, gangling middle aged man, with a grey complexion and wispish greying hair, receding at the temples. Wearing half moon spectacles, perched at the end of his nose, a baggy grey two piece suit and the most enormous pair of black shoes, with two inch thick soles, he stooped over Toby with the air of an inquisitive school master.

'Oh bearing up Bill, like all of us I guess,' Toby responded.

Witherspoon guided the way towards his office. Inside, Toby

related the details of his problem child, without mentioning his parenthood involvement.

'We could take him of course Toby, but you know our set up. The parent would have to pay. We can only take them on assistance if there is no parent at all. Do we know who the father is?'

'Not at this stage,' Toby said sheepishly.

They discussed fees, residential requirements and the like. Mark could reside in the school Monday to Thursday night. They concluded their meeting by talking about the problems of Toby's work. When he left Witherspoon's office he felt like a complete fraud.

Toby drove home depressed, dwelling on his stupidity. The money involved to pay for a terms fees wasn't totally prohibitive. But anything more than a year would make a big hole in his life savings. And how would he ever explain that to Margaret he thought.

'Are you all right?' she asked when he was back inside their house. A woman's intuition had spotted something had been wrong for the past few days.

'Yes. Just a heavy caseload at the moment,' he replied.

She looked at him again, she was sure it was more than that. She waited for him to explain. Usually they discussed things fully but this time he wasn't forthcoming.

'Don't you think at your age you should give up some of these commitments. We haven't had a holiday for nearly two years. You're no good to me dead, Toby Ballard.'

* * * * *

Stan had arranged to meet Anne at a supermarket car park on the way to the coast.

'Why do I feel as though I'm playing truant?' he said to her when she opened the window of her Range Rover when it drew up alongside. Fortunately the warmth of her smile injected him with courage. She was wearing a canary yellow jumpsuit that accentuated all the colours of her body.

'We'll take mine if you like,' she said pointing at the Rover. 'This will drive on a beach or up a rough lane if we need to.'

And so they set off, like a couple of newlyweds about to embark on their first exercise in house hunting. The sun was shining, the sky was clear blue. Anne alongside him looked like a Hollywood film star and it all made him feel like a young beau again.

'I've drawn the money out,' he said. 'It'll be in my bank account in three days.'

She looked across at him.

'You haven't. How much?'

'Five thousand,' he said hesitatingly. 'I can cover that from my existing balance.'

For a moment he didn't know if she was going to mock or praise him, but suddenly the glowing smile was back on her face.

'Oh Stan, that's great.' Her left arm stretched out and with her hand she rubbed his right thigh. For the rest of the journey they talked excitedly. She described the bays they could look at, the private caravan sites she knew, the best pubs, the nicest restaurants.

'Did you bring your little red note book?' Stan inquired.

'Oh yes, I made sure to bring that,' she replied.

They eventually stopped at a rocky cove, with a beach just big enough for half a dozen people to sit on at low tide without getting in each other's way. The narrow road they'd just travelled along skirted the coastline, connecting one village to the next. She parked the Rover in the access way and while they sat admiring the view, she extracted from her handbag the red notebook. Meticulously she went over again how her system worked; tirelessly trying to explain all the nuances. First time round Stan was just as confused as he'd been before. 'I really don't follow that at all,' he said in an embarrassed tone.

Anne sighed, picked up a biro and began to illustrate each point again. On the third attempt Stan had just about grasped the rudiments. 'I don't know whether I could do that in a casino though, under pressure,' he said.

'You don't have to,' Anne replied, 'You just leave it all to me. As long as you have some idea of what I'm doing that's all that matters.'

'H'm,' he snorted.

To attempt to clear his head they'd decided to walk down to the sea. At that precise moment Jimmy was travelling along the same coast road on his way to meet up with Dougal. The race date was nearing. It was time to put their syndicate together and the trip was another opportunity for Jimmy to train his pigeons. The little road behind the beach was the route Jimmy took to Dougal's village. Instantly he recognised Anne's personalised number plates. He pulled up behind the Rover, then he saw the two figures on the beach, down near the shoreline. Initially thinking it was Anne and Scott, he was just about to toot his horn when he noticed that the man wasn't Scott. The couple were moving around, almost playing, like a couple of teenagers. Stan was chasing her. When he caught her he put his arm round her waist and they walked along the shoreline hand in hand.

Jimmy couldn't believe his eyes. 'Stanley you old devil,' he said to himself. 'You bloody lucky old devil,' he repeated.

For a second he thought again about sounding the car horn; embarrass the two of them to death. His hand hovered over the steering wheel, but something somewhere in the dark enclaves of his devious little mind stopped him. A cynical thought flashed through his brain, preventing his hand from making contact with the horn. Maybe, just maybe, he thought, I could use this to my advantage. So he drove slowly on, looking across to the beach all the time, watching the two of them frolicking down by the sea-shore.

The narrow road twisted up a steep hill away from the bay and at the top he pulled into a gateway, stopped the car and ran back to the edge of the cliff. From there, the high vantage point meant he could see down onto the beach, where Stan and Anne were still wrapped up in each other, arm in arm. They were walking along the edge of the tide. Briefly they stopped and then Jimmy saw Stan turn his head sideways to kiss Anne on the lips.

'Well now won't you look at that,' Jimmy said to himself. 'There's a pretty sight, if ever there was.'

For some minutes he crouched and watched the two of them, just to make sure they really were alone. A car approached, so he made his way back to his own vehicle, talking to the pigeons when he got inside.

'Well now my beauties,' he said. 'There's a thing or two going on down there I would never have believed. You're not the only ones trying to fly.'

* * * * *

When he arrived home Stan's mind was still encased in fanciful cliff top caravan sites and quaint seaside pubs.

Rosemary remarked on it. 'You look miles away Stan. Is it all those nice kitchens you've been looking at? You were gone a long time.'

'Yes dear,' he lied. 'I couldn't find the timber I wanted so I went into Swansea. By the time I got there it was lunchtime and I was hungry so I stopped for a bite to eat. But I still couldn't find any timber. That's why I was late.'

'What about my kitchen?'

'I looked at some of those as well.'

'Well?' Rosemary asked questioningly.

'It's all changed a lot since we last bought a kitchen.'

'Shows you how long ago it is then doesn't it.'

He suddenly realised he had never actually told Rosemary a deliberate lie before. Many times he had bent the truth, changed the facts around slightly, to avoid a nagging, but never a complete and outright lie.

In the evening he telephoned Colin.

'I'm sorry to disturb you Colin,' he began.'But there's a mathematical formula I've got to get my head around and the only person I know who can help me is you. Would it be possible to call on you some time?'

For Colin, any chance to get his mind into a new set of figures was like tempting a wine taster with a new vintage. The opportunity to test his brain against any formula was just too irresistible to turn down.

'Why don't you come over this evening,' Colin replied. 'Veronica is going out to one of her meetings.'

'I've got to nip out to see Colin,' Stan told Rosemary later.

'You're out a lot these days Stanley Richards. If I didn't know you better I'd think you had another woman.'

Stan felt his cheeks redden. He tried to cover it with a chuckle. 'There's something Colin's going to show me on his computer. I won't be long.'

There, he'd lied again. He was worried about it becoming a habit. He'd written his own notes regarding Anne's formula on scraps of paper whilst at the pub they had visited for lunch. In his car he smoothed them out on the front passenger seat before starting the engine to drive off to Colin's house.

You approached Colin's property along a narrow lane that weaves through a wooded valley. Rain had arrived earlier that evening and a gusty wind was scattering the first leaves of the autumn. Stan's headlights illuminated the swaying gold, greens and yellows of the foliage. Something moved in the hedgerow. Stan slowed and a fox loped out in front of his wheels, causing him to brake hurriedly. He drove on feeling slightly shaken. The outside lights of the house were on. The ivy clad walls and tall chimneys gave the rambling old structure a mystical quality. Stan got out of his car and pulled on a wrought iron bell, half expecting a coat tailed butler to answer. He was disappointed when only Colin, in his horn rimmed glasses, pulled back the door.

He led the way to his study. The curtains were drawn; a plethora of small table lamps gave the room a warm atmosphere. Dudley was sprawled out on one of the leather chairs. Sleepily he lifted his head when Stan entered the room and quickly dropped it back down again onto his paws. Stan's immediately noticed the array of calculators. He moved towards Colin's desk inspecting closely those within view.

'And they all work,' Colin said. 'A toddy for the brain?' he asked holding up a decanter of brandy.

'Oh I don't know, I'm driving,' Stan said.

'A little one won't hurt,' Colin replied, and half filled two balloon glasses.

He gave one to Stan and they both settled in leather chairs in front of Colin's desk. In his left hand Stan was clutching the scruffy bits of paper he'd scribbled Anne's formula on.

'Now what have you got there my boy?' Colin said, pointing at them after they'd supped at their brandy.

'I'm not sure,' Stan began, flattening out the bits of paper on the desk. 'I'm told it's a system that'll guarantee success on a roulette wheel. I've only just got the basics of it, but I can't see how it's guaranteed. That's why I've come to you.'

'That sounds unlike you, gambling on a roulette wheel. You know what Einstein is reputed to have said, 'You cannot beat a Roulette Table, unless you steal money from it.'

Stan sat back in his chair. 'At this stage I don't know that I will be doing any gambling. I've seen this system in action at a casino. The person involved made one hundred and thirty pounds from a hundred quid in under an hour. Now whether that was just luck or for real is what I'm trying to establish.'

'H'm,'Colin said and rubbed the side of his nose. 'Well let's have a look at what you've got.' He took the pieces of paper from Stan and moved behind his desk, donned a different pair of horn-rimmed spectacles and picked up, from the shelf behind him, one of his many calculators.

For the next quarter of an hour or so Stan tried his best to explain what Anne had told him. There were many facets he couldn't remember. In attempting to unravel the system, he sometimes confused himself further. Colin listened, without saying much more than 'H'm' or 'Oh'. He wrote down many figures on a foolscap sheet of paper as Stan talked. Occasionally he reverted to his calculator. When Stan finished his description, the sheet of paper was full. Very interesting,' Colin said, put down his pen and took off his glasses. He began his analysis using words like operands, averages, trends and others Stan had never heard of before, let alone understood. It became too technical so Stan was forced to interrupt.

'Hang on a minute Colin,' he said. 'That's far too complicated for me. I don't understand any of that. All I want to know is, is the system fool proof?'

Colin rubbed the side of his nose again, then began polishing his horn-rimmed glasses with the end of his tie.

'No system is completely foolproof,' he said. 'This is a formula based on the Fibonacci sequence. If you feed in the right variables it could be ninety per cent accurate. But if you put in the wrong variables the whole thing will go haywire.'

Stan sat back again in the leather chair and sighed.

'Were you thinking of using this for that money of yours?' Colin asked.

Stan hesitated. Up until then he'd kept everything to do with this matter to himself. Firstly he didn't want to be implicated with Anne and secondly having rejected all the other's ideas and said the whole thing was too risky, he really didn't want to reveal his change of heart.

'I'm going to swear you to secrecy on this Colin,' he said and looked across at him. ' If I do anything I'm not going to dabble with anything like the full amount on that statement. I already have a few thousand pounds of my own legitimate money in that account and I was perhaps thinking of taking a chance with a similar sum, that's all. But you are the only one who knows that and I'd ask you to keep it to yourself.'

They looked at each other, eye to eye.

'Of course dear boy. Just as you wish,' Colin said. 'Only if you don't understand completely how this system works you're never going to be able to use it in a casino. There just isn't the time in between bets and if you don't bet on the next roll you'll lose the trend.'

'I might get the person who devised the system to bet for me,' Stan said and gulped down the remainder of his brandy.

'H'm,' Colin said. 'Would you like me to set something out for you, something you could follow?'

'Oh Colin would you?'

'I'll see what I can do. Mind you it won't be the same system as this.' Stan looked puzzled. 'It'll be simpler for you to understand. I'll set it out on paper. You'll have to learn it parrot fashion though and if you're going to use it you'll have to apply it to the letter and be able to do it with your eyes closed. You can't deviate from it, even when you're losing. This system here,' Colin said, holding up the sheet of foolscap, 'has room for a margin of error, if you change the variables. But if you get the variables wrong you'll go down the Swanee.'

Soon after that Veronica returned from her meeting. Colin agreed to write out his system for Stan to have on Monday. That night, with variables and averages swirling round in his brain, sleep for Stan was difficult. By three o'clock he wondered if the whole thing was too much for him. Then, a vision of Anne's smiling face projected into his subconscious and gradually a sleepy tiredness overpowered him.

CHAPTER TWELVE

That weekend was our groups monthly foray into the club's competitions. The third Saturday of the month is always the day of the Monthly Medal; a club competition for single players, where every shot played counts towards your score. That means there are no 'gimmees' on putts and at the end of the eighteen holes each player has to add up his total gross score for the round, then deduct his handicap. The best or lowest net score, gross less handicap, wins the competition. In addition, the round is played from the competition tees, which are usually situated twenty or thirty yards behind the yellow tees, which most players play off during the week; thereby making the holes longer. There are usually prizes for the winner and the four best scores behind him.

By and large most of the members of our group don't enjoy playing in the Monthly Medal. Firstly, it involves paying an entry fee, which for nearly all of them goes against the grain. Secondly, the prize winners, those usually placed first to fifth, don't actually receive cash as a prize. To comply with amateur status, any prize money is awarded as a credit in the club Professional's shop, for the purchase of equipment or golf clubs.

'Bloody swindle', Jimmy always says, 'just another way of lining the pro's pocket'. And thirdly, the competition involves counting every shot, unlike the stableford scoring system our boys use in the week. The pressure therefore involved in avoiding a high score often gets to the player's nerves. Sometimes causing the symptoms of high blood pressure and cardiac arrest.

'I don't know why I put myself through this punishment,' Ginger remarks when he arrives at the course that day and begins unloading his clubs from the car.

'It's the only way your handicap can be accurately assessed,' Colin replies.

The format used involves recording the details of all scores incurred in the competition being entered into the club's computer and afterwards handicaps are then adjusted, upwards or downwards, depending on the net score achieved.

'I think sometimes you lot deliberately play badly in competitions so you can get a higher handicap,' Ginger says.

Having a higher handicap means that players receive more shots to deduct from their gross scores when they play each other in their weekday matches for money.

'He's sussed you out at last Colin,' Jimmy cut in, grinning from ear to ear. 'I always knew there was some ulterior motive behind those mathematical calculations of yours.'

'Huh. I wouldn't waste my time on such frivolities. I enter the competition because it is the only properly structured game of golf we play. Which means, unlike when I play with you bandits, I do have an even chance of winning,' Colin replied.

Stan who had arrived and parked in a space alongside them, said, 'Quite right Colin.'

'Thank you Stan,' Colin replied, while he heaved his golf bag onto his trolley. Colin's trolley was a battery driven affair, equipped with almost as many sophisticated attachments as his computer. He operated and guided it by a remote control unit, not unlike a mini version of the type you use for a television. His regular party piece once he'd loaded and wired everything together, was to set the trolley on a path for the clubhouse while he remained seated on the beam of his car's rear bumper tying up his shoe laces.

'I once had a dog who would do that, 'Jimmy said, watching the trolley whizz past him like a mad dalek on the loose. 'Trouble was he'd never come back.'

'I bet you wish you could get your golf ball to obey you like that,' Scott said, having just arrived alongside the others.

A ritual among our group that proceeded a medal round was the habit of imbibing a mouthful of 'Dutch courage'. Jimmy was usually the provider. 'Just to settle the nerves,' he said as he unscrewed the top of his hip flask. The blend he'd concocted was a mixture of his best Irish malt, with an added liberal quantity of Cointreau. He took a large swig before passing the flask to Scott.

'Bloody firewater,' Scott said after taking a mouthful.

'Put lead in your pencil that will,' Jimmy said.

'He doesn't need any lead in his pencil,' Toby said smirking. The others looked at each other and nodded.

And so they made their way to the Pro shop, to pay their entry fees. Byron Curtis, the club's Golf Professional was often the butt of Jimmy's tongue. He'd a lesson with him once, which turned into a disaster and Jimmy never tried again. 'Put ten shots on my game,' Jimmy said at the time. Jimmy also thought Byron was tight. 'He never gives discount on anything you buy,' Jimmy said regularly.

They gathered around the till in the Pro-shop.

'I expect you get commission on these fees,' Jimmy said as he handed his four pounds entry fee to the pro. Two pounds was for the competition, one pound for the holes you finished in two shots and another pound for a bag draw. In that instance all the cards entered, are thrown in a hat and whoever is drawn out wins a cash equivalent prize.

Byron was used to Jimmy's carping.

'If I did Jimmy, I wouldn't be standing here listening to you lot on a Saturday morning,' he replied to Jimmy's barb.

'You'd be on the European tour, I expect Byron,' Jimmy retorted quickly. He knew Byron had once competed in one of the qualifying events for the main European tour, but hadn't made it through.

'Oh I could think of somewhere better than that to be,' the Pro said, while passing out their score cards. Byron was a big man with fair straight hair and a build like John Daly. 'You boys try and keep out of the bunkers today,' he continued, 'you know how they make a mess of your scores.'

'Tight fisted bastard,' Jimmy said when they were outside.

A medal competition was the one occasion when some of them would practice before a round. Toby never bothered. Jimmy sometimes would roll up a few putts on the practice green, but on Medal days, Colin, Scott, Stan and Ginger always went to the practice ground first. There, for ten minutes or so, they'd attempt some chipping shots, coerce some mid irons and swish at a couple of drives.

This often meant that one of them was late on the tee for their starting time. That day Colin was paired off with Jimmy and Ginger and Jimmy was waiting impatiently. 'I don't know why you blokes bother to practice,' he said trying to hurry the other two. 'You'll wear yourselves out before you start.'

'If it's good enough for Tiger Woods, it's good enough for me,' Ginger said, a little out of breath as he walked up the steps of the first tee.

'If you played golf one tenth as good as Tiger Woods you

wouldn't need to practice at all,' Jimmy said.

'Now don't get me angry before I begin,' Ginger replied taking out his driver. 'I've paid good money to be in this.'

Ginger took two big deep breaths, then embarked on numerous violent practice swings. There followed a lot of posturing and lining up behind the ball, before he eventually took his stance. Jimmy looked at Colin and shook his head. There was a moments pause then Ginger attacked the ball with the same vigour as his practice swing. Basically he mis-hit it, topped it, causing the little white object to trickle down the fairway about twenty yards in front of him, before coming to a forlorn halt alongside the yellow tee they normally played off in the week. The other two looked at each other and worked hard to suppress their laughter.

'Seems like a bit more practice might have been in order there Ging. We're playing off the white's today, not the yellows,' Jimmy said.

'Now I blame you for that,' Ginger replied pointing at his ball.

The other two made respectable drives and they were away. Now, as I mentioned before, in a competition the rules of golf have to be applied to the letter. When our guys are playing amongst themselves, sometimes the rules are bent. Not necessarily to cheat in anyway, more to get the game over with in a reasonable time and without incurring too many lasting arguments. You might say certain rulings are glossed over.

On competition day however, the rule book is applied and there isn't more of a stickler for its application than Colin. On the fifth hole Ginger's drive took a vicious kick to the left when it landed on the fairway. As a result the ball came to rest in a hacked out hollow on the edge of the fairway. The other two had driven to the right hand side of the fairway and they looked across to see Ginger eyeing his ball warily.

'I think I'm in a rabbit scraping,' Ginger bellowed across at them. To obtain relief from that type of lie it has to be verified by your playing partners. If the ball has indeed come to rest in any animal scraping, or hollow, you are entitled to drop the ball outside it, without penalty. The other two walked over. Ginger was still postulating over his ball, which had come to rest in a spot where the turf had been removed to a radius of about five inches, making his next shot extremely difficult.

'Looks like a rabbit scraping to me.' Ginger said pointing, when the other two arrived.

Colin and Jimmy circled around the golf ball, like two drainage inspectors come to check on a burst water main.

'H'm,' Jimmy said, scratching his chin. 'I'd say that was a divot wouldn't you Colin.' A divot is where a clod of turf has been removed by a golf club striking the ground and leaving a bare patch and that doesn't have the benefit of a free drop, if your ball lands in it. At that stage Colin wasn't committing himself.

'Of course it's a bloody scraping,' Ginger said glaring at Jimmy. 'There's bloody rabbit droppings all over the fucking place.' He pointed to the copious pellets of the animal's toilet that decorated the edge of the fairway.

'I'll grant you there's droppings Ging. But they're from over there. You can see where their feet have removed the grass,' Jimmy replied and pointed to a spot more into the rough, where there had obviously been rabbit activity. 'This divot has the shape of a big golf club, a three wood I guess. The rabbit scrapings are narrower and deeper and the muck isn't anywhere near the divot. This is a golf club divot.'

'Absolute bloody rubbish,' Ginger said. 'What do you think Colin?'

All this time Colin had been pondering on the situation. This was a vital stage of the game; a medal round is all about achieving a par score on each hole. If Ginger had to drop an extra shot here, it would spoil what had the makings of a reasonable round. Also, it would destroy the fragile non-contentious relationship that had prevailed so far that morning. But the conscientious application of rules and regulations had always been a dominant factor in Colin's life.

'I grant you it has the look of a rabbit scraping Ginger,' Colin began cautiously. 'But,' he added, reached into Ginger's golf bag and extracted his three wood, 'the marking here is identical to the format of a three wood.' He removed the club's head cover and inserted the club head into the point of impact on the ground. It was a perfect fit. 'See what I mean. I think we would have to say that's a divot.'

Jimmy said nothing, just nodded his head. Ginger made no reply, but glared at Jimmy, then snatched the three wood from

Colin. The two walked back to their balls on the other side of the fairway. All the while they could hear Ginger thumping practice swings into the ground.

'That'll be an even bigger hole by the time he's finished there.' Jimmy said to Colin, who just smiled.

In due time, they heard Ginger's three wood make contact with his ball. There followed a barrage of expletives, as it dived into the rough, some hundred and fifty yards ahead.

For the next hour or so they played on in near silence. Jimmy tried to placate matters by complimenting Ginger's every good shot and sometimes his mediocre ones as well, but Ginger played on stoically, almost ignoring the other two.

By the time they reached the fourteenth green Colin had the makings of a good score. Ginger had continued to bemoan his luck, mostly to himself, on almost every hole since the fifth. That day he certainly wasn't going to win any prizes. Jimmy was also on the way to a score that was unlikely to win anything either, but Colin had kept quietly plugging away. There had been no birdies for him, but a steady succession of pars had put him in contention for a prize.

By then the wind had got up and the incoming tide was accompanied by a damp south westerly, the kind of weather that makes playing golf difficult and takes the enjoyable edge off the game.

The fourteenth green is the most westerly point on the course, facing directly out to sea. From there on in, the holes lead back to the clubhouse, with the prevailing conditions usually behind you. On the fourteenth green however, you get the full brunt of whatever the sea throws at you.

They had all donned caps and waterproofs. On the green, while he was standing over his ball, preparing to putt, Ginger's peaked baseball cap was blown from his head by a tornado-like gust. 'Fucking weather,' he said, as he watched his cap blow thirty yards across the green. Jimmy ran to retrieve it, while Ginger continued with his putt, and of course, he missed. More mumbled expletives were heard as he picked his third putt from out of the cup. Jimmy handed him the cap, which he snatched without saying a word.

Colin was next to putt. The wind gusted, his trousers flapped, flecks of spray off the sea whipped across the green. Colin cleaned his ball on his towel and replaced it in front of his marker. Then he lined up; he was about eight feet from the hole and needed this putt to go in for a par. The wind was still gusting, he took a few practice strokes. The fine drizzle on his glasses was making it difficult to see. He took a long time steadying himself, trying to keep his body still. Carefully he put his putter down behind the ball. Then, just as he was about to putt, Ginger called out.

'That ball moved.'

· Now, the rule is, if a ball moves when you address it, having grounded your club, the ball must be lifted and replaced before it can be putted. In a strong wind, on a closely cropped putting green, the ball will often move marginally, or sometimes sway in its resting-place. Colin was in the middle of his putting stroke, but Ginger's intervention caused him to stop.

'I didn't see it move,' Colin said, looking across at Ginger.

'It definitely moved,' Ginger said dogmatically. Colin looked at Jimmy.

'I never saw it move,' Jimmy said. 'Mind you, in this wind my eyes are watering so badly I can't see much anyway.'

'It definitely moved,' Ginger repeated. 'You'll have to replace it before you can putt.'

Colin sighed. He hadn't seen the ball move and he'd been standing right over it. Rules were rules however and in Colin's mind the integrity of your opponent in golf was unquestioned. So, he marked the spot, lifted the ball and replaced it again before putting. You've guessed it. He missed the putt and dropped a shot.

The weather deteriorated further over the remaining four holes. From there on in conversation became sparse. Colin continued to drop shots, like an erratic fielder in the slips and finished with a score that was one shot worse than Ginger's. By the time they walked off the eighteenth green communication was non existent. They were cold and wet. Only a cursory handshake was exchanged before they trudged off to the sanctuary of the clubhouse.

'Pity about the weather. Spoilt it a bit,' Ginger said, as finished cleaning up in the changing room. The other two remained silent.

Ginger didn't stay for a drink. Colin and Jimmy retired to the bar, to await the others, muttering evil condemnations about their playing partner.

* * * * *

With every day Toby's pangs of conscience deepened. Each morning, after golf, he journeyed over to see Catryn. Every visit however, invoked more pain, brought more despair. It was as though he had just awakened from a memory lapse and couldn't understand how he had got himself into such a mess.

Catryn's continuing resentment only added to his misery. Suddenly, she appeared to look upon their relationship in a jaundiced light. Gone, was the bright cheerful girl, whom he'd seen restored to full health. Gone, was the warm, affectionate lover he'd developed a comforting relationship with. All those feelings were becoming a distant memory. In its place, he was discovering a surly, argumentative little madam. He'd noticed a change in Mark as well. A once happy and contented child, he now appeared to cry a lot. Catryn put it down to a cold, but Toby wondered. He wondered if Catryn was permanently back on drugs again. Each time he asked, she denied it, but the boy from the village was often around the house. His enquiries in that respect were always challenged, by Catryn, with the words, 'what's that got to do with you?' The situation was beginning to prey seriously on his nerves. Up until then he had been able to compartmentalise the whole saga of their relationship into a little box and place it somewhere in the corner of his mind. Now, it was running wild and free in his head, like a forest fire, contaminating all the other precincts in which he had felt safe and secure.

That Saturday afternoon, after the medal round, he was in the kitchen of Catryn's house, with her and Mark. His questions as to their well-being had been mostly met with taciturn responses. Toby was sat at one of the rickety chairs by the small kitchen table. He remembered buying the pair of them at a car boot sale.

'I visited the school in the week,' Toby said. Catryn was at the sink, tackling what looked like more than a day's washing up.

'And?' she replied insolently. Toby noticed her hair had lost its sheen. Her clothes looked as though they'd been on for most of the week.

'They are prepared to take him, although it will involve having to pay,' he said patiently.

110

'And?' she repeated, thumping each dish down on the sink noisily.

'Well what do you think?' Toby said. She turned and scowled at him.

'Well I haven't got any money. What do you mean what do I think? You know what I think.'

'What I meant was, are you happy for him to be away for four nights in the week?'

Catryn turned to face him full on. Her wet, soapy hands went to her hips. her elbows stuck out in a demanding posture; a furrowed frown creased her forehead.

'Toby, I just want to get a job. So I can keep myself and live a normal life.'

To avoid her agitated countenance, he found himself brushing the crumbs on the table in front of him into a neat and tidy pile. 'I know you do dear,' he said. 'I just don't want you to be unhappy if he isn't around you all day. You've had him here all the time since he was born.'

'I *know* I've had him around me since he was born,' she said vehemently and turned back to continue with the washing up, slamming more dishes down on the drainer board.

'All right, all right. I'll get it organised this week. I am trying to do what's best for all of us Catryn.' She made no reply.

A few moments later the back door opened and the youth Toby had seen sitting on the settee the other day, slouched in. Toby inspected him carefully. He was a lad, not much more than twenty, of medium height, wearing a grubby white T-shirt, with the words 'Sid Vicious Lives On', written on the front, baggy fawn slacks and a pair of scruffy sneakers. His hair was dark and closely cropped. Three brass rings pierced through his left ear lobe and a brass stud was at the side of his nose. He totally ignored Toby.

'Come on Catryn, are you ready,' he said.

'I've just got to finish this first,' she replied, reached for the tea towel and began wiping the dishes. 'Darren and I are going out for the afternoon Toby. Will you have Mark?' Catryn said, turning her head over her shoulder to half look at him.

The youth was slouched against the door frame. Toby was taken aback by her words. 'My wife's expecting me,' he said defensively. The youth scoffed. Catryn said, 'I thought you might say that,' and continued wiping the dishes. Toby rose from the chair.

'I'll make the arrangements in the week,' he said. Catryn made no reply. Darren remained standing in the doorway. Toby had to brush past him to get out. The youth hardly moved. Toby could detect the sweet smell of pot on his clothes.

For the rest of that day Toby was in a low mood. Later in the afternoon he went to the harbour, to clean up his boat, but his depression prevailed. For the first time in his life he felt his age. In the evening, sitting in their lounge, Margaret remarked on his quietness.

'Are you all right Toby?' she asked. 'You're very quiet.'

'Yes I'm fine,' he replied.

All that night he hardly slept. At Church in the morning he prayed. What he was praying for he really didn't know. Forgiveness, fortitude, strength, guidance, they all swirled through his head, but not one of them seemed applicable in his case. The vicar chose adherence to the Ten Commandments as his sermon and that only seemed to rub salt in Toby's wounds.

He spent most of the day attending to his Church duties. After dinner that evening he slumped in the armchair in front of the television and fell asleep. Something Margaret had rarely seen him do before.

* * * * *

On Sunday Jimmy met up with Dougal at The Myrtle Inn. The horse they were backing was running that week at Kempton Park and they needed to organise their money. Slowly, their cash commitments were coming together. Already, they had decided to split the pot into two bets. One, Jimmy would take to a betting shop in Haverfordwest, where he wasn't known. The other, Dougal would place at a similar establishment in Cardigan.

'They're different firms as well,' Jimmy said, when they were sitting together in the pub, 'so that way we shouldn't attract any attention.' They had decided it would be better not to put down a very large bet at one office, there might be a problem.

'With that amount of cash though we'd better go in half an hour before in case there's any questions. We'll liaise on our mobiles and go in through the door of each shop at the same time,' Dougal had said. He lit up another cigarette. A downdraft from the gale outside belched a cloud of smoke into the room, adding to the fug. He took a draw on the cigarette and coughed a rattling smoker's hack. 'Is there any more on that big amount of money?' he asked when he had finished spluttering. 'Is he likely to come on board?'

'Doesn't look like it,' Jimmy replied, then hesitated. 'There is one thing I haven't tried though which may work.'

'What's that?' Dougal said. Eamonn was sitting on the upright bench alongside him and shifted himself arthritically into a more comfortable position.

'Blackmail!' Jimmy said.

Dougal's eyes lit up. 'Tell me more.'

Jimmy related the details of his sighting on the beach.

'Get away with you,' Dougal said. 'How will you threaten him,' his voice croaked with excitement, his face was alive; the weathered wrinkles, veins and warts protruded like the granite pinnacles on a mountain, as he sucked energetically on the butt end of his cigarette.

'I can't really threaten him with anything. I told you he's a mate and his wife's a nagger. But just letting him know that I know may be enough. I mean two women cost a lot of money, one's bad enough.'

'Ach James you're just an old softy. If it was me, I'd threaten him with exposure.'

'I don't think that would work. He's such a stick in the mud. That's what is so amazing about what I saw. If I threatened him with anything he'd run a mile. Then we certainly wouldn't get any money and my man wouldn't get his nooky, and she's a cracker.'

A raucous cackle emitted from Dougal's mouth. The aperture revealed a cavern of fractured, decaying teeth, aligned haphazardly between innumerable worn gum gaps. 'Come on let's have another,' he said draining his pint. Eamonn sat up.

CHAPTER THIRTEEN

Over the weekend, while Rosemary was out of the house, Stan used the telephone to check the balance on his bank account. He hadn't been aware before that you could do such a thing, but fishing around in all the paperwork he discovered the relevant number and their last bank statement. A recorded voice on the phone read out a balance. It was approximately five thousand pounds greater than the balance on their last statement. Straight away he telephoned Anne.

'My money's come through,' he said excitedly when she answered. 'We can arrange a date for the casino whenever you like.'

'Stan that's marvellous. What about Tuesday afternoon?'

Stan took a deep breath. 'Sounds OK to me.'

'Wonderful. We'll go to Bristol. I haven't been there for a while.'

On Monday he told Rosemary he was going to be out on Tuesday afternoon. 'I still haven't found the type of wood I want. I'm going to have to look further afield. It may take a few hours.'

'You and that old woodwork of yours,' she replied. 'What about my kitchen?'

'I've told you, I'll think about it,' he said firmly. Rosemary looked at him. He didn't usually speak to her with such authority. 'I'm making enquiries with my Pension people, to see if it's possible to get hold of some cash out of that.'

* * * * *

On Monday afternoon Toby visited the school in Carmarthen and met up again with Bill Witherspoon.

'I'd like to get the boy I mentioned in here as soon as possible,' he said in Witherspoon's study. 'He's not picking up any words at all and his mother's not well. I'm worried about him.'

'Just as you wish.' Witherspoon replied stiltedly. 'We can start him next week, if that's what you want. As I mentioned there's the question of the fees.'

'I've said I'll help the mother out with that. She's a sort of friend of a friend. Can we pay by the term.'

Witherspoon was sitting behind his large cluttered wooden desk. He had very large hands, like table tennis bats, and he placed the tops of the fingers of both hands together as though he was praying.

'Of course you can, but are you sure you're doing the right thing. It's going to be of no benefit to the boy if he doesn't spend at least a year, or maybe more, with us. If you say she's got no money, she's not likely to have any in the future either. You're taking on an awful lot yourself in this instance, if you don't mind me saying.'

Toby looked flustered. His cheeks reddened.

'I think we've got a lead on the father,' he said. 'What we can gather is he's in a well paid job, so eventually we should get some lien on his salary. I'm just tiding them over until then. As I said, the family's known to me, so there shouldn't be a problem. And the child really is going to be backward if something isn't done soon.'

Witherspoon looked at Toby dispassionately. He was about to repeat his previous warning, but he didn't. 'Just as you wish,' he said and reached in his desk drawer for the requisite forms. In completing them they had to scotch over many questions. Toby actually knew the real answers as they all related to him, but such was his relationship with Witherspoon, that he got away with it.

'I'll need the mother to give her consent at the bottom here,' Witherspoon said, pointing to the spot on the form when they reached the end.

'I'll bring it back with the boy and a cheque on Monday,' Toby said and then made an excuse about a pressing appointment and left quickly.

When he'd gone, Bill Witherspoon sat behind his desk for a long time, with his big hands together as before. He'd known Toby Ballard for over ten years and in that time he'd come to respect him greatly. He knew he was a fit, intelligent man, who'd been a pillar of the community. But he'd never known Toby look so flustered, or brush over so many imponderables. He just couldn't imagine Toby doing anything silly, but at that moment he did wonder.

On the way home Toby called in on Catryn. When he arrived at the house Mark was cavorting around on his small bike in the garden. Toby bent down to talk to him.'And how are you today Mark?' Toby asked. The child didn't respond jumped off the bike and ran away into the house.

Catryn was in the kitchen, wearing the same clothes she had worn the other day. Toys and washing were scattered about the floor, dishes were again unwashed around the sink.

'Hasn't he been to school today?' Toby asked.

'No, he wasn't well enough,' she replied in an off-hand manner.

Toby took a long, hard look at her. Mark was now with them in the kitchen, leaning against her legs looking warily at him. Catryn bore the similarities of the young girl he'd seen on their first meeting, four years ago.

'I've arranged for him to go into the special school next Monday,' he said.

'Good,' she replied.

'Will you be able to take care of him until then?'

'Haven't I taken care of him up to now. Where would he be now if I hadn't taken care of him?'

They stared at each other.

'I'm only enquiring Catryn. You said you hadn't felt good.'

'Well I don't feel good. What are you going to do about it?'

Toby sighed.

'I'm doing my best. I need you to sign this form, if you want him to go to the school.' He held out the form Witherspoon had given him. She snatched it from him with her wet hands. Suddenly Mark began crying.

'There, look now you've upset him as well,' she snapped. 'Where have I got to sign?' She moved over to the kitchen table. The form became wet at its edges from her hands. Toby gave her a pen. When he stood next to her, close like that, the yearning was just the same. Would it ever go away he thought. Toby moved towards the child, to pick him up, but Mark's snivelling turned into a scream.

'Toby, just go please,' Catryn said after she'd signed the form. She moved between them, picked the boy up and he stopped screaming.

Toby said nothing more, he just looked at the two of them, mother and child, and felt his heart sink into his boots. He made for the door. 'I'll call in later in the week,' he said when he reached it. Catryn made no reply.

* * * * *

For most of that weekend Scott had been flapping about his forthcoming golf trip to Spain. During those two days he'd spent most of his time trying to persuade Jane Kirby to accompany him. He was flying out from Cardiff on Tuesday morning, which suited Anne fine as it would give her the rest of the week to indulge herself with Stan, without having to account for her every movement.

Jane however, was resisting Scott's pleas. On Saturday morning they'd been in bed together, as was their habit, if Bill was out fishing, and all through their lovemaking he kept relating the benefits of an Iberian break.

'Everybody will know I'm not your wife,' Jane retorted when he'd raised he subject. 'And some of them might have been in the pub and seen me.'

'You won't be coming as my wife. You'll have your own room, but we can meet up when we like.'

'I don't know,' she said, panting, while her arms grappled with his body. For both of them their Saturday morning indulgences were like shots of cocaine to a pair of addicts. Downstairs in the bar, after opening time, sitting on a bar stool, Scott continued to harangue her.

'I won't know anybody, and what about this place?' Jane said, while wiping down the bar counter with a dishcloth.

'You'll know me, that's all that matters. And there'll be other women as well. I promise you, you won't be the only woman. Surely Bill can run this place for four days. Come on Jane, you'll enjoy yourself. A bit of warmth, a few games of golf and whatever else takes your fancy. Do you good to have a break from here.'

'If I leave this place for four days, there won't be a pub to come back to.'

Scott placed his beer glass back down on the bar.

'Of course there will,' he said. 'You worry too much. Anyway, how would I cope without your gorgeous body for four days.'

'S'sh. Somebody will hear you,' she said. 'I just don't know. I've got a business to run,' she half whispered.

For over an hour he sat on that bar stool pouring his heart out. In the end he was forced to leave without conclusion. His luncheon date with Anne was pressing.

* * * * *

'What time are you leaving for the airport on Tuesday?' Anne asked when they were sitting opposite each other in the restaurant, eating anchovies as a starter.

'About eight in the morning I guess. Why?'

'Oh nothing. I was going to arrange a hair appointment that's all.'

'You look beautiful enough to me,' he said, toasting her with his glass of white wine.

'Flatterer,' she replied. 'And you're flying from Cardiff?'

'That's right. On the eleven o'clock flight.'

'Boys week away?' she said, tilting her head to one side to look at him. 'And a bit of nooky on the sly?' she added.

'Won't be time for anything like that,' he replied instantly. 'We're playing golf every day and looking at the course they've chosen, we'll all be too knackered for anything but sleep after a few drinks.'

'Ha!!' Anne laughed coarsely. Scott looked down quickly at his plate and carried on eating.

Later on, in the afternoon, back at home on his mobile phone, he rang Jane again. Anne was watching something on the television and he'd gone out to the garage to make the call.

'You know you really would be doing me a big favour if you could come on this trip, Jane,' he said. 'I've gone and bought the tickets for the two of us. I don't really get on much with the other people. I'd be pretty much on my own if you don't come.'

'Scott I'm busy right now. I've got a bar full of people here. Can't you take your wife?'

'She wouldn't want to come. And it would be much more fun with you. We'd have a great time.'

'I'll let you know tomorrow. I'll have to talk to Bill first.'

Sunday morning, before opening time, he slipped round to the back door of The Ship Inn. Bill had gone out fishing and Jane was still in her night things. It didn't take long for him to wheedle her back into bed. 'We could do this all night,' he pleaded between groans. 'And again in the morning.'

'What about the golf?' she said, breathlessly.

'Sod the golf,' Scott said.

Later that day, after his third call on the mobile, she agreed to accompany him. They'd meet up at Cardiff Airport in time for

118

the flight.

* * * * *

On Sunday evening, at home in his study, Ginger was completing the application form for the share issue he'd mentioned to the others. Alongside the prospectus on his desk was Saturday's Financial Times and a couple of issues of the Investor's Chronicle.

Ginger's study wasn't at all like Colin's. To begin with it was much smaller, being the third bedroom of the house. There was just enough room for a small desk, a leather, high backed chair and a couple of cupboards, which Ginger used as filing cabinets. On the top of one of the cupboards was a small portable television and there was a telephone extension. It was a room he could escape into, to smoke his cigars and watch the sport without disturbing his wife. As yet he hadn't graduated to computers and all the gadgetry of modern technology.

The more he'd read about this investment, the more convinced he became of its attraction. Completing the application form he'd hesitated when he reached the block for the number of shares to be applied for. He was about to enter one hundred. Dearly, he would have loved to put another nought at the end of the figure, but at that time he just couldn't afford it. He tapped his pen on the desk as he pondered. If only there was a way he could apply for more shares. In time, his thoughts came back to Stan. Normally, Colin was his best bet on anything like this, but he'd already cried off, pleading lack of money. Jimmy's spare money was going on the horse. Toby pooh-hoed such things and Scott, well he wouldn't trust Scott with his grandmother. So he was back to Stan. Despite his reluctance before, Ginger was prepared to make one more approach. Stan was in his lounge, watching television with Rosemary, when he answered Ginger's call.

'Stanley old chap,' Ginger began. 'Sorry to disturb your evening, can you speak?'

'Just a minute,' Stan replied and carried the phone into the hall.

'I've just been reading an article in the Investor's Chronicle on the share issue I mentioned,' Ginger began, applying his bank manager's tone of voice. 'They're very bullish about it and the FT's given it quite a good write up. What can I do to persuade you to come in with me old chap? We'd make a fortune.'

'There's nothing you can do Ging. I'm going to write to the building society about the mix-up. I'm most grateful you've thought of me, but I've decided to let the matter rest.'

There was a pause on the line. Stan heard Ginger sigh. 'Oh well dear boy it's your decision. Let me know if you change your mind. I won't post the form off until after golf in the morning.' They finished their conversation by talking about the likely weather prospects for the morning and then Ginger rang off.

'You men are phoning each other a lot these days,' Rosemary said when he was back in the lounge. 'What's going on?'

'Oh nothing, just golf talk.'

After he put the phone down Ginger's pen still hovered when he came back to filling in the application box on the form. 'To hell with it,' he said and wrote the number five hundred in the share application box. He hadn't been a bank manager for nothing. He'd apply for an overdraft to cover the shortfall in his own money. It shouldn't be a problem to talk young Bevan, the new manager, into the idea, over a slap up lunch. Once the market had taken up the shares, he would sell and pay off the debt. Feeling pleased with himself, he signed the form and wrote out the envelope.

* * * * *

Colin Mordecai was still wallowing in a state of gloom regarding his investments. Over the last week there'd been no break in the Stock Market's fall. Having made some minor adjustments to his portfolio he was hesitant to dabble too much in case of a turn around. The usual investment advice was that the Market would right itself in the end, and if you were in it for real, you should be in it for the long term. That was standard procedure, but for once Colin wasn't too sure. Hour after hour he sat in his study, brooding over his computer screen.

Stan's visit the other evening however, had set his mind off on a different tack. After Stan had left, he sat down and dissected the formula he had created with a fine tooth comb. Time and time again he ran the figures through his calculating machines until he was satisfied the system was foolproof.

The sudden shortfall in his own balances had caused him to reconsider his personal situation. His opinion was that this bear market was likely to be around for a while. With hindsight, perhaps he'd been foolish to put so much money into this new form of investment, but normally there was some predictability to it. You could bet on a rise or a fall, but now total mayhem had broken loose. Without a trend there was nothing he could pick up on apply his calculations to.

As yet he hadn't mentioned anything to Veronica about the situation. Pretty soon though, she'd be champing at the bit about this world cruise they'd talked about. So perhaps a change of tack was required. He wasn't the sort of man to suffer losses without doing something about it. The reduction in capital created not only a serious hole in his retirement plans, it was also a major blow to his pride, as though his life's work had been undermined.

On the Monday, at golf, he was partnering Stan. Ginger was playing with Jimmy and Scott. For some unknown reason Toby hadn't turned up. On the fifth hole Colin's drive had careered off into the right rough. While they were stomping about in the long grass looking for it, Colin turned to Stan and said; 'Have you done anything with that formula yet?'

'Mum's still the word on that,' Stan replied and put his index finger in front of his mouth. 'I might have a go this week, but I'm not going to risk too much. Please don't say anything to the others.'

'You know you can rely on me, but would you like some help. I'd really be interested to see if the system works in operation.'

Stan's feet were getting wet in the long grass. Colin's interest had taken him by surprise. For a moment he was stuck for a reply. He was desperate not to reveal anything about Anne's part in all this. 'What ball are you playing?' he said to Colin, trying to give himself time to think.

'Titleist,' Colin replied and added. 'If I came with you I might risk an odd flutter myself.'

'Here it is,' Stan said bending down. The little white object was buried in an entangled mass of grass. 'Don't fancy your lie much.'

'Need a shovel there, not a club,' Colin said when he reached the spot.

Colin walked back to his bag for a pitching wedge. Stan

remained by the ball, marking the spot. 'I've promised the friend who showed me the first formula I'd do it with him,' he said, when Colin got back alongside him. 'I think he's a bit coy about the whole matter. I don't think I could bring someone else along at this stage, although I'd be happy to come with you on another occasion.'

'Just a thought,' Colin said while trying out a few practice swings. Then he hovered over the ball. Stan watched his forehead crease into a frown. He swung the club at the ball and removed the most enormous clump of grass, which flew away to his left on the prevailing wind. The ball only shifted about four inches. 'I don't know why they bloody well can't cut this rough,' Colin said. 'It's stupid to let it grow this long.'

'Shortage of staff,' Stan said. 'If you moan to the Secretary about it, he'll tell you they haven't got the staff. He told Jimmy, when he was carping about it the other day, that more staff would mean putting up the fees.'

'Typical,' Colin said and realigned himself alongside the ball's new position.

Stan was glad that nothing more was mentioned about the formula. Already he felt embarrassed about it and he didn't want to get the others involved.

Later on, when they were leaving the clubhouse, Jimmy collared Stan in the car park. By then the others had all driven away, giving Jimmy the opportunity to say his piece in private.

'You remember that horse we talked about,' he said just as Stan was about to get into his car.

'I do James.'

'Well it's running next Wednesday. There's time enough to come on board with us if you want to.'

'No thanks Jim, I don't think so. I'm not really a gambling man. Not to that extent anyway.'

'Oh, I just thought the winnings would come in handy with your new expenses.'

Stan smiled. 'What new expenses are those Jim?'

'On your new lady friend.'

Jimmy watched a look of horror spread across Stan's face. In an instant it turned white. Stan was so shocked by Jimmy's remark that he slumped into the front seat of his car.

'What's that supposed to mean?' he said eventually.

'Don't worry,' Jimmy said. 'Your secret's safe with me. It's about time Scott got his come-uppance anyway. I just thought a little bit of cash would come in useful. I promise you Stan this horse is a cert. The price is still forty to one. We'd all make a lot of money. I absolutely assure you I wouldn't be on it myself if that wasn't the case.'

Stan's face still looked as though he'd just been told about the death of a relative. 'Well I thank you for the offer, but the answer's still 'no' and I haven't a clue about what else you're talking about. I'm going to have to go, Rosemary is waiting for me to take her out.'

Jimmy said nothing more, just smiled. He kept smiling as he watched Stan close the car door, start up the engine and reverse erratically out of the parking space. When the car was alongside him, Jimmy beamed and gave Stan a thumbs up before he drove away. He kept his thumb in the air while he watched Stan's car disappear at speed down the driveway.

* * * * *

That morning Toby left home at the normal time, as though he was heading for golf. But instead of taking the coast road to the course, he drove inland to Catryn's house. On Sunday, after Church, he'd called there just to make sure they were organised for Mark's trip to the school, next day. He'd found there wasn't much organisation about anything in that house anymore. All the rooms looked a mess. Unwashed clothes were littered everywhere; Mark's toys were scattered about; used coffee mugs sat untidily on the small tables. Catryn was in the lounge cuddled up to Darren on the settee, watching television when he arrived. Mark was playing upstairs by himself in his bedroom. Getting any sense out of them was difficult.

He tried to coax Catryn into the kitchen. 'I'm watching this at the moment,' she said pointing at the television.

He climbed the stairs to Mark's bedroom and the little boy gave him a cold stare. The child looked grubby, his clothes unclean. Toby made some meaningless remark that Mark ignored and so he returned downstairs.

'Catryn I have to see you,' he said, standing in the hallway. In his right hand he held out the fifty pounds he gave her each week. Lethargically she untangled herself from Darren's arms and shuffled across to the lounge doorway. All the while her head was still turned in the direction of the television. She snatched the fifty pounds from Toby's hand without looking at him.

'I'll be here at eight in the morning, to take him to the school,' Toby said. Can you make sure he's properly washed and dressed and has a bag for the four nights stay.'

Slowly she turned her head way from the television to face him.

'Yes sir,' she said, while making a mock salute with her right hand.

'I'm serious Catryn. You're the one who wanted him off your hands. Can you please make sure he's in a fit state to go.'

He watched an expression of scorn spread across Catryn's face. 'Haven't I always ensured he was in a fit state to go anywhere,' she said.

Now they both looked at each other eye to eye.

'Yes,' he said. 'But tomorrow's important. We want him to make a decent impression on his first day.'

She continued looking into his eyes.

'Of course I will. What do you think I am, stupid or something?'

There was contempt in her every word. He turned and walked away to the back door. 'Eight o'clock,' he stated firmly as he pulled the door closed.

When he arrived on Monday morning the first thing he noticed was that the front garden had been tidied. Mark's play things and the litter were gone. He knocked twice on the front door but there was no reply. He was becoming angrier by the second. If Catryn hadn't got him up in time he was going to blow his top. He went round to the back door and looked in through the kitchen window. There was still no sign of anybody. He tried the door handle and it opened, so he strode in.

At that moment Catryn appeared from the hallway with Mark holding onto her hand.

'Why didn't you answer the door?' Toby said angrily.

'I was seeing to him in the bathroom,' she replied just as brusquely. 'You said you wanted him clean and tidy well here he is. Why have you got to be so unpleasant all the time?'

'Me? Unpleasant?' Toby scowled, 'pah,' he exhaled in disgust.

Mark, who looked nervous, was wearing a clean white shirt, a red tie, a blue v-neck pullover and grey short trousers. His curly fair hair was combed for the first time in days and his face was clean.

'Come on young man,' Toby said and reached out his hand for Mark. 'We're going to take you to a brand new school, with a nice new teacher.'

Mark huddled closer to his mother, retreating behind her legs.

'You've got to go with Tiad,' she said and bent down to pick up the small suitcase she had brought in from the hall. While she was bent she kissed Mark's cheek and straightened his tie. 'You must be good now.' The boy gripped tighter onto her leg.

'I want to be with you,' he said beginning to snivel.

'You'll be back on Friday,' Toby said. 'By then you'll have made lots of nice new friends.' He bent down and picked up the case.

'Go on,' Catryn said encouragingly, taking the boy's hand and leading him towards Toby. Mark began to cry. Toby stretched out his arm further. The child screamed, 'I don't want to go.' Toby put down the case and picked him up.

'Come on now young Mark, it'll be all right, I promise.'

The child screamed himself into a tantrum. He kicked out with his feet, pummelled Toby's chest with his fists and continued in the same manner all the way out to the car. Catryn followed on behind carrying his case. It proved difficult, but after a few attempts Toby managed to strap him in the back seat, put on the child lock and closed the doors. Mark's tantrum continued unabated inside the car. The decibels of his screams rose higher. Toby took the case from Catryn and looked at her.

'Will you pick him up on Friday or do you want me to?' he said, while Mark still screamed vehemently.

'I can't afford the petrol to go that far and back.'

He looked at her with a resigned expression.

'All right,' he said. 'I expect we'll be back about five.'

Their eyes still held, but she made no reply.

Toby walked around to the driver's side and got into the car. Mark's wailing continued. Catryn remained on the pavement, watching his tear-stained face through the car's window as they drove away. The boy's howls of anguish could still be heard when they reached the end of the road. She waved briefly, when they were nearly out of sight, then turned and walked back into the house.

* * * * *

By Tuesday morning Stan was in a fractious state of nervous exhaustion. A hundred times he'd almost telephoned Anne to call off their planned visit to the casino. Once he'd even gone as far as lifting the receiver before replacing it back again. Around the house, he'd been getting under Rosemary's feet.

'Stanley Richards I don't know what's the matter with you today,' she berated eventually. 'Wherever I turn you're in my way. Haven't you got any woodwork that needs doing?'

So he moved out to the garage. But instead of sawing, planing and chiselling, he found himself staring into space, going over and over in his head Colin's formula. He kept re-reading the pieces of paper Colin had given him, desperately trying to remember every possible nuance, as the clock agonisingly ticked towards midday. The same questions however, kept re-appearing. Did he really have the courage to carry this out? And if he did, would he ever have the bottle to see Anne again on his own, even if they won any money. Jimmy's insinuation had also cut deep. He just couldn't think where the little Irishman had seen them together. He knew that in this town, gossip spreads like an infectious disease. Unfortunately, it's a disease everybody locally wants a share of. Most of the businesses wouldn't survive if the accumulation of gossip didn't provide an excuse to call in. If details of his flirtation got out, how would he ever face anybody locally again? And how would he deal with his golfing pals, knowing they knew? And Scott? My God, the imponderables were too horrendous to contemplate.

The morning took an eternity to pass, fuelling his doubts, stimulating his indecision. Gobbling his lunch gave him indigestion. Washing up afterwards he accidentally dropped a plate from the sink, onto the floor.

'I've just cleaned that floor,' Rosemary berated. 'Will you please go and get your pieces of wood or whatever it is you're going out for. You're getting on my nerves.'

Still bearing his reticence like a cross, he set off for the bank. Despite his doubts, he was, by then, on auto pilot; having just about convinced himself that his destiny lay in seeing the project through.

Never before in his life had he cashed an amount of money like five thousand pounds at a bank. On his way through the car park he wondered if perhaps he should have checked first. What if they wouldn't cash his cheque? What if they had to phone Rosemary for confirmation? She'd always dealt with the banking transactions. He couldn't even remember the last time he'd been in the bank. How would they know him? Would he need identification? All these thoughts mingled with his reservations as he walked across the carpeted banking hall. At the back of his mind, a small part of him hoped that perhaps they wouldn't be able to give him the cash. Then at least he'd have a viable excuse to just walk away, ring up Anne and say it was all off. Couldn't get the money out. Let's bottle the whole thing. Much the best idea, he thought. All this gadding about, gambling at casinos, with loose women was not really his style at all.

But he did keep walking towards the cashier and she did cash his cheque, with a minimum of fuss. Yes, they wanted some identification, but he had his driving license. 'How would you like the money?' she asked. He'd never thought of that. The girl looked at him quizzically while he pondered. At that moment he couldn't think clearly at all. Panic mode prevailed in his brain. 'Oh I don't mind, some tens and some twenties please,' he replied eventually, trying to cover his embarrassment. The cashier counted the money out in front of him and within minutes he was on his way out. How the devil was he going to remember the formula, if he couldn't even work out what denomination of money was needed, he thought. All the way to his car the words 'shall I, or shan't I', kept revolving in his head.

Having allowed a good half hour for the bank, which only took a matter of minutes, meant he was much too early for his clandestine meeting with Anne. For what seemed like a lifetime, he sat in the car park at their agreed rendezvous, working himself into a state of hyper-tension. Visions of divorce, financial ruin, fights with Scott, even arrest for fraud raced through his head as he gazed perpetually at the entrance to the car park. To try and concentrate his mind he pulled out the pieces of paper from his pocket, and went over, again and again, Colin's formula, while his stomach churned.

To make matters worse Anne was late. By the time she arrived his palms were sweaty, his hands were shaking and he was almost hyper-ventilating.

'Don't look so worried, this is supposed to be fun,' she said when she saw the distraught look on his face. 'Nothing can go wrong, I promise.'

He clambered into the Rover alongside her. She looked class. A cream, fluffy polo neck sweater, a red skirt and tan boots should have been an inspiration for any man. But his first words were, 'I don't know if I can go through with this.'

'What do you mean you can't go through with it? We're on our way. Did you get the money?'

'Yes, I've got the money.'

'Good. Well we're going through with it then.' She placed her hand on his thigh. Her touch made him shudder.

The journey to Bristol took about two and a half hours, providing plenty of time to talk.

'I think we've been spotted,' he said to Anne when they were under way. A gale had got up. Trees, still in their autumn leaf, were swaying precariously; gusts rocked even the sturdy Rover sideways, clouds scudded ominously. When they joined the motorway, the computorised road signs announced that the Old Severn Bridge was closed, although the new crossing remained open.

'Seen by whom?' Anne replied to his statement.

'Jimmy I think. The other day he made some snide remark about me needing money for expenditure on my new lady friend.'

'That was probably a joke. Men's banter.'

'I don't know. He said something about, it's time about Scott got his comeuppance.'

'You know how you guys rib each other. Come on, relax, we're supposed to be enjoying this. Anyway, we're not doing anything wrong. I'm taking my husband's friend to Bristol, to show him how he can make a bit of money on a roulette wheel. There's nothing wrong with that. If somebody's seen us together before now, we were just meeting up, to talk about the system. Nothing wrong with that either.'

The further they journeyed, the more they talked the easier his palpitations became. Why, oh why, did he always feel better in her company, was a point he conjectured on as she confidently dealt with the aspects of driving.

Ahead of them, the sky was blackening, a storm looked imminent. The new Severn bridge is an improvement on the old, in that it rarely completely closes in times of gales. However, as they approached the crossing, a traffic queue was forming. Cars and lorries were being diverted from the old bridge to mingle into this route. High-sided vehicles were being stopped in the inside lane. All of which was causing a delay. Anne's Rover taxied to a halt in the middle lane. By then, a veritable gale was gusting up the channel, hitting them sideways on, shaking the Rover with its force. Slowly they inched forward in the queue. Rain was spattering on the windscreen. 'I hope there hasn't been an accident,' Anne said.

Ahead, all the traffic was being channeled into the central lane. As they progressed, cars were filtering in, in front of them. A few impatient drivers, trying to jump the queue, continued to speed by on the outside. Suddenly, a red Porsche Boxer whizzed past them.

'There's always some clever clogs,' Stan said.

'That's Scott!!' Anne exclaimed. 'What's he doing here? He's supposed to be in Spain.'

Even Stan could read the yellow number plate, emblazoned with SL1 in bold blue letters. Subconsciously he contracted further down into his seat.

'What's he doing here?' Anne repeated.

Gradually they inched forward in the queue. Scott's car was still stranded in the outside lane, nobody was letting him in. When they were about thirty yards away Anne reached for the mobile phone which was in a consul by the gear lever. She pressed a button, Stan heard the dial tones ring. They could both see, through the rear window of the Porsche, Scott pick up a similar mobile and put it to his ear.

'What the hell are you doing here?' Anne barked into her phone.

'Who's this? Oh, Anne, where are you?' they could both hear Scott reply.

'At this moment about six cars behind you in the central lane. I repeat, what are you doing here?'

They could see Scott's head half turn backwards to look behind. At that moment Anne also noticed a blonde woman sitting alongside him in the passenger seat.

'It's this gale Anne,' Scott said, over crackling on the line. 'Our plane wasn't able to land at Cardiff, 'cos of the storm. It's been diverted to Bristol. So we're all having to bomb over there.'

'Who's that woman sitting next to you?' Anne hollered.

For a few moments Scott didn't reply.

'Oh just another poor stranded passenger like me. I'm giving her a lift to Bristol. Look sweetie, I'll have to put my foot down or we'll be late for the flight. Take care of yourself. I'll phone you when I get there.'

Stan and Anne both watched the Porsche thunder away in a cloud of black exhaust fumes. When it was a long way ahead, near the cut off barrier, they saw it gate-crash its way into the queue. While the car was sideways on, cutting in, Anne could just about make out the woman in the passenger seat. She couldn't be sure, but she would swear it was Jane Kirby from the Ship Inn.

'That bloody man,' she said.

'What's the matter?' Stan asked.

'He's got his damn girlfriend in there with him and he's taking her to Spain. No wonder the rat was anxious to go on this trip. I'll bloody well kill him when I get my hands on him. I've got a good mind to follow them to the airport.'

Stan said nothing. He could see Anne was perturbed. To him it all seemed a little ironic. Here she was playing patsy with him, while at the same time fuming about her husband doing the identical thing with somebody else. Somehow it eased Stan's conscience; if anything it relaxed him a little. At that moment the fear aspect of the whole charade changed. His mind began to rationalise the escapade for what it was. A harmless, meaningless bit of fun.

* * * * *

For the rest of the journey into Bristol Stan was inwardly amused as Anne continued to verbally curse her husband. Over the bridge and all the way into the city her vexed tirade was unrelenting. And with it, gradually, the stiffness in Stan's shoulders began to ease. The tension in his arms relaxed and in a peculiar sort of way he began to relish the challenge ahead. They never saw Scott's car again. Once they were over the bridge the traffic flow improved, although the gale still blew. Soon they were hurtling under the Clifton Suspension bridge, on their way into the city centre.

The main room in the Casino was twice the size of the one in Swansea. Roulette and card tables littered the centre of the floor area. Comfort seating was spread evenly round, one-arm-bandits jingled merrily along the side walls, while piped music droned surreptitiously in the background. Whereas the Swansea venue was like a private club, this room had more resemblance to an entertainment centre; people bustled everywhere.

Anne continued to harp on about her wayward husband as she began to organise herself. Stan was getting concerned. Her diatribe was beginning to effect his concentration. He also began to wonder if Anne was really in the right frame of mind to tackle what they had come to do. Evidence of her distraction was plain from the outset.

They arrived at a roulette table, almost haphazardly, whereupon Anne extracted the notebook from her handbag.

'Aren't you going to get any chips?' he asked.

'Oh my God,' she said instantly. 'That damn man's put me completely out of my stride.'

Stan tried his best to calm her down. He suggested a cup of coffee.

'No, let's get on with it,' was her instant reply.

They both exchanged some cash for chips. Once she started betting it was clear things weren't right. To begin with she insisted on using her money until they got a roll going. They joined a table where four other people were betting, but to Stan, Anne appeared to be slapping money on any number without thought. After every bet the croupier whisked the chip away. Quickly the pile dwindled. Within a few minutes most of her money had gone.

'I don't like this table,' Anne said. 'Let's try another.'

They moved further down the room. She stopped at two or three other tables, looked across at what was happening, then moved on. Stan followed behind. A table at the end of the room was crowded, twenty or more people were gathered around. Anne moved in closer. Only five couples were actually betting, the rest looked to be friends. One of the group was winning money. Cheers erupted each time the ball landed on the woman's number. She wasn't betting for big stakes, but she was winning.

'We'll try here,' Anne said and laid what was left of her chips on the table. First, she put a small bet on black, but just as before, the croupier whisked the chip away. The other woman won again. There were more whoops from her companions. Anne consulted the little red book.

Without speaking to Stan she put another bet on black with the same result. Another few roles of the wheel her money was all gone. She turned to look at Stan. His chips were still untouched in his pocket.

'Let's take a break,' he said.

'No, it'll come right in a minute,' she replied and held out her hand, demanding some more money. Reluctantly Stan delved into his pocket, fished out a small handful of chips while trying to disguise a grimace and handed them over. This time she put two chips on even, but the result was the same. Two more followed on a number, thirty six. Surprisingly it won. 'Now we're away,' she said. Stan smiled weakly. She consulted her notebook, put two more chips on black which lost. The onlookers whooped again. The other woman had won.

For the next quarter of an hour Anne continued to lose money like water swirling down a drain, cursing to herself at each loss. Stan could see this wasn't going to be her day. When the chips he had given her were gone, he said 'Let's stop there and have a coffee.' Anne already had her hand outstretched demanding more, but Stan walked away. She caught up with him at the bar.

'If you'd just give it a few more minutes the system will work in,' she said when she was alongside. He didn't reply. He ordered two coffees. When they arrived he guided her to a table.

'Anne I think this business with Scott has upset your composure,' he began. 'Perhaps we should call it off for today.'

'Nonsense,' she replied. 'I'm fine. We've just had a bad run. It'll change. These things happen in this game.'

'Well I don't particularly want it to happen with my money,' he said. 'Or perhaps I should say, somebody else's money.'

While they drank their coffee they continued to bicker. By the time they'd drunk it Stan agreed to risk another two hundred pounds. 'That will be seven hundred in total,' he said. I'm not prepared to lose any more and that's final,' he added firmly.

Anne stomped off to the toilet. While she was gone he took from his pocket the crumpled notes he'd made of Colin's system. In his own mind, while watching Anne losing, he'd been mentally attempting to apply the things he could remember from his notes and by and large with the numbers that came up he guessed it might have worked. But with the noise around him and trying to figure out what Anne was up to, he couldn't be absolutely sure. So while he was alone he read and re-read his notes.

When Anne returned they moved to another table. Only three people were playing on this one. Anne bet on black and it won. Then she bet on a corner and that won as well. A split bet followed, which also won. Then a straight sixteen was next, right in the slot.

'There, what did I tell you,' Anne said. Stan smiled.

But soon she started to lose again. The pile of chips in front of her was dwindling again. Then she won a couple more times, but just as quickly lost and within half an hour, the two hundred pounds Stan had given here, plus her winnings were gone.

'I think we'd better stop there,' Stan said.

She looked at him with a resigned expression.

'I am sorry Stan. I just don't know what happened. Using this system I've never lost like this before.' He put his arm round her shoulder and they moved away from the table.

'Don't worry,' Stan said. 'I think you were probably upset by what you saw on the way here.'

'Maybe you're right. I'll make the loss up. I'll draw some money from my bank.'

'You'll do no such thing. It was my gamble. Before we leave though I just want to try something.' She looked at him quizzically.

He moved over to another table where there were only two people playing. Then, from his pocket he took out a chip and placed it on even. It lost. He put another chip on even which won and he got his first chip back. Then, desperately, he tried to make his aged brain work. Could he recall Colin's system without looking at his notes. He bet his winnings on a corner, which won, at odds of eight to one. Anne moved in closer and held onto his arm. He kept going, betting on a five number. That won at six to one. The few losses he suffered were more than compensated for by the winnings. Sweat began to form on his brow. In what seemed to him like seconds he'd won back the two hundred pounds.

'Stan that's wonderful,' Anne exclaimed excitedly, pressing her body into his side, but he was determined not to lose his concentration. He didn't reply and continued to bet on high tariffs. Six number bets, split bets, trio bets and lots of straight up bets. Soon the formula became etched in his brain and from it he extracted the numbers to bet on. Suddenly he was confident the system worked. Standing by his side Anne shrieked joyfully at each big windfall, but he kept his head down. He could feel the sweat on his body. He wiped his face with his handkerchief. Anne gave him a Kleenex. News of his winnings had got out. A small crowd was gathering around his table. The croupier's face bore a sickly smile each time he paid out. He was Asian maybe, with thin lips and coiffured dark hair. The pile of chips in front of Stan grew and continued to grow; by how much he hadn't a clue. For a second he stopped, thought about counting them, made a move to do so, then one of the spectators said, 'Keep going. Don't stop while you're winning.'

So he kept going. The chips in front of him piled high. Anne kissed his cheek after each winning roll. The crowd around the table had swelled. Now he was playing the croupier by himself and it was like printing money. In front of him the chips had become an untidy pile, some spilt on the floor. Every time Anne picked each one up as they fell. He looked down. There was one more big win and then suddenly everything in front of him was a blur.

'Time to take a break,' he said and wiped his forehead with the Kleenex. The spectators groaned. 'I'm sorry,' he said joking with them. 'I can't go on.' They began moving away. Some shook his hand. One lady remarked, 'if you want any help spending it, give me a call.' Stan laughed. Anne cut in. 'That's my job,' she said and kissed him again on the cheek.

They moved away to a table by the bar and he slumped down on a chair. A waiter came over. 'What would you like sir?' he said. Stan looked up at the guy and thought. His mouth felt dry like sandpaper, his shirt was wet with sweat, his hands were shaking uncontrollably, people passing by continued to stare at him.

'Champagne,' he said. 'A magnum of champagne please.'

When it arrived, in an ice bucket and with two glasses, he gulped at the first pouring like a man struggling in the desert for liquid. In front of him, on the table, his winning chips were scattered in an untidy heap.

'You were marvellous,' Anne said and planted yet another kiss on his cheek. 'How on earth did you manage that?'

'A friend gave me another system. How much have we won?' he asked, pointing to the pile of chips, and took another large gulp of champagne.

Anne began to stack the chips into neater, tidier piles of equal numbers. It took her some minutes. While she was counting Stan sat back in his seat, supping on the champagne, while continuing to wipe his brow.

'You're never going to believe this,' she said.

'Go on surprise me.'

'There's getting on for twelve thousand quid here.'

'And there's still the four thousand or so I've got in my pocket,' Stan replied.

'And you did it all by yourself,' she said, put her arm round his shoulders and hugged him. 'Stan you really are the man.'

He swallowed some more champagne, wiped his mouth with the back of his hand, then said, 'Come on, we'd better get out of here before they arrest us.'

CHAPTER FOURTEEN

It was late in the day by the time Stan got home. After Anne had dropped him off at the supermarket he telephoned Rosemary to say he'd been delayed. Deliberately he drove very slowly to give himself an opportunity to think and allow his high state of euphoria to settle.

'I don't know how a few bits of wood can be so difficult for you to sort out,' Rosemary had said on the telephone.

'I can't find what I want. So I have to keep going further a field,' he replied patiently.

Rather than invent any more lies he put the phone down quickly. Once he was on the quieter, green hedged roads of Pembrokeshire he allowed his mind to wander. Having all that cash stuffed in his pocket had quickly created a new found sense of freedom in his head. The more he conjectured however, the more constraints that particular freedom seemed to bring. When it's impossible to do something, you can only dream and fantasise about it, he thought. But when your dreams are suddenly within arm's length, a veritable hornets nest of side issues suddenly come into play.

To indulge with Anne in anything more licentious than sitting by her side, holding hands, making polite conversation, up until then, had been a pipe dream; a schoolboy fantasy; something for his mind to play with on a humdrum day. Now though, with all that cash in his pocket, the possibilities of their relationship turning into something more physically engaging was real. Unfortunately, by then, a mess of dubiety had also crept into the susceptible corners of his brain.

Jimmy's supposed sighting of them together had unnerved him. If that happened again it wouldn't take long for the whole peninsular to know about it. Stan was a well respected member of the community; a popular churchgoer; a stalwart member of the golf club. My God, the shame he thought. Then there was Rosemary. Despite her nagging, despite his weariness with her ways, he was still her husband. They'd been married for thirty odd years, produced two healthy upstanding children. How would he explain it all to them? The thought of it was pitiable. The closer he got to home, the more the reservations piled up into furrows of doubts.

'Stanley Richards I just don't know what you have been up to,' Rosemary berated when he got in. 'I've had this dinner on for over an hour. It'll all be dried up by now. Where have you been?'

He saw the concern in her eyes, the worry on her face. A face, despite it's almost permanent agitated expression, he had come to accept. A belly full of contrition was now beginning to dull his appetite.

'I'm sorry,' he said. 'I needed to see somebody about this pension of mine. For that I had to go to Bristol.' Rosemary looked at him in astonishment, so he continued. 'I know you want this new kitchen, and I didn't want to say anything for definite until I was sure I could get the money.' The expression on Rosemary's face began to lighten. He could still feel the cash weighing down his right hand trouser pocket. 'We can start looking properly now, if you like.'

'Oh Stanley, you are the most marvellous man,' she said excitedly and flung her arms round his neck.That was the second time that day he'd received a similar accolade and he was beginning to like it.

Later in the evening he sidled off into the garage to regroup his thoughts. Planing large pieces of timber has therapeutic qualities. The smooth regular motion of his hands and arms, aligned to the grain, induced a calming sensation into his body. While shaving four large pieces of wood, he ran over and over, in his head, the events of the day.

The excitement and elation he'd encountered with Anne at the casino were sensations new to him. The cheers of the onlookers at each successful roll of the wheel provided immense exhilaration. During those brief moments he felt as though he was floating on air, as though anything was possible. But to see Rosemary's unhappy face when he got home reinstated reality. He was a family man, the provider; that's how it always had been; that's when he was happiest; only the elongated years had eroded the gloss. He would have to explain it to Anne of course, but he guessed she'd understand. He desperately hoped they'd still remain friends; closer now, but friends. What pleased him most of all though, was that for once he'd succeeded at something by himself. Without Anne's encouragement, without Colin's formula, it wouldn't have been possible. But the decision to try out that formula was his and on the day he was the sole operator. That made him feel good. Within an hour there were four perfectly planed pieces of wood.

Next day, there were many things to sort out. Going early to golf gave Stan the opportunity to get out of the house before Rosemary was really up and running. Already she was champing at the bit about kitchen showrooms. 'Later, probably tomorrow,' he said on his way out through the door; he kept moving, without listening to her reply.

On the course, amongst his pals, he was back on form. His drives unerringly found the middle of the fairways; his pitches peppered the holes and his putts dropped into the centre of the cup, with a satisfying clunk. That morning he was partnered with Jimmy and Colin. All through the round Jimmy kept up a running dialogue about his horse. 'Not too late to come on board if you want,' he began, on the second hole. 'It's running at three thirty this afternoon,' he continued.' 'You could make your fortune,' he added many times.

'Thanks again Jim, but no thanks.' Stan replied repeatedly.

When they were alone, he was able to talk to Colin. 'That system of yours does work,' he said quietly when Jimmy was out of earshot. 'Keep it to yourself, but I tried it out for real yesterday.'

'Did you by jingo. How much did you win?'

'S'sh, I don't want Jimmy to hear. Let's just say I won enough. But it certainly works. I used it myself and I'm very grateful.'

'Well done old chap. I knew it would work. Good luck to you,' Colin said and pulled a six iron out of his bag for his next shot.

That morning Stan won the money. The group only stayed for a drink and lunch. All of them claiming things to do that afternoon, so snooker was ruled out. After he'd left, they all remarked on how Toby didn't seem to be himself. Ginger, who'd played with him, said his golf was awful. During lunch Jimmy tried cheering him up by talking about the horse he was going to bet on. Partly to shut Jimmy up, Toby gave him a tenner to place on it as a bet.

'You won't regret it Toby. It can't lose,' Jimmy said.

* * * * *

From the golf club Stan drove straight into town. His first call was at the bank, where he deposited fifteen thousand pounds into his current account. Afterwards, walking along the High Street, he stopped outside the betting shop and peered in through the door. It didn't look crowded so he went inside.

Although Jimmy had never revealed the name of his special horse, he had let slip, in various discourses on the subject, that the horse was running that afternoon at Kempton Park at three thirty. In the betting shop Stan scoured the racing journals for the likely animal. Looking down the list of runners in that race, he decided it had to be Galway Boy. The horse was from Ireland, television screens around the room confirmed the price was still forty to one, so Stan put a fiver on it to win and left. From the stationers, next door, he bought a writing pad, some envelopes and a book of stamps and made his way to the library. There, in the dark, narrow reading room, amongst the old men, reading newspapers and doodling at crosswords, he wrote to the building society. In his letter, he said that he noticed, when recently making a withdrawal, his account showed a balance in excess of two hundred and fifty thousand pounds. He said, he didn't see how that could be possible, as he'd never deposited anything like that amount in his life. He also enclosed a cheque for five thousand pounds for credit. Could they kindly confirm and explain, he asked.

After the library he found a phone box and telephoned Anne. 'Are you in this afternoon?' he enquired.

'Yes,' she replied expectantly.

'Can I call round to see you?'

'I've been hoping you would.'

'I'll be there in quarter of an hour.'

From the telephone box, on his way to the car park, he called in at the florist and purchased a dozen red roses.

* * * * *

Meanwhile, Jimmy had raced home from the golf club to pick up an old, black, Gladstone bag he had owned for years and then drove like the wind to Haverfordwest. In the town car park, amongst the weekday shoppers, he used his mobile to telephone Dougal. 'Are you right?' he asked when his pal answered.

'I am that. How much have you got?' Dougal replied with a croak.

'About six thousand in all. I have it right here by my side.' He picked up the Gladstone bag and shook it near the phone. 'And you?'

'Just short of five,' Dougal said. 'What time shall we do it.'

'I make it a quarter past two. I can see the betting shop from where I'm sitting. If we leave the cars at a half past two, that should be about right.'

'That's it then,' Dougal said. 'I'll phone you again when I'm at the shop door.

Jimmy sat in his car, humming something tuneless to himself while tapping his feet in time. This was going to be his big day. If they won, he'd organise a massive party to celebrate; a proper hoe-down. He rubbed his hands together at the thought of it and puffed even more energetically on his cigarette.

At precisely two thirty he got out of his car and with bag in hand walked the hundred yards or so to the betting shop. When he was about twenty feet from the doorway his mobile rang.

'I'm going in now,' he heard Dougal say.

'And me. Good luck,' he replied, then pressed the disconnect button and walked into the shop.

Inside, a small group of punters lingered at the far end, smoking cigarettes, reading racing journals, and watching the action from various courses around the country on TV screens. The atmosphere was thick with tobacco smoke. There was no one at the counter, so Jimmy moved forward and gave his instructions; 'a straight bet on a win,' he said, then added the horse's name and the race. When he lifted the Gladstone bag onto the counter the clerk looked at him warily. Jimmy tipped out the contents and confirmed the amount. He'd tied the money up in neat bundles of tens, twenties and fifties, all held together by elastic bands. The clerk held his hands up in horror and looked straight Jimmy. 'You want to bet all that now?' he asked.

' I do that,' Jimmy replied, feeling his heart pounding.

The clerk stared at the money for some more moments before saying. 'I'll have to check with head office. We don't normally accept large cash bets this close to a race.'

'As you wish,' Jimmy responded hearing his heart pounding louder.

The clerk scribbled the horse's name and the race on a scrap of paper and went back into an inside office. Through a glass screen Jimmy could see him talking on a phone. He was there some time; by then Jimmy was palpitating. After what seemed like an eternity the clerk returned. Jimmy held his breath and tried to smile pleasantly.

'We'll do it on this occasion, but I can't guarantee we'll do it again,' the clerk said gruffly.

Jimmy repeated the attempt at a smile and felt his shoulders loosen. It took a few more moments for the teller to check the cash and agree the amount before handing Jimmy the receipt. Jimmy then moved away to stand near a TV screen showing Kempton Park and looked at his mobile. A text message from Dougal said, 'Money bet'. Jimmy typed back the same message. Now all he could do was wait. He lit up a cigarette and sucked hard on it repeatedly.

* * * * *

Anne was waiting at her front door when Stan drove up the driveway. The bright sunshine dazzled on the whitewashed facade of the house. Her smile was evident from a distance. She was wearing a swirl print blouse, with long fluted sleeves, tight denim jeans and was barefoot. When he stopped the car he reached into the back seat for the roses. Her smile widened when she saw the flowers.

'For my favourite girlfriend,' he said, handing them over.

'Stan these are beautiful. You continue to surprise me.' She bent her head to sniff the blooms.

Inside the front porch she closed the door and stretched her arms around his neck then kissed him full on the lips. A kiss full of passion, accompanied by a clasp of longing. Stan was totally unprepared for the intensity. Straight away he knew what he had come to do wasn't going to be easy.

'Have you heard from Scott?' he asked when they were together in the lounge. Anne was standing very close. The incandescent blue of her widened eyes was making his task harder.

'Oh I had a quick phone call the other night, to say he'd landed,' she said offhandedly. 'But why do I need to think about Scott when I've got you alone here and all to myself.' She moved in closer again. Her perfume and the affinity of her bare flesh was intoxicating. All he had to do was reach out a matter of inches and she would be his. Desperately he grappled with his desires and took a step backwards. Suddenly he found himself blurting everything out.

'What I've called round to say Anne, is that I don't think I can go ahead with our plan,' he stammered quickly

They were both standing perfectly still, eyeball to eyeball. Hers searching for some sign, some weakness, his, still dazzled by her radiance.

'Why is that Stan?' she asked, almost pleaded.

'Can we sit down,' he said. They moved to the large white settee and there he did his best to try and explain. 'I know you'll think me a coward,' he began. Then, one by one he carefully and slowly listed his reasons. He began with Rosemary, then their kids, their home, her kitchen, his beliefs, his shame if anybody really found out. He spoke for a long time; Anne barely interrupted. She just nodded at each point, occasionally she said 'Right,' but nothing more till he'd finished. 'But I want you to know I've had the most marvellous time doing what we have done,' he said at the end.

She turned her head away from him and sighed. 'But we could still go on having fun. I don't want to break up your marriage, or your home. What we have is just a bit of light relief for two middle-aged people.'

'I know. It's just the way I am I'm afraid. It's the way I was brought up I suppose. It's the way I've always lived my life. Unfortunately I can't alter now. I perhaps believed I could, but I know now I can't. I am sorry.'

She looked straight at him again. 'Never mind,' she sighed. 'And there's me thinking I'd found my perfect man. I did have fun with you at that casino though, when you were winning.'

'And me,' he said.

* * * * *

Jimmy's nerves were stretched as tight as the strings on a cello as he waited for the half hour to three thirty to elapse. Watching the TV screen his frustrations multiplied as the horses at Kempton Park made their way down to the starting gate. Galway Boy, with his bright roan colouring, had cantered happily that way, but there was a straggler, who just wouldn't obey its jockey's commands. The rest of the field, Galway Boy included, were walking patiently around in circles at the start, but further down the track, half a dozen arm waving, yellow jacketed marshals, were trying to coax the errant horse in their direction. Jimmy impatiently tapped his feet, sucked feverishly on another cigarette, and thought about the amount of money he had just handed over. Never before in his life had he risked such a sum on a bet. The fact that a lot of the money wasn't his only added to his concern. For the first time in this venture, he wondered if he had done the right thing. Perhaps he should have bet the pot each way, he conjectured as he watched Galway Boy's mane fluffing up in the breeze, on the TV screen.

The minutes passed, the wayward animal still balked. The starter told the others to get into the stalls. 'We'll go without him,' Jimmy heard the man shout from his rostrum. Then suddenly, the stray was cantering, head in the air, towards the start, as though his previous misbehaviour had never happened. With some effort, and a certain amount of pulling and shoving the marshall's managed to get the animal into his stall. All the while Jimmy's already fractious nerves deteriorated further. Another cigarette was already down to its butt end. He noticed Galway Boy was sweating up.

At last the starter was ready to let them go. 'They're off,' Jimmy heard the commentator shout from the TV. He stubbed out that cigarette and lit a fresh one. There were twelve runners in all. A grey galloped into the lead, the rest were bunched together in a pack. The race was over two miles. Jimmy recognised the blue and white stripes of Galway Boy's jockey somewhere near the back. And that's how it stayed all the way around to the finishing line on the first circuit. The grey still in the lead by about two lengths, the rest following at a gentle gallop. Jimmy was fretting. His favourite was still well in the middle of the pack, at the back. Would he get boxed in? Would he leave his break too late? Why wasn't he making any moves? Were the questions revolving in Jimmy's brain as he fretted.

Round the top bend nothing changed, still a gentle gallop, still the grey out in front; farther ahead if anything. Jimmy was getting worried. 'Come on boy, time to move,' he muttered to himself.

Second time down the back straight the pace quickened. The front runners of the pack were catching the grey. All the horses were now into a full gallop. Galway Boy though was last. 'Come on boy. Time to shift your arse,' Jimmy called out.

A gap opened up between him and the others. Jimmy sucked ferociously on the cigarette. All that planning, all that coercing, all those risks, for this, he thought. Gradually as the bend tightened, Galway Boy began to catch up. Jimmy watched intently as the jockey's arms started to pump back and fore on the horse's shoulders. Up front the grey had been caught. There was now a group of five in the lead, then a short gap to the rest, with Galway Boy still near the back.

Jimmy could see the jockey pumping his arms harder. They were rounding the bend into the straight when Galway Boy made his move, he was coming on the outside. The horse's mane was fluttering with its own velocity, his legs were flowing with grace. He caught the pack and in the space of half a furlong, like a Porsche accelerating away, he'd passed them all as though they were standing still. 'Come on my beauty,' Jimmy called out.

Inside the final two furlongs the front five were coming back at him. He was on fast wind, they seemed in slow motion. The grey was now the back marker of the five. Galway Boy passed him with a furlong to go. There were three up front, spread across the track, vying for the lead. A gap, just about the width of a horse, developed between each of them. By then Galway Boy was really flying. Daringly, the jockey went for the gap between the middle horse and the one on the outside. There wasn't far to go and it saved going the long way round. The jockey's head was down low, his arms pumping like pistons, the horse's ears were angled well back. The crowd at the trackside were roaring. 'Go on,' Jimmy shouted. The other people in the shop looked at him.

Like an outside half, dissecting an opening in centre field, Galway Boy shot through the gap. There seemed some contact with the horse on the outside, but he was through, away and clear of the others. Jimmy whooped, threw his arms up. Boy crossed the line in full flow, a length ahead. 'Yes!' Jimmy exclaimed and pumped his fist in the air.

He looked at his mobile. 'We've done it,' was messaged, in text, from Dougal.

Jimmy wanted somebody to hug. He virtually hugged himself, then sent a text back to Dougal. 'Drinks all round,' he typed. Then he moved to the counter to present his ticket. 'My lucky day,' he said to the clerk, who put the ticket in the machine.

There was a delay. The ticket held in the machine. 'There's a stewards inquiry on this one,' the clerk,' said.

'What?' Jimmy yelled. The clerk gave Jimmy his ticket back and pointed towards the TV screen. In his enthusiasm to text Dougal he hadn't heard the announcement. Jimmy went back to the screen. They were showing the final furlong, this time, front ways on.

He watched, horrified, as he saw Galway Boy bump the horse on his right, sideways, when he went through the gap. It wasn't so noticeable on the side-on camera, but from front on you could see it clearly. The bump caused Galway Boy to veer left, so that when he passed the two horses on his inside, he cut right across, causing them to almost stop. You couldn't see that either from the side on view. Jimmy's heart sank. He lit up another cigarette and paced the floor.

Five minutes went by. Another text from Dougal. 'Trouble,' was all it said. Jimmy continued to pace, threw away that cigarette, lit another. The final furlong continued to be re-run on the TV screen. He listened hard to the commentary.

'Galway Boy is disqualified,' the voice on the TV said eventually. Jimmy couldn't believe his ears. It had been a bump, yes, but he'd outrun the other three horses by miles. 'Bloody hell, how can they do this to me,' he cursed under his breath. He waited, then the result was confirmed in the shop. The three in the line were placed first, second and third. 'Bloody hell,' Jimmy swore out loud.

He moved back to the clerk and held out his ticket. 'Do I get anything at all for this?' he asked. The man looked at it and reinserted it into the machine. 'I'm sorry sir,' he said. 'The horse has been disqualified and placed last.'

'Some bookmakers pay out on a first past the post basis?' Jimmy enquired.

'I'm afraid that's not the policy of this company,' the man said and pointed to a plastic sign on the wall, behind the counter, that spelt out the company's rules. He handed the receipt back to Jimmy, who stared at it for a long time.

The amount printed on the ticket was for six thousand four hundred and thirty five pounds and that included Toby's tenner. Now it was all gone. Every last penny. Lost for good, in a matter of minutes. He felt completely numb, as though all the juices in his body had been sucked out and drained away. Slowly, dejectedly, he plodded back to his car, all the while thinking about the people whose money he'd gambled; feeling he'd personally let them all down.

In his car, on his mobile phone, he dialled Dougal's number. 'We've been stitched up there all right old son,' he said when Dougal answered.

'The bastards,' Dougal replied. 'He won it by a mile. It's an inside job if you ask me. They didn't want him to win, 'cause he's from across the water. Bastards!!'

In the same manner, they commiserated with each other for some minutes, then Jimmy drove slowly home.

CHAPTER FIFTEEN

Stan's mind and body suddenly felt clear of the self-imposed restrictions he'd foisted on himself for most of his life. Flirting briefly with fantasies that had tantalised him for years, took away the yearning, leaving his mind free to pursue more practical matters.

'We can go into Swansea and look at some kitchens today if you like,' he said to Rosemary over breakfast.

For the first time in a long time she looked at him with admiration. 'I'll get ready right away,' she replied. When she'd gone upstairs Stan slipped into the lounge and tuned the television into the previous days racing results on Ceefax. He laughed when he saw the result of Galway Boy's race.

In contrast, Jimmy's demeanour that morning was full of despair. Last night he'd tried to anaesthetise his pain by consuming large tumblers of his best Irish whisky. Unfortunately the guilt and pain about other people's money he'd gambled and lost soured every sip. An internal argument in his head had raged continually about betting the pot each way, but that was now superfluous. The horse had been disqualified; it wasn't even placed second, third or fourth; so whatever he'd done in that respect wouldn't have changed anything. But he still felt responsible. All evening he'd cursed about, 'the useless f****ing jockey.' It wasn't the horse's fault, he told himself. He'd run well enough to win the race. It was that 'bloody clod on board, who'd guided him the wrong damn way,' who was to blame, Jimmy lamented.

By eight o'clock in the morning, the depressing reality of dehydration and it's consequent headache had forced him to take a large cup of black coffee up to his pigeon loft. As yet, he hadn't spoken again to Dougal or any of the other punters, although he guessed, by then, that most of them would be aware of the result, except perhaps Toby who wasn't really into such things.

* * * * *

That morning Toby had more important matters on his mind. The previous evening he'd called round at Catryn's house, partly to see how she was and partly to make sure she'd be at home when he brought Mark back from school. When he arrived there

147

the house looked closed up, her car was not outside. He knocked the front door two or three times without an answer, then went round to the back. On his way there he peered in through the windows, before hammering on the back door. There was still no response. Usually he could hear Mark shouting or screaming, or the television, or Catryn playing music on the radio, but that morning everything inside was silent.

He knew the people next door, by sight anyway. They'd never been all that communicative but he thought he'd try, so he rang on their doorbell. After some moments, a tall unshaven man in his late twenties, wearing a coloured shirt covered in cement dust and pale blue jeans with the same dusting, pulled the door open.

'I'm sorry to trouble you, but I'm wondering if you've seen Catryn from next door, at all today?' he asked.

The man peered at him for some seconds. 'Dunno mate,' he replied. 'I've been out working.' The smell of alcohol was on his breath.

'What about your wife?' Toby asked.

'She ain't my wife. Gloria have you seen Catryn today?' he shouted back over his shoulder into the house.

'No,' a yell returned over the sound of the television.

'Sorry mate, can't help,' the man said and began closing the door before Toby had an opportunity to say anything else.

On an off chance he drove over to the pub where Catryn used to work. He spoke with the landlord, but he said he hadn't seen her since she'd left his employment and he didn't know much about the lad either.

'He might live over on the council estate but I can't be sure,' the landlord added.

By morning Toby was worried. Early on, he again visited the house, but just as he'd found the previous night, the property was shut up with no sign of life. Perhaps she'd gone away for a few days he thought, but where and with what money? He knew she had no cash to speak of and the lad certainly didn't appear the sort to have any capital. What would he do tomorrow if she wasn't there when he got back from the school with Mark. The school wouldn't keep him; it shut down at the weekend.

For the rest of the day he tried to busy himself with some of his many duties. All the while though, his mind was running riot on the possible consequences of what may happen on Friday afternoon.

* * * * *

Ginger had also spent the last day or so in a stew. The price of shares had continued to free fall. The bear market that caused Colin so many problems was now well and truly set in and any chances of Ginger making a profit on the share issue was diminishing by the hour. Each time he switched on his television and keyed into Ceefax, another ten points or more had been knocked off the Footsie index.

Only three days before, over lunch at the golf club, he'd been extolling the virtues of the company concerned to young Bevan, the current bank manager. Usually it wasn't his custom to get involved socially with members of his former branch, they were all so young nowadays. When he'd been Bevan's age he was still a clerk; so what could this young whippersnapper know in comparison to his years of experience. Still, he thought he'd better go through the process of treating the guy to lunch. He certainly wasn't going to attend at the branch for an interview to obtain his overdraft.

Throughout lunch Tony Bevan mostly smiled and listened as Ginger lauded it over him. Unfortunately nearly all of Ginger's reminiscences were about practices the bank had long ceased to adopt, but Bevan wasn't going to spoil his fillet steak by disagreeing with the old man. By the time they reached the coffee and brandy stage Ginger was into an eulogy about the company whose shares he wished to purchase.

'The managing director is a personal friend and I've got this opportunity to buy in,' Ginger remarked, as he swirled the brandy round and round in the bulbous glass in his hand.

Bevan worked hard to suppress a smile. Only that week he'd read about the issue in the Financial Times, where the correspondent had written it down as a risky venture.

'I want to get in for as much as I can,' Ginger continued. 'Trouble is, most of my capital is tied up in other ventures at the moment. I just need a small amount to top up my own liquid money. Once the shares are on the open market, I'll take the profit and pay it off. It'll only be for a week or so.'

'What happens if they don't make a profit?' Tony Bevan said and looked enquiringly at Ginger.

'Can't fail old boy,' Ginger said without hesitation. 'I tell you, I have it straight from the horse's mouth on this one.'

They talked some more about the amount Ginger required.

'Well I'm perfectly happy to lend you the money Mister Rearden,' Bevan said. 'But you must have noticed what's happening in the market. In the last week there've been record falls.'

'Temporary blip old boy,' Ginger replied and knocked back the remains of his brandy in one mouthful. 'Quality shares won't be affected in the long run. I'm sure you know shares are the best long term bet. First thing they taught me when I joined the bank,' Ginger added condescendingly.

'Up until now they have, but things change,' Bevan said, sipping assiduously at his brandy. He kept his eyes on the liquid as he spoke again. 'For the first time in years America has a big current account deficit. That'll affect the market.' He paused for a moments thought. 'Anyway, as it's you I'm perfectly happy to lend you the money. You know, of course, that now you're a pensioner I can no longer charge you the staff rate.'

Ginger looked at him with an expression of astonishment.

'I'm afraid my hands are tied on that,' Bevan added. 'Bank policy unfortunately. Still as you say, it should only be for a few weeks.' He added a smile designed to placate.

They finished their coffee and made to leave. In the car park they shook hands.

'Thanks for the lunch. I'll drop you a line to confirm our arrangement,' Bevan said to Ginger, then drove away in his own car.

'Cocky young bastard,' Ginger said to himself as he got into his own vehicle.

* * * * *

The day before the issue was due the Footsie 100 dived by another one hundred and fifty points. The financial press was full of rumours that 'Makepeace', the name of Ginger's company, was considering cancelling the issue. That afternoon things looked uncertain. Sometime before five o'clock the company issued a statement, stating that the issue price would be dropped by thirty pence. That meant more shares for Ginger, but less chance of any major profit.

When the day of issue dawned Ginger spent a worrying

morning glued to the Ceefax screen. The flotation had gone ahead, but the shares opened up forty pence below the offer price. Ginger slumped in his chair and cursed. Periodically, through the day, he reverted back to the screen, but each time it was bad news. By four thirty in the afternoon, the price was down seventy pence and Ginger had lost a lot of money.

* * * * *

Jimmy's mood hadn't improved either. He'd spent the morning replacing some rotten battens in the pigeon loft roof and repainting the main struts. Eventually he decided he needed some fresh air to clear his head. So he stowed the birds into their carriers and prepared to take them out for a training session. Perhaps he'd drive out to see Dougal for some mutual commiseration, he thought. On his way there, he called in on Toby to tell him the worst. The look on his friend's face when he answered the door suggested Toby already knew about Galway Boy.

'I guess you know then,' Jimmy said, before Toby had a chance to say anything.

'What's that then Jim?' Toby said and twirled the end of his moustache with his hand.

'That we lost.'

'Lost what?'

Jimmy hadn't seen Toby look so wan before. His normally robust, colourful face looked pale and drawn; his eyes, usually sparkling, appeared tired and strained as though he hadn't slept. For the first time since Jimmy had known him, Toby looked his age.

'Our horse lost, I'm afraid,' Jimmy said. 'Well it won actually but then it was disqualified, so I'm afraid you lost your money.' The news still didn't seem to sink in. 'I'm sorry Tobe,' Jimmy added.

'Oh that. Oh gosh, I'd forgotten all about it.' Toby replied and stroked his moustache again, but a smile was still a long way off his face.

'Are you all right Tobe?' Jimmy asked. 'You don't look well.'

Toby rubbed the other end of his moustache.

'I've just got a difficult case on at the moment that's all. It's causing me a few problems I'm afraid.'

'You shouldn't still be involved in that sort of thing at your age. You've done enough. Do any good to tell me about it?' The two men stood on Toby's front door step, looking at each other.

'Well if you've got time,' Toby said and ushered him inside. Margaret was out, so Toby was able to take him into the lounge. He brewed some tea, then recounted the whole story of Catryn and Mark, without mentioning that he was the father.

'You're wrong to get so personally involved Toby,' Jimmy said as his pal came to the end of his tale. 'It seems to me she's taking advantage of your good nature.'

'I know. But I thought she'd really turned the corner this time. Up 'til now she's been one of my real success stories. There you are, that's life I suppose,' Toby said in a resigned tone

They talked some more, then eventually Jimmy had to leave; his pigeons would be 'fretting', he said to Toby.

Driving to the coast he was still worried about his pal. Their conversation had aired most of the aspects of Toby's dilemma, but Jimmy was convinced there was still more to it than Toby had let on. A dark cloud seemed to hover over Toby's head all the time he talked.

* * * * *

Colin had spent the last two days deep in purdah. His study door was shut tight and he only came out to walk Dudley, eat his food and go to bed. Veronica was getting worried. Inside the room Colin was actually testing his system for roulette. On the internet he'd discovered he could download a roulette wheel game and for hour after hour he put his formula through every conceivable scenario possible. Not once did his system fail him. He began to conjecture on how much Stan had actually won at the casino. On his downloaded wheel, in imaginary money, Colin had won over a hundred thousand pounds. Suddenly, reclaiming the deficit in his hedge speculation became a distinct possibility. He decided to telephone Stan. Rosemary answered his call.

'How are you my dear?' he asked.

'I'm fine Colin,' she replied. Colin was shocked. Never before in his life had he heard Rosemary utter such a statement, without in some way contradicting it. Usually, there was an added rider about some aspect of her health, or about Stan or a domestic problem. This time there were no added riders. When he asked if Stan was there, she brightly said, 'I'll fetch him now'. Normally she would have made a contrite remark about him being out in the garage, whilst she was stuck in the lounge on her own, but this time there was no such tirade.

'All seems well in the Richard's household?' Colin said when Stan came to the phone.

'We've been looking at kitchen units all day,' Stan replied with a sigh. 'It's kept the missus happy. I don't know about me.' Colin guffawed.

'I'm ringing up about that formula I gave you,' Colin said. 'I'd like to give it a go for real myself and I was wondering if you would accompany me? Just as moral support you understand. I wouldn't expect you to risk any money yourself.'

Stan was taken aback. He had always considered Colin way above his mental stratosphere. After all he was a Professor and so obviously clever. Never in his wildest dreams could Stan have imagined Colin ringing him up for help on anything to do with something like a mathematical formula.

'Well I'm happy to help if I can, what have you in mind?'

'This is strictly between the two of us old chap,' Colin said in a hushed voice. 'Veronica knows nothing of this and I wouldn't want it to get out amongst the other lads.'

'No, of course,' Stan said. 'And the same goes for me with Rosemary.'

'What about us both going to the casino you visited?'

Stan hesitated before replying. It was Anne who had been a member there, not him. He wasn't sure. 'Let me find out a bit more about it,' Stan said. 'You have to be a member to use it. I went with the friend I was telling you about, who is a member. I'll let you know.'

After they'd finished talking Stan sat in the chair in his lounge and thought. He'd got away with it once. Pushing his luck again might be a step too far. He decided to ring Anne on his way to the golf course in the morning.

Next day the skies were laden with cloud, but those who were available decided to risk the golf. Anne was still in bed when she received Stan's call. She'd been painting her toenails when the phone rang and she lay back on the pillows while she listened to Stan's soft husky voice.

'Stanley you old devil, how are you. You've caught me in bed. Are you coming over? Scott's still away.' Her tone caught him off guard. He wished then he hadn't phoned.

He mumbled defensively, 'I was telephoning about the casino actually.'

'Do you want to go again?' Anne interrupted. 'I'd dearly love to give my system another go. I just can't think what went wrong the other day. And you've got your method as well. We could make a real killing this time.' Her voice sounded excited. 'Oh do say you will Stan, we had such fun last time,' she continued.

'No it's not for me,' Stan cut back in. 'It's for a friend. He wants to have a go, but I guess he needs to become a member first. How does he go about that?'

'If you come round here now I'll tell you.'

'No Anne, I can't do that. I'm on my way to golf.'

'Oh you're such a rotten sport. I'm so lonely here by myself and that cheating husband of mine is off cavorting with his girlfriend. If you won't help me, why should I help you?'

CHAPTER SIXTEEN

His telephone call to Anne caused Stan to be late for golf. He caught up with the others in the changing room. That morning Toby was absent. Scott was still away, so it was only the four of them who were playing.

'I'm worried about Toby,' Jimmy said to the others as they were putting on their shoes.

'I went to see him yesterday and he didn't look well. Has anybody else spoken to him?' Nobody else had.

As they pushed their trolleys down the slope towards the first tee Jimmy told them about Catryn and her son Mark, just as Toby had told it to him. Out on the course a gusting wind was blowing which was obviously going to be a factor in the day's proceedings. Trouble was, on that course you could never be sure how bad the gale would be until you actually got out onto the headland. Jimmy regularly said, 'if the wind is against you on the outward journey, by the time you reached the headland, it'll have probably changed direction and be against you on the way home as well'. More often than not he was right.

'I think there's more in that relationship than meets the eye,' Ginger said as they walked on referring to Toby and Catryn.

'What do you mean by that?' Jimmy replied.

A veritable gale, hit their faces straight on when they reached the tee.

'Bloody hell, here we go,' Colin muttered.

'My gardener lives on the same estate as the girl and he's much of the same mind,' Ginger said while donning his waterproofs. 'He tells me Toby was around there quite a lot when the baby was born.'

He took his driver from his bag and engaged in a series of energetic practice swings. Then reached into the bag for a ball.

'Surely not our Tobe?' Jimmy responded. 'He's the last one I would have thought of in that respect. Well perhaps the next to last,' he added and looked across at Stan, who looked away.

'Well I'm only telling you what I've heard. I can't confirm anything,' Ginger said.

Colin, who was searching for some tee pegs in his bag said, 'I'd have thought Toby was too old for that sort of thing.'

'You're never too old,' Ginger said. 'We'd better have a balls up,' he added and arrogantly held out his hand for the others to place a golf ball in it.

'You're on dangerous ground jumping to conclusions on something like that,' Stan said and looked straight at Jimmy.

'Bet I end up playing with Jimmy,' Ginger said as he threw the four golf balls in the air. His ball landed next to Stan's and so Colin was to partner Jimmy. 'Thank heavens for that,' Ginger said as he picked his ball off the ground.

That morning the strong south westerly made golf difficult. After a few holes a persistent drizzle also intervened to dampen proceedings. A film of moisture formed on Colin's glasses. Before every shot he had to stop and wipe them clean with his handkerchief.

'This is the one time I envy that bugger Lambert,' Colin said, stuffing his handkerchief back into his pocket. 'Somewhere in Spain is the place to be on a day like this.'

'Aye and tucked up with some bird if I know him,' Jimmy said. 'If Ginger had said it was him involved in something furtive, it wouldn't have surprised me at all.'

At that moment, the seventh green was a good one hundred and fifty yards away from where they were. While they'd been talking Ginger had been visualising his shot to the pin, conjecturing on which club to take. Eventually he took a six iron from his bag and began brandishing it vigorously alongside his ball. 'That should do it I guess,' he said then settled into his stance.

Very slowly he swung the club back before unleashing it smack into the centre of the ball. It soared like a sky rocket towards the right hand side of the green. However, at the peak of its trajectory, the wind caught the ball and drew it unerringly inwards. With one bounce it hit the flag stick and came to rest not more than three feet from the hole.

'Great shot,' the other three exclaimed.

Ginger turned and looked at Jimmy. 'Now you try and get inside that young man,' he said and pointed towards the green.

Jimmy and the other two tried their best, but none of them could get within ten feet of Ginger's ball. Even using his good luck charm, 'I have a feeling this is going in Ging', phrase, Jimmy's ball still ended up twenty feet from the hole.

As they walked forward, into the gale, Ginger recounted at

least two or three times the exact format he had used to play the shot. When they were about twenty yards away a big black crow began to circle above their heads. A couple of times it landed on the green, pranced around, took off again, then continued to circle above them.

'Watch that little bugger,' Jimmy said pointing upwards.

By then the four of them were quite close to the green. The crow however, was unperturbed by their presence and it made one more swoop onto the putting surface. This time it dived straight for Ginger's ball and like picking a fish out of a pond, the bird grasped the ball in its beak, then hovered tantalisingly, about twenty feet above the four players, flapping its wings, showing them the ball.

'The bastard's got my ball!!' Ginger shouted while clapping his hands to try and distract it. Alongside him the other three were doubled up laughing. Ginger took his putter out of his bag and waved it in the air at the crow, which continued to hover defiantly. In desperation he threw the club up at the bird, but it was way off target and landed, like a spade, with it's head buried in the ground. They all watched as the crow flew away with Ginger's golf ball firmly grasped in its orange beak. Clearly you could see the round white object against the bird's dark black feathers, till it landed in the sand dunes, almost a quarter of a mile away. Jimmy couldn't contain himself. Tears, caused by a mixture of the gale and his laughter ran down his cheeks. 'I'm afraid you'll have to go back and play that shot again Ging,' he said.

'Like hell I will.' Ginger replied.

'What's the rule on that one Colin?' Jimmy asked.

'The rule is, if you see a bird pick up your ball and fly away with it, you can replace it with another ball on the same spot,' Ginger cut in.

'Are you sure you're right?' Jimmy replied; his face still creased with a smirk. 'How do we know you're right?'

'Because I'm telling you I'm right. If you think I'm going back there,' Ginger said, pointing back at where he had played the shot, 'and try and replicate that shot again, you know what you can do.'

Ginger marched up to the flag stick, repaired his pitch mark, which was two foot from the pin and put down a ball marker six inches nearer the hole. The others watched in silence. Jimmy looked at Colin who said nothing and then they all putted out without saying anything further. Ginger and Stan won the hole.

'I bet he couldn't make that shot again if he tried,' Jimmy said to Colin, but loud enough for them all to hear as they walked off the green.

The rest of the game proceeded without further ado. Stan and Ginger won the match, three and two, although for the remainder of the game Jimmy muttered constantly about them winning by default. 'I'm going to ask that miserable bugger of a pro about that rule when we get in,' he said as they all shook hands, when the match was over.

In the changing room afterwards Colin cornered Stan about the casino.

'There's three I know of,' Stan began in reply. 'You can join any of them, for not very much, on the day you go, as long as you have some form of identification with your name and address on it.' Anne had eventually relented to his questions on this aspect.

'Would you come with me Stan? You know the form,' Colin asked.

'It's not something I really want to get involved in again. I've had my bit of luck and I'd be loath to push it again.'

'I wouldn't expect you to bet,' Colin said. 'Just sort of hold my hand. Metaphorically speaking that is.'

On their way to the clubhouse bar, Jimmy detoured via the pro shop. At the time Byron was in his back room, fixing a new grip on a putter.

'I'm sorry to wake you up Byron,' Jimmy called out.

Byron didn't respond until Jimmy was alongside the counter, where he could see him. 'Did you have a good round?' the pro asked, while remaining in his room.

'Not bad,' Jimmy countered. 'Now Byron, you're supposed to have passed all those exams about rules and things, perhaps you'll answer me this.' Jimmy then went on to describe the situation with Ginger's ball.

'If you all saw the bird pick the ball up, you can put another ball down where you consider the first one was taken from,' Byron replied without hesitation.

'H'm,' Jimmy said. 'Ginger hasn't been in here has he?'

'No,' Byron replied.

* * * * *

Toby's Friday was a completely different affair. That afternoon he had to pick up Mark from the school in Carmathen. First thing in the morning he drove over to Catryn's house to see if the situation there had changed, but the house was still empty. For some time he sat outside, in his car, wondering what to do. Up until that time, Catryn had never actually let him down as far as Mark was concerned. Yes, she'd prevaricated a lot. Regularly she was petulant, but always she'd kept to her side of the bargain. Perhaps she and the boy had gone away together for a few days, he thought. It would be her first opportunity to do that in a long time. This time Toby decided to try the neighbours on the other side.

A large, obviously pregnant woman in her early thirties answered the door. She had tangled auburn hair and a floral smock. 'I'm the social worker involved with Catryn, next door,' Toby began and showed her his identification badge. 'She seems to be away and I was wondering if you might know when she was coming back?' he added.

The woman looked at him with an air of disinterest. She wore glasses that appeared to make her squint.

'I think she has taken off with her young man,' she said.

'Oh, was that recently?' Toby asked.

'They were packing her car to the roof the other day. Looked like everything but the kitchen sink went in.' The woman sniffed and wiped her nose with the sleeve of her smock.

'What about the child? Have you seen Mark?'

'No, he hasn't been around for a few days now.'

'You wouldn't, I suppose, know where they have gone?' Toby asked hopefully.

'Na,' the woman said. 'She used to say the guy who got her pregnant s'married. So I dunno. Perhaps he's got the kid.'

Toby took a step backwards. 'Thank you anyway,' he said, turned and walked desolately back to his car.

Afterwards he drove home very slowly. All the way he wondered what else Catryn had divulged to all and sundry about their relationship. By then the enormity of everything he'd done, every sin he'd committed, every lie he must have told, was burrowing deeper and deeper into his mind. Throughout his

159

journey, he didn't notice the road, the traffic or the familiar scenery. His head was filled totally with the catastrophe he had conspired to devise. The shame, the conceit of it all, filled him with horror. He just couldn't envisage how he would reconcile it with Veronica, with his children and with all his friends in town. He'd never felt so low, or so desolate in his life.

Tragically, the continued inward humiliation caused him to miss the red light on the only set of traffic lights in town. He never saw the red light and he certainly never saw the Spar delivery lorry, hurtling down the hill, from the side road. The light had been red for some moments. The lorry was in a hurry; on its way to the store at Pembroke Dock. And the lorry driver never saw Toby's car until he ploughed straight into the driver's door, shunting it into a ten foot high wall on the other side of the road. Toby certainly never knew a thing about it.

CHAPTER SEVENTEEN

That afternoon Scott arrived home from Spain to a welcome as acrid as a squirt of lemon on a finger cut. By the time he got into the house Anne was brooding sorely. Stan hadn't been back in touch about any proposed trip to the casino. In fact all she'd done for the past few days was mooch around the house and then when her cleaner appeared, visit the gym.

When Scott walked into the lounge she was stretched out, with her feet up, on the white leather settee, wearing a black see-through sequined jump- suit and sipping a Martini. 'Have you been all right?' he enquired tentatively.

'What *do you* think?' she replied with scorn. 'While you've been away indulging yourself, I've been alone in this great barn of a place for nearly a week.'

'You tell me you love the house. It was built to your design. And you said you hate these golf trips.'

'I do. The house was designed with the two of us in mind.'

Scott sat opposite her. He hadn't seen that angry look on her face in a long time. Over the years his golfing trips had become a regular occurrence, but his homecoming had never been like this before. Usually he brought back some expensive present to placate her. This time it was a pair of Gucci leather boots. On all the other occasions something like that and a bottle or two of champagne, followed by a quick roll around in bed and things were soon back to normal. This time he guessed Anne had seen Jane Kirby with him in the car. It wouldn't have been the first time she'd seen him with another woman. For that matter neither of them had been exactly angels during their marriage.

'You wait till you see what I've bought you,' Scott said bending down into the luggage he had dropped on the floor beside the chair.

'What did you buy your floozy, or did you give her enough while you were there?' Anne said caustically, then took a large gulp of her drink, tilting her head back, as it ran down her throat. Scott looked at her.

'Anne I don't know what you mean. The lady you saw in the car was scrounging a lift. I told you the flight was altered to Bristol. There was a bus, but neither of us wanted that so I gave her a lift, that's all. The rest of the time, honey, I've been playing golf. You look at these,' he said, handing over the bag containing the boots. 'Let me go and get a drink, darling. What about some champagne?'

'I'm fine with what I've got here,' Anne said holding up her glass of Martini. When Scott moved off to the kitchen she picked up the package and began unwrapping it. The boots were impressive. She ran her hand delicately down their smooth, shiny surface and smiled to herself. By the time Scott returned to the room she had discarded the boots, thrown the packaging back on the floor and regained her former pose.

Scott was carrying a silver bucket filled with ice and containing a magnum of Krug. 'There we are,' he said placing the ice bucket and two glasses on the table beside her. 'Things almost back to normal now.' Extracting the cork caused a minor bang and some effervescent champagne spilled on the table. 'Nothing like the bubbly eh!' he said, chuckling, then poured out two full glasses.

'Come on Anne,' he said. 'I know you've been lonely. I apologise for that. Let's have a glass of this, then take the rest to bed. What do you say? Come on old girl. Time to make up.' He held out one of the glasses for her.

She looked at him with utter disdain, ignored the offered glass and said, 'piss off.'

He took a big gulp of his drink. As he was doing so the phone rang. It was Stan.

'Scott. Thank God you're back. I've got some awful news,' he said.

'Bloody hell!' Scott said when Stan told him about Toby. 'Bloody hell!' He kept repeating as Stan related the details.

Anne could see Scott's suntanned face had turned ashen. 'What is it?' she asked sitting up straight in the settee. Scott shook his head while Stan was talking. 'Do the others know?' he said. It was Jimmy who'd phoned Stan. 'Bloody hell,' Scott said again as Stan finished relating the details.

'What is it? What's the matter?' Anne repeated again when Scott put the phone down. By then she was on her feet.

'It's Toby. He's been killed in a car crash, in town,' Scott said.

'Oh Scott,' Anne retorted and dived into his arms.

* * * * *

Toby Ballard's death hung over the town like a damp sea

mist. Being such an integral part of nearly every organisation in the area, his passing affected everybody. Suddenly, a huge chasm appeared in the day to day workings of the community. Decisions, which he normally took, were delayed. Events, on which he was the guiding light were postponed. Conversations, locally, became centered on only one subject. Most of the time the townsfolk talked to each other in half whispered tones.

At our groups golf gathering next day the atmosphere was similarly funereal. The club's flag hung limply at half mast on its pole outside the clubhouse. The faces of each one of them, as they entered the changing room, were identically glum. Even Ginger talked to Jimmy on his arrival. 'This is a rum business,' Ginger said when he'd extracted himself from the toilet cubicle.

'Makes me wonder,' Jimmy said. 'I told you the other day, he looked wan. I mean it's so unlike him. For God's sake the man's sailed a boat, more or less by himself, around the world. Unless something desperate was on his mind I can't see him missing a set of traffic lights he knew like the back of his hand.'

'Well I told you the rumour I heard,' Ginger replied. 'I'm sure it wasn't just malicious gossip. The person who told me is just not like that.'

'What about poor Veronica?' Jimmy added. ' If you're right, how will she fare in all this. It so unlike our Tobe. He was a pillar of the community.'

'Well there you are. You never know,' Ginger said and sighed.

One by one the others arrived and expressed similar words of incredulation.

'We must call on Veronica and see if there is anything we can do.' Colin said.

'Best if Ging and you go,' Jimmy said. 'She won't want to see all of us. We'll all help, but you and Ging would be best. He's used to that sort of thing in his work and well, Colin you're better educated than the rest of us.'

The others grunted their approval and Ginger and Colin agreed to call at her house after their game.

Once they got going that morning's golf was a muted affair. For once there was no wind to speak of, but apart from the odd, 'good shot', or 'hard luck', each player was too wrapped up in his own thoughts to say much. In the still air, a late autumn mist was rolling gently in off the sea, creating a surreal atmosphere. Every time he teed up his ball, Jimmy kept expecting to see Toby's walrus moustachioed face alongside him. When he was around you could rely on Toby to tell some tale about one of his activities. Usually there was a humorous element to it, which he would exaggerate to perfection.

Stan won the match that day, but it was of little consequence. Afterwards they all trooped off to the bar, still wrapped up in their own thoughts. A toast 'to absent friends' with their drink before the meal did little to ease matters. When they had eaten, Ginger and Colin drove off to see Veronica, leaving Stan, Jimmy and Scott to idle away their time, without much enthusiasm, in a snooker match. Colin had promised to let the others know afterwards if there was anything they were required to do.

A feeling of trepidation clouded their journey to Toby's house, but fortunately Veronica's face was filled with a calm acceptance when she opened the front door. They had phoned ahead to say they were coming. Her eyes still retained their sharp blue, but her fair hair seemed to have acquired a little more grey since the news. She wore a blue jumper, with a gleaming string of pearls, Toby had given her for their fortieth wedding anniversary. A check skirt with an ornamental safety pin in the small slit at the hem, completed her smart attire. When Toby was about you tended to forget what a capable person, in her own right, Veronica was. The two men presented their condolences then they all moved through to her comfortable, well furnished lounge.

'The lads want to know if there is anything we can do to help,' Ginger said after they had all sat down. They'd refused tea. 'I mean, anything financial, business, home, or to do with the funeral,' Ginger began. 'We've all had to sort those things out at one time or another.'

'You're all very kind,' Veronica replied. 'But in that respect we were quite well organised. With Toby being older than me and him sailing off around the world, I made sure he'd sorted those things out a long time ago. And I'm pretty tidy in that way myself.' She paused. 'There is one thing however, that baffles me,' she said and brushed a loose hair off her face with her hand. The other two sat back and looked at her enquiringly. Veronica continued.

'For the past few weeks Toby had been worried about a case he had with his social work. A girl, I understand, who he helped when she was on drugs. It seems lately there was a problem with her again and it looked outwardly as though it was getting on top of him, which surprised me. You both know Toby, nothing used to beat him for long.'

The two men nodded in agreement.

'Well, this morning I had a call from the special school in Carmarthen, about a boy Toby had taken there. It was Bill Witherspoon, the headmaster who called. He was very upset about Toby and didn't go into a lot of detail. But I had been worried about this matter and I got him to tell me a little more.'

The two men on the sofa kept nodding.

'It seems that the boy in question belonged to this girl and Witherspoon told me Toby paid for the child's first terms fees at the school. It's a private school, I understand, for children with learning difficulties. When was this I asked? Oh, only last week the headmaster said. Well, naturally I was astounded. Toby hadn't said anything to me about it. So I looked up our bank statement and there, sure enough was the cleared cheque for over five thousand pounds. I was astonished. Have you chaps any idea what this may be about?'

Ginger and Colin looked at each other and both shook their heads at the same time.

'Well,' Veronica went on. 'Witherspoon told me not to worry. He said they'd sort it out.' She paused again. 'But now I am worried. What on earth possessed Toby to pay out an amount like that for some boy whose mother was one of his cases.' She paused once more and swallowed hard. 'I was wondering if I could ask you, his close friends, to find out a bit more for me. I mean who is this girl? Where does she live? What's it all about? Have I lost that money? With the funeral and everything else I haven't the time at the moment. But I am curious now, as well as being five thousand pounds lighter. Would you do that for me, please?'

Outside, afterwards in the car, Ginger turned to Colin. 'I told you there's no smoke without fire. Something's happened there, none of us, including Veronica knows anything about. I'd better take a trip out to see my gardener friend. He lives round the corner from this girl. Will you tell the others?'

For the time being Colin and Ginger put thoughts of casinos and share issues onto a back burner. After Colin phoned Jimmy with the news, he stopped brooding about his betting loss. Jimmy phoned Scott and he and Anne put aside their bickering. Stan received a call from Ginger and decided to leave negotiations in respect of the new kitchen in Rosemary's capable hands, while he phoned Veronica to offer his condolences.

'I've been very lucky,' he said after their initial dialogue. 'I've had a bit of a windfall,' he continued, 'and I've decided, in memory of my dear friend Toby, that I'm going to make a contribution to the Scout Hall roof.'

'Oh Stan, I'm sure he'd be pleased,' Veronica replied. 'He was so worried about it. But you shouldn't spend your money on that. You're a pensioner like us.'

'No, I've given it a lot of thought. I was going to do it anyway, before Toby's accident. The money has been acquired completely by chance, so some of it has to go to a deserving cause and I can't think of a better one. I'll get in touch with the Scouters.'

'You've all been very kind,' Veronica said. 'I saw Colin and Ginger earlier on and I told them of my little problem.'

'Yes, I heard,' Stan said. 'We'll see what we can find out.'

After she'd thanked him some more, they finished their call.

* * * * *

Ginger waited until the late afternoon then drove over to see his gardener friend, Duncan Thomas. His timing was right. Duncan was cleaning out the days rubbish from his white transit van as Ginger arrived. He looked up when he saw Ginger.

'Oh hello Mister Reardon. I know, I know, you're next on my list. It's this bad weather, I'm all behind.'

Duncan Thomas, like his father and brother, had tended gardens in the area all his working life. The Thomas family were reliable. They would turn up, do a proper job and remove the rubbish afterwards. Two large council contracts were part of their work, but by and large they gardened predominantly for the retired local pensioners. Duncan was wearing a mud stained white t-shirt, filthy blue jeans and a light blue baseball cap, when Ginger approached. He had fair features and a pointy, spotty face.

'No it's not that I've come to see you about Duncan, although my lawn does need a cut,' Ginger replied.

Duncan tipped his cap back on his head and wiped his nose on the back of his arm.

'You've probably heard about my golfing pal, Toby Ballard, being killed,' Ginger said.

'Yes, I did Mister Reardon. It's a bad business. Casper on the ambulance said he was in a terrible mess when they pulled him out. One of the worst he's seen. He never had a chance I'm told.'

'Yes, a good man too.' Ginger said and moved closer to Duncan. 'There's been a bit of a problem though and I've come to you for some help,' Ginger said and looked at him intently. Duncan wiped the sweat off his face with a dirty handkerchief. Ginger continued. 'A few weeks back you told me something in confidence,' Ginger began, then went on to tell Duncan some of the details he'd learnt from Veronica.

'Well it doesn't surprise me Mister Reardon. Barbara, my wife knows more about it than I do. She's seen the girl around with the little boy, in the shops and things. They've passed the time of day, chatted a bit, that sort of thing. You'd better come in and see her.'

Inside, the house was untidy and cluttered. Every space was filled with plant cuttings, seedlings and potted-on geraniums. Barbara was a tall buxom woman, with red hair. She admitted responsibility for the cuttings. 'I sell them at the car boot,' she said to Ginger. 'You'll have to excuse the mess, I'm sorry.'

Ginger remained standing and related some of his tale again.

'From what I can gather Mister Reardon,' Barbara said, 'Catryn's gone off with the Williams's boy, from down the road. Mind you what she sees in him I can't think. Right little layabout. Always in trouble, just like the rest of the family and on drugs I'm told.'

'Was this recently? The going away together, I mean?' Ginger asked.

'This last week, so Vera who lives next door says. Packed the car one evening and just disappeared. I bet she's not paid the bills.'

'And the child, Mark?' Ginger queried.

'He didn't go with them. Vera says that Mister Ballard took him away on the Monday morning in his car. There was a bit of a to-do. Funny business all round, if you ask me. But I'm sorry he was killed in such a way. He did a lot of good in the area.'

'Well I've got to try and trace them. Do you think I'd get anywhere with the Williams'?'

'Ho, you could try Mister Reardon,' Duncan cut in. 'But I wouldn't count on it. We fell out with them years ago. An odd lot for sure. You be careful if you go there.'

Ginger left it at that. He found out where the Williams' lived and the number of Catryn's house. He thanked them both, then drove to the Williams' address. Duncan promised to 'be round to do the lawn next week'.

Ted Williams was an unemployed labourer, who did odd jobs, for cash, nobody else wanted to do. A smell of alcohol was on his breath when he stood in front of Ginger on his front step. He was a tall, gangling man, with straggling grey hair, an unshaven face and unkempt clothes. Ginger handed him a business card which he'd had printed on his retirement. It read ex-bank manager, that sort of thing, with his name and address and included his designatory letters, FCIB. Williams looked at it unimpressively and made no reply.

'I'm trying to trace Catryn Wallace, who lived down the road at number thirty eight, on a matter of urgency,' Ginger started. 'I'm told by the neighbours she may have gone away with your son.'

Williams scratched his chest and made as if to shrug his shoulders.

'Would you happen to know where they've gone?' Ginger asked firmly.

'Don't know and don't care Guv. Just to get that little bleeder from under my feet is a blessing. He owes his mother a lot of money, so I expect he's gone away to get out of paying her. So there's no way he would tell us where he's gone.'

Ginger tried a few more brief questions about Catryn and the boy Mark, but got nowhere. Williams slammed the door closed as soon as Ginger moved away.

Finally, Ginger drove over to Catryn's house. There was still no sign of life, the house was closed up.

Later in the day most of the group spoke to each other on the telephone. Jimmy was anxious to know what Ginger had found out. It was at times like these, times of crisis, involving something serious, that Jimmy and Ginger actually talked to each other like normal human beings. On those occasions, the nit picking and the one-upmanship were absent, just as it had been absent when Jimmy drove Ginger's mother-in-law to hospital for treatment.

'If we could find out her car number we could get the police to try and trace it,' Jimmy said to Ginger. 'You know the Inspector down there. Isn't he one of your Rotary mates?'

'We could try,' Ginger replied. 'Mind you I don't know we'd get much help from the neighbours on the number and where would the police start looking? She could be anywhere in the country, or abroad?'

'Well they could put out a 'Missing Person'. She is missing and there is an abandoned child at stake. Surely that's a good enough reason?'

'You have a point there James. I'll have a word with Holyoak of the Yard.' That was the locals nickname for their top policeman. Sometime in his career, Inspector Graham Holyoak, who was from Llanelli, had worked in Scotland Yard, although only in an administrative capacity. So behind his back, he was generally referred to by his nickname.

Meantime Colin had been phoning around with details of the arrangements. 'The funeral's on Tuesday at eleven o'clock, then up to the Crem,' he told Stan. 'And there's a bash afterwards at the Marine.'

'I just can't believe we won't see Toby with us again on the course,' Stan said to Colin. 'Something must have been tearing his mind apart for this to happen. I mean he's normally such a good driver. In his working days he used to drive the fire engine and he's been through those traffic lights ten thousand times. This business with this girl must be at the bottom of it all. I tell you Colin, it's upset me.'

'And me, but we've all got to do what we can for Veronica at the moment,' Colin said. 'It's bad enough losing her husband without having his funeral desecrated by a scandal.'

'Yes, yes. But I'd like to get the bottom of it for Toby's sake. You know what this place is like for rumours.'

'Innuendos become embellished with fantasy,' Colin said in reply.

'Exactly. For his sake I feel we have to try and establish the truth. I just can't believe he'd carry all that around with him for all those years.' Stan said. 'Ginger's found out that this child is nearly five years old. That's a hell of a long time to carry something like that around in your head. Veronica obviously didn't know and we his mates didn't know, so it would amaze me if it's true.'

'There's nowt stranger than folk though Stan. I expect we've all got some skeleton in the cupboard. What's yours?'

Stan laughed.

'Your bloody gambling system. Don't you dare tell Rosemary.'

Colin laughed and they ended their call.

* * * * *

Next day Ginger called in to see the Inspector Holyoak.

'I see your handicap's coming down Graham,' Ginger said to him when he was ushered into his untidy, cluttered, small room at the town's police station.

Graham Holyoak was a tall thin man with dark features, a long nose and a receding hairline. Ginger had seconded his application when he joined the golf club; the policeman being a customer of his at the bank.

'Well I get it down in a match, then I go into the Medal and it goes back up again,' Holyoak replied. 'I think at twelve, I'm about as good as I'm going to get.'

'It's an imperfect game,' Ginger said, then explained why he had come.

'Surely not Toby,' Holyoak said after he'd heard Ginger out. 'He's the last one I would have thought of being involved in that sort of thing.'

'Keep it under your hat Graham. We don't want too much getting out at this stage, the funeral's on Tuesday. But it's important we find the girl. That's why I've told you.'

'Yes, yes of course,' Holyoak replied. 'I owe Toby more than one favour. He was the guy who'd sort the problem kids out for us. I'll see what I can do.'

'There's the Spoons competition this weekend. Are you going in that?' Ginger said as he was leaving the room.

'Yes I suppose so,' Holyoak said with an air of resignation. 'That'll get my handicap up again.'

They both laughed.

* * * * *

Over the weekend both Ginger and Jimmy made periodic visits to Catryn's house. Ginger to see if she had returned, Jimmy with every intention of effecting an entry, until one afternoon Ginger caught him nearly in the act of doing so.

'Just what do you hope to achieve?' Ginger asked, when he found him round by the back door with a jemmy in his hand.

'If I could get in, there may be some clue as to where she had gone,' Jimmy said. Ginger looked at him incredulously.

'James you really have been reading too many crime novels. Do you honestly think this girl is going to leave a note on the kitchen table, saying if you want to find me I'll be at such and such a place? Sometimes you really do astound me.'

'No, I don't think that Ging. But there maybe a telephone number on a pad, or a brochure or something.'

'Somehow I doubt that very much. This girl has obviously run away. If that's the case she's not going to leave any clues, is she? And if you were caught breaking in, how would you explain that one to the police. Tell me that?'

'I'd get you to have a word with your friend Holyoak of the Yard.'

'Do me a favour, will you please,' Ginger said and led Jimmy away.

The weekend passed without any real progress on the matter. Scott was busy trying to placate Anne, who still hadn't forgiven him for his indiscretions. This time it was going to cost him more than a slap-up meal and a pair of expensive Gucci boots. After the disappointment of Stan's rejection she had her eyes set on a Caribbean cruise, at the very least.

Stan was busy with Rosemary looking at kitchen estimates. During one of their many discourses on the matter Rosemary raised a subject Stan had been dreading. 'Stanley, I've been meaning to ask you something for the last few days. But what with all the trouble surrounding Toby and these kitchen things, it's kept slipping my mind.'

'What's that my dear?' Stan replied, having already guessed what was coming next.

'The other day our Building Society statement came in the post,' Rosemary said. Stan looked down at his feet. 'Have you looked at it?' Rosemary asked.

'No my dear. I've been been busy with other things, as you know.'

'Well let me go and get it,' she said.

While she was gone Stan worked desperately to get his brain into gear. By the time Rosemary had returned, clutching the statement, he'd fixed his face into a false smile. Rosemary unfolded the statement in front of him on the kitchen table and pointed at it.

'It shows here a credit of two hundred and fifty thousand pounds and then later on it's reversed.'

'That must be a clerical error,' Stan said quickly. 'I haven't paid in anything like that, have you?'

She looked at him suspiciously. 'Of course I haven't,' she replied cautiously. 'But also it looks as though our five thousand pounds was drawn out. Then a few days later it was paid back in again.' She stood back and waited for his reply.

Stan was in real dilemma. Should he tell her the real truth, or should he lie. He knew if he told her the truth, she would never trust him again as long as he lived.

'Well if you really want to know, I drew it out to buy you this new kitchen you've been going on about for so long. Then I realised, when I shopped around, on all those trips I went on, it wasn't going to be enough anyway, so I put it back and went to sort out some cash from my pension fund.'

Rosemary looked at him wide-eyed. 'Stanley Richards, you did that without asking me?'

'You wanted a new kitchen.'

'Yes but that is our nest egg, our only savings.'

'Seems I'll do anything to make you happy. Beg, borrow or steal. Anyway, I didn't use it and you're having your new kitchen, so what does it matter.'

They looked at each other for a moment.

'Don't you ever do anything like that again,' she said eventually and wagged her finger at him.

'No dear,' he replied, pushed the statement to one side, then quickly reverted her attention back to the kitchen plans.

* * * * *

On Sunday morning, at Church, Stan caught up with David Archer, one of the men involved with the Scout Group and told him about his idea of a donation for the hall roof.

'If we could get that underway before the winter it would be a real bonus,' Archer said to Stan outside the Church porch, after the service. 'I'll phone you with our bank number,' he added.

'Perhaps we could name the hall after Toby, when the roof's finished,' Stan said.

'That's an idea,' Archer replied. 'I'll put it to the committee.'

'Don't do that,' Stan said. 'We'll need a decision before the decade's out.'

They smiled at each other.

* * * * *

Colin spent most of the weekend in his study, scouring the net and searching the pages of the financial press; attempting to devise a rescue package for his depleted capital. The Far East and China appeared to be the only areas that possessed any real potential for the sort of growth he was looking for. Both, however, were long shots, riddled with the possibility of unmitigated disaster. He was getting desperate. The markets were still in a perilous state and he was running out of ideas. At the end of the day, after he'd switched off his computer, he began to re-read the sheets of paper he'd written out on the formula he'd given to Stan.

* * * * *

On Sunday morning, Jimmy took his pigeons out for a training flight, en route to see his friend Dougal. They hadn't met up since the disaster of the race, although most of the other punters had been in touch. None of them actually said so, in as many words, but nearly all of them, by inference anyway, blamed Jimmy for their loss. The horse was, after all, his tip, from his sources and they had all backed his judgement. All that, coupled with Toby's demise and the associated problems, left him feeling pretty low.

He found Dougal in his usual spot in the corner at The Myrtle Inn. It looked as though he hadn't shaved for a week, the straggled end of a rolled cigarette hung from the side of his mouth and he also bore a melancholy expression. Eamonn was sat on his lap.

'I swear to you Jim, I sometimes wonder if the devil himself isn't involved in this horse racing game,' Dougal said as Jimmy sat next to him. 'I'm sure he invented gambling, so wasters like us would pay for our sins.'

'Ay, I reckon you're right there.' Jimmy replied. Dougal continued.

'Jimmy, lad, that horse of ours won that race by a mile. But the outcome was the work of the English and the Devil that took our money from us. They weren't going to let him win, no way, I tell you that now for a fact now.'

'Yes,' Jimmy said and supped at the beer he'd bought on the way to his seat. 'He hardly touched the horse he was supposed to have bumped. And as for cutting across, well that was pure invention. The Bloody English as you say.'

'And the Devil!' Dougal retorted.

They spent the next two hours consoling each other with beer and whisky. The pigeons beat Jimmy home by hours.

Meantime, Ginger had given up all hope of making any money out of the Makepeace' share issue for the time being. Sitting on his sofa, at home, after Sunday lunch, swirling a twenty year old Highland Malt, round and round in a glass, he conjectured on how he was going to explain everything to Margaret. His only hope of salvaging his capital was to sit tight for the duration of this bear market. Knowing that could take years only added to his depression. At his age, a big drop in capital would curtail their life style dramatically. His bank pension was inflation linked, but over the past couple of years that had only been somewhere around two per cent, certainly not enough to keep them both in the jollies they'd become accustomed to.

* * * * *

When the five of them gathered for golf on Monday morning a shroud of gloom continued to hang over the proceedings. Their minds were not only preoccupied with the following days funeral, but except for Stan, the other four were also bedevilled by the precarious state of their finances.

Conversation therefore, was sparse as they donned their golf shoes. Each one of them loath to upset the delicate bond of empathy they shared about their recently departed colleague.

'You know I miss Toby already,' Colin said, trying to cut the ice, as he tied up his shoe laces. 'By this time of a morning you could guarantee he would have said something to cheer us up.'

'He would that,' Jimmy said.

'I suppose we are no nearer finding this girl?' Stan cut in, leaving the question in the air.

'Not so far,' Ginger answered. 'I'll call in on Holyoak on my way home after golf. But I expect he would have phoned me by now if there had been any news.'

The delicate mood prevailed as their studded golf shoes clinked down the concrete path to the first tee. That morning, to each of them, everything felt odd. There were now five where there used to be six; five is an odd number. Quite often, the six of them weren't always present. Usually, someone was away, or couldn't make it for one reason or another, but in their minds, their group was made up of a round half dozen. If there was one missing, it was always commented on. The others would then conjecture on where the missing one had gone, what he'd be doing and with whom and they'd laugh and joke on the possibilities. But now and for the foreseeable future there would only be five. Which meant, that most times they'd have to play as a three and a two, not a rounded format at all. The concept was irregular, lopsided, uneven.

Ginger put his golf ball on a tee peg on the first tee and sighed. 'Let's get on with it then,' he said. 'The quicker we get on with it, the quicker we'll get it over with.' And without any of his customary exercises or practice swings, he whacked the ball, as though he didn't care about its outcome, straight down the first fairway.

The others followed pretty much in the same spirit, and without much enthusiasm they wended their way around the course. Colin was playing with Ginger and Stan, while Jimmy and Scott were together, in a two ball. The standard of golf was mixed. Somewhere in the first nine holes, when they were almost out of Ginger's earshot, Colin broached to Stan the subject of his formula for roulette.

'I've discovered that the system's virtually flawless,' he said to Stan when they were on their own together. 'I've tried it out on a simulated game on the net and won every time.'

'Well that's how it was for me,' Stan said. 'Except for at the beginning, when I wasn't sure of what I was doing. After that I don't think I lost on any roll.'

'Well there you are then. Why won't you accompany me? I'm not asking you to risk your money this time. It'll be my money we're risking, but I'll give you a cut. Let's say ten per cent of what I win, if you'll come with me.'

Stan looked at him. There was a stiff breeze off the sea which was making his eyes water. 'I don't think so Colin,' he replied and dabbed his handkerchief at his liquid eyes. 'I've had my share of fortune. Lightning doesn't strike twice. If I came with you I'd probably bring you bad luck.'

Ginger who was having a miserable time with his golf had been ear-wigging while they were talking.

'What's all this about gambling,' he interrupted.

Colin briefly explained about his formula.

'Colin my old friend, we're all mates here,' Ginger said and moved towards him. The three of them were stopped in the middle of the fairway. Suddenly their game of golf became a secondary consideration. Jimmy and Scott were well ahead and at that moment there was no one behind. 'You know that whatever you say to me is in complete confidence,' Ginger continued. 'You forget I was a bank manager.'

Stan scoffed. 'That's what would worry me,' he said.

Ginger ignored him and turned to Colin. 'What you're saying Colin, is that you have devised a system for winning at roulette?'

'That's about it,' Colin said. Stan stood to one side and looked embarrassed.

'My dear chap,' Ginger said and put his arm round Colin's shoulder. 'Let me share your burden,' he added.

That day Stan played the best and won most of the money. After the game, in the clubhouse bar, Ginger was quick to relate Colin's exposé to Jimmy and Scott. They both listened eagerly, then leered at Colin as though he was the man who held the keys to the Bank of England.

'Let's hear some more,' Scott said.

They all moved to sit at the far side of the room, away from the other members and John the steward, who's ears usually flapped at the mention of money. There, overlooking the eighteenth green, with calm patience, Colin began to recount the bare bones of his system. In those surroundings it was impossible to go into detail. Even if he had the others wouldn't have understood much of it. During his discourse, Stan sat slightly aback and said nothing. Ginger, Scott and Jimmy however, remained wide-eyed as Colin recounted his theory.

'Well I can't see how we can go wrong.' Scott said, downed

some of his beer and slapped Colin on the back.

'Well, all we've got to decide on then is a date when we can all go to the casino,' Jimmy interrupted. 'Are you in with us Stan?'

They all looked at him. 'Not for me,' he replied.

'Oh come on Stan, don't be a spoilsport,' Scott said.

While they scoffed their lunch, all of them, except Colin, continued to harangue Stan, but he refused to budge. 'I've made my mind up on this one and I am sticking to it,' he repeated firmly at each attempt to involve him.

In the car park afterwards the others began to make tentative arrangements to go to the casino at Swansea. Colin had guided them that way, knowing of Stan's success in Bristol.

'The funeral's tomorrow. What about Wednesday?' Jimmy said. 'That way we won't have to tell our wives anything. Swansea's only an hour. We can say we had a late game and stayed on longer for snooker.'

They all looked at each other. Stan was already on the way to his car. Amongst the others there appeared to be a consensus of agreement about Swansea and Wednesday. 'I'll phone before, to check if we can get in,' Colin said.

On his way home Ginger called in at the Police Station, but Holyoak had no word on Catryn.

CHAPTER EIGHTEEN

When Ginger pulled up outside his house, Duncan Thomas was in the front garden cutting the grass.

'You were right Mister Reardon, it badly needed a cut,' Duncan said.

'I knew you'd get here as soon as you could,' Ginger replied as he made his way to the front door. He was just about to go inside when Duncan stopped the mower and called after him.

'I nearly forgot,' Duncan said as he unhitched the full grass box. 'My wife told me to tell you that the girl you asked about the other day is back at the house. She saw her this morning in the Spar.'

Ginger stopped in his tracks and stared at him. 'Good God,' he said. 'Thank you Duncan. Are you going to the funeral tomorrow?'

'Hope to,' Duncan replied while emptying the grass from the box into a plastic bag. He went back to the mower, restarted the engine and carried on cutting.

Ginger phoned Jimmy and Stan as soon as he was inside the house. 'I think the three of us should go over together and confront her,' he said after he had explained. 'Strength in numbers is better for something like this.'

They agreed to meet up in half an hours time at a lay-by near Catryn's road. When they'd all arrived they got into Ginger's BMW for the short journey to the house.

'If she is there, what are we going to say?' Stan said in the car. 'She may not know Toby has died.'

'Well that's a good starting point,' Jimmy said. The aroma of expensive leather in Ginger's car and the purr of the powerful engine, was far removed from his scruffy old Merc. Ginger drove slowly while the three of them continued to speculate on their modus operandi.

At Catryn's house they cautiously approached the front door. Ginger rang the bell. When Catryn opened the door they all took a step backwards. To their surprise, in front of them, stood an attractive, intelligent looking young woman; not at all what they had expected.

'We are sorry to descend on you like this,' Ginger began, 'but we are friends of Toby Ballard and we are wondering if we could see you for a few minutes.'

Catryn blinked, looked at them defensively. At first they thought she was going to refuse. She made no immediate reply while her eyes took in each of them in turn. Eventually, she stood back, opened the door wider and gestured for them to enter. She still hadn't said anything.

In the lounge, they all stood awkwardly looking at each other. Ginger then introduced each one of them in turn, explaining how they had been Toby's golf friends for years. Catryn still remained silent, eyeing each one up and down, and nodding her head as their name came up.

'The first reason for us calling was, I'm afraid, to bring some bad news. I don't know if you know, but unfortunately Toby has been involved in a road accident. Had you heard?'

For the first time Catryn's face expressed some emotion. She averted her eyes and looked down.

'Yes, I had heard,' she said. 'That's partly why I've come back. I understand the funeral is tomorrow?'

'Do you think we could all sit down?' Ginger said.

Catryn pointed to the chairs in the room and fetched one for herself from the kitchen.

'Well,' Ginger continued, when they were all sitting, 'we know you and Toby were very close friends. From what I understand he was very kind to you when you were going through a bad patch.'

Catryn looked at him almost defiantly.

'That's quite right. He was very kind. I owe him a lot.'

'You see, the other reason we are here is actually on his wife's behalf. We are all old pals as I've tried to explain.'

Catryn nodded her head but said nothing, so Ginger continued.

'Well, the other day Toby's wife received a telephone call from the school for children with learning difficulties, in Carmarthen. They said a few days before his death, Toby had brought a child into the school, who we are given to understand is your son, Mark.'

Catryn nodded her head. 'Yes, Mark is mine.'

'Mrs Ballard also says, and the school confirm, that Toby paid the first terms fees for the child, out of his own money. What do you know about that?'

Catryn looked at Ginger and then again at each of the others in turn, before looking down at her hands, which were spread out on her lap. She began to rub her fingers together, then she spoke.

'It's all a complete mess,' Catryn said, sighing. 'I repeat, Toby was very kind to me. He did help me a lot when I was in a bad way. He could see Mark was struggling with his reading and his vocabulary.' She sighed again, folded her arms, unfolded them and folded them again across her chest. 'I'd met up with a boy recently. Dylan Williams, who was no good for me whatsoever. He got me involved in drugs again. I'm afraid I couldn't help myself. The last few years have been one big struggle. Just recently I lost my job. That sent me off the rails again. Toby could see what was happening. That's why he put Mark in the school. I wasn't in a fit state to cope.'

'Where's Williams now?' Stan asked.

'Oh I don't know and I don't care,' Catryn replied. 'He was a complete waster. I sent him packing a few days after we went away together. He was stealing money to pay for drugs. As soon as I found that out I kicked him out. I've spent the last week cleaning myself up. I assure you I'm ready to face the world again, and my child.'

'Where is the child now?' Ginger asked.

'He's with the Social Security. During the week he stays at the special school. I'm told he's got on well so far. I'm going to see him after the funeral and on Friday he'll come home to stay with me. For the first term anyway. After that we'll have to see where we stand.'

'Who is the father of the child?' Jimmy cut in. Ginger looked at him angrily. He had been trying so hard to be diplomatic. Catryn glowered at Jimmy. She folded and unfolded her arms again. For a moment it looked as though she wasn't going to reply. They all waited. What followed was a long explanation.

* * * * *

On Tuesday morning a large crowd gathered at the old Norman church in the centre of town. Many churches in that part of the world display classic Norman towers. This one is similar, but also sports a searing spire on top, which provides a prominent landmark for miles around.

A funeral locally usually guarantees a big turnout, being one of the few events when there is something to dress up for. Inside the church they were packed shoulder to shoulder in the hand carved pews.

Veronica, with her children and family alongside, was up front and veiled in black. To begin with the congregation chorused resoundingly into 'Jesu, Lover of my Soul'. By the time the Canon was into his address, tears of compassion were evident on the cheeks of the majority. There was a reaching for handkerchiefs, and a clearing of throats before the hymn 'Cwm Rhondda', brought temporary relief.

When Stan reached the pulpit to deliver his eulogy, silence had enveloped the congregation. Everybody in that church had heard the rumours. When he looked up from his notes Stan could see Catryn sitting just five pews from the front. She looked proud, defiant, dressed in comparable black. Not a tailored smart black like Veronica's suit, but everything black and matching.

Stan listed a history of Toby's achievements. His Fire Service record, his around the world sailing and then a veritable catalogue of local social and functional positions. The CV was impressive. Stan's reading of it clear and concise. He coughed before continuing.

'In fact I would go so far to say that Toby Ballard has the most unblemished record of helping people, particularly locally, that I have ever known,' Stan said forcefully. There were murmurs of approval from the congregation. At that moment he looked straight at Catryn. 'In fact I would challenge anybody here today to contradict that assumption.' He stopped speaking and looked around the packed church. His words were greeted with a wall of silence. He scanned the congregation. He knew almost everyone there, some closely by association, others by acquaintance. His dalliance with Anne, his success at the roulette table, his new found affinity with Rosemary, had all given him a confidence he hadn't possessed before. So from the superior height of the pulpit he looked down on the congregation for some moments, holding the eyes of many of them, until his rested again on Catryn's. She bowed her head.

'And so I commend you all to the life and work of Toby Ballard,' he continued eventually. 'May God rest his soul and preserve his memory.'

'Amen.' The congregation chorused, in unison.

The service didn't take long. The majority were going on to the Crematorium, but they all paused on the steps outside, on their way out. Taking time to shake hands, offer kisses and affection to each other, as though they were greeting long lost friends, not people they saw almost every day.

Catryn stood to one side and watched it all with calm detachment. Nobody approached her. Stan caught her eye and they exchanged a smile. What she told the three of them last evening was enough to satisfy his concern for the time being. She'd taken a long time relating her story. Once it was said however, they all agreed to keep in touch and do whatever they could to help her.

Ginger knew most of the business people in the town from his bank days. He promised to see if he could find her a job in town, to fit in with school times. Stan would deal with the Social Security, to try to get young Mark permanently into a school for special needs. Jimmy would speak to Colin about arranging a savings scheme for her, to put by some money, when she was working, to try and repay Toby's debt. She appeared grateful. They'd parted on good terms.

What she told them was that Toby had saved her from a life of drugs and petty crime. She'd said that Mark's father was a lad who'd disappeared when she became pregnant. The last few months had completely got her down. Mark wasn't improving with his vocabulary. Then she lost her job, which depressed her further. Toby had paid for the boy's school fees when he saw the state she was getting in, she said. She went out with Dylan to try and cheer herself up, but he was on drugs and encouraged her to start again. She was so depressed she thought it might help. But when they went away together, she saw straightaway, he was no good. He was stealing from cars to pay for the drugs. She dumped him and came home. She knew now life wasn't any greener on the other side of the fence, there was no fast lane; she'd learnt her lesson, she admitted; Toby had been right all the time. She didn't know how she was going to cope without him. That's when the other three offered their assistance.

The funeral ended as funerals do. There was a wake at the Marine Hotel. Veronica braved it out. By the time a drink or two had been consumed, a semblance of a smile emerged from the previously grim faces. Tales were swapped about Toby's good deeds. Eventually chuckles of laughter gradually seeped around the room. In time, they all drifted away to continue with their various tasks and duties in the community.

* * * * *

The following day, Wednesday, the five gathered for golf as normal. The sombre mood of their previous game was absent. They'd all talked together a lot at the funeral wake. Matters amongst them were for the most part back to normal. Jimmy called out 'Fore, keep your bowels open Ging,' when he arrived in the changing room. Ginger ignored him and remained in the cubicle until Stan arrived.

On the first tee there was an argument about who was playing with who. When Stan threw the five golf balls in the air, Ginger's landed next to Jimmy's. 'No I just couldn't stand that,' Ginger said and turned away. And so the bickering began again.

Colin won the money that day, with the best stableford score. Still quibbling, they retired to the clubhouse bar to argue over the monetary spoils. They had one drink, ate lunch, then, afterwards, Ginger, Colin, Scott and Jimmy, set off, in Ginger's BMW, for Swansea and the casino. Stan smiled to himself and sighed as he waved them away. And life carried on.

THE END

ABOUT RICHARD F JONES

If you have enjoyed this book Richard has published five other novels: **A FLIGHT HOME-DANCING WITH THE DEVIL-EXPLOSIVE VOYAGE-WAR TO THE DEATH-BEN'S BOAT and MOUNTAIN INTRIGUE**, details of which can be viewed on his web site: www.richardfjones.net

Richard was born in North Wales, but has also lived in the highlands of Scotland, the Wye Valley, Spain and Majorca. All his page turning novels are set in places where he has had a home.